ONE

AMERICAN

DREAM

Bernard Beck

Amberjack Publishing
New York, New York

Amberjack Publishing
228 Park Avenue S #89611
New York, NY 10003-1502
http://amberjackpublishing.com

Publisher's Cataloging-in-Publication data
Names: Beck, Bernard, 1938-, author.
Title: One American Dream / Bernard Beck.
Description: New York, NY: Amberjack Publishing, 2017.
Identifiers: ISBN 978-1-944995-09-6 (pbk.) | 978-1-944995-10-2 (ebook) | LCCN 2016950331
Subjects: LCSH Immigrants--Fiction. | Jews--Fiction. | American Dream--Fiction. | Depressions---1929--Fiction. | Depressions--1929--United States--History--Fiction. | BISAC FICTION / Historical | FICTION / Jewish
Classification: LCC PS3602.E26845 O54 2017 | DDC 813.6--dc23

Cover Design: Red Couch Creative, Inc.

Printed in the United States of America

To my wife, Judy, with whom I have shared more than half a century of Kavanah.

GLOSSARY

Baal Shem Tov: Jewish mystical rabbi, considered to be the founder of Hasidic Judaism.

Bar Mitzvah: Confirmation: the religious initiation ceremony of a Jewish boy who has reached the age of 13 and is regarded as ready to observe religious precepts and eligible to take part in public worship.

Bubba: Grandmother

Bubbe meises: Old wives tales

Chasidism: A Jewish religious sect which arose as a spiritual revival movement during the 18th Century and spread rapidly through Eastern Europe.

Cohen: A person from the priestly class

Daven: Pray

Derash: Intensive investigation

Dybbuk: The dislocated soul of the dead

Ein Sof: Literally "without end"—another name for God

Frum: Religious

Goy: Non-Jew

Hashem: Literally: "The name"—another name for God

Kabbalah: An ancient wisdom that claims to reveal how the universe and life work.

Kavanah: Spiritual intensity

Kliphos: Hindering spirits

Maimonides: A brilliant medieval Spanish Jewish philosopher and mathetician.

Mamzer: Bastard

Mein Liebe Rivka: My Darling Rivka

Mezuzah: A piece of parchment in a decorative case that is mounted on door-posts and is inscribed with the Hebrew verses from the *Torah* that begin: "Hear, O Israel, the LORD (is) our God, the LORD is One".

Minsk: A city on the Russian Polish border that once contained a large Jewish population.

Mishnah: The oldest authoritative post-biblical collection and codification of Jewish oral laws, systematically compiled by numerous scholars over a period of about two centuries.

Mitzvah: Good deed

Pale of Settlement: The term given to a region of Imperial Russia in which permanent residency by Jews was allowed and beyond which Jewish permanent residency was generally prohibited.

Peshat: Simple meanings

Pogrom: An organized massacre of a particular ethnic group, in particular, that of Jews in Russia or Eastern Europe.

Rashi: A medieval French rabbi and author of a comprehensive commentary on the *Talmud* and the *Torah*.

Rebbitzen: Rabbi's wife

Remez: Research

Shabbos: Sabbath

Shaina Maidel: Pretty girl

Shema: The central prayer of Judaism that begins: "Hear, O Israel, the LORD (is) our God, the LORD is One"

Shmatas: Rags

Shnops: Whiskey, usually Scotch

Shtarke: Big shot

Shtetle: Small town, usually with a substantial Jewish population.

Shul: Synagogue

Sod: Divine realm

Talmud: The central text of Rabbinic Judaism that contains more than six thousand pages of discussion and debate on all aspects of Jewish life

Tefillin: Also called "phylacteries," are a set of small black leather boxes containing scrolls of parchment inscribed with verses from the *Torah*. They are worn by male, observant Jews during weekday morning prayers.

Torah: Or the *Pentateuch*, is the central reference of the religious Judaic tradition.

Vus macht a yid?: How's it going?

Yarmulke: Skullcap

Yeshiva: Jewish religious school

Yiddishkeit: Jewish spirit

Zayde: Grandfather

Welcome to our house. Come freely, go safely, and leave something of the happiness you bring.

—Bram Stoker

PROLOGUE

From the time that we are born, we invent and reinvent ourselves—reducing our options and narrowing the perspective as we age. And as we continue to invent ourselves—responding to external stimuli and internal struggles—we shape and reshape our impression of what we have achieved, what we still expect to achieve, and what we hope to get out of life at the end of our days.

My grandfather and I are at either ends of our days: I'm just starting mine, and he's been reviewing his. I am going out into the world; he is retiring from the world. I have the advantage of a life ahead of me; he has been burdened with retrospection.

The best that I can hope for is to live a good, moral life and not to do too much damage. The best that my grandfather can hope for is that the good that he has done outweighs the damage.

My grandfather was blessed—or perhaps cursed—with a passion: to be an authentic American. This passion often clashed with his determination to also be a good, Orthodox Jew. These two passions often pulled him in opposite directions, and he was so conflicted and insecure that he would either under-think or over-think nearly every decision he made.

Of course, we are all blessed with twenty-twenty hindsight, and I'm sure that, had my grandfather been able to anticipate the consequences, he would have made different choices.

Is it ever possible, I wonder, to accurately balance the scales? Does a good intention compensate for a foolish act? Does naiveté compensate for arrogance? Do acts of goodness later in life compensate for earlier damage done?

Hard to say.

CHAPTER 1

Rose and I had not expected this. We had expected a battle, and we had been prepared to relent. I took my glasses off and slowly folded them and put them in my breast pocket. I suddenly felt older— tired. I had fought a battle and won, but somehow, I didn't feel good about it. I felt that there was something missing—that there should be something more—but I couldn't tell what it was. It had been too easy, something was off kilter, but I couldn't tell what. I stared at Rose, hoping for inspiration. Something was wrong, very wrong, and Ruthie, I sensed, was at risk. I needed time to think, but they were here now, and they were waiting for my answer, and I had to give it. But still, I needed time to think.

"Ruthie is our pride," I said aloud. "You must promise to take care of her always. She is a special person with a special gift. You must honor that gift.

"Here," I said, standing up, "give me your hand. Promise me now."

I stood and Harry stood and we shook hands. Formally.

"Harry," I said, still holding his hand, my mind racing for guidance, trying to buy time. "You have pledged to learn the Orthodox way. I don't expect you to do everything that you promised. But I

am a businessman, and I want to make sure that you are going in the right direction, so here is my offer: you study and show me that you are serious, and I will give you and Ruthie my whole-hearted blessing. We should make a deadline. How about Chanukah?"

Harry freed his hand and looked at Ruthie, who was anxiously watching him. "That sounds like a good plan, Mr. Rubin. We can then arrange for a spring wedding, maybe in June."

"Chanukah, it is," I said, taking Harry's hand once more. And then Harry and I embraced, and then we all hugged each other. And Rose began to cry.

Looking back, this was the turning point in all our lives. Was he right? Wrong? Guilty? Innocent? Maybe a little bit of each. You really need to know what happened before this to understand where he was coming from and the intensity of the impact that his choices had on his family and the lives of those close to him. He wasn't proud of the events that his decision ultimately created, but he thought he was doing what was best for Ruthie and our family . . .

I don't remember much about that time, only feelings. The engines had stopped, and the ship was cruising quietly. There was excitement in the front of the ship as word came back that you could see the Statue of Liberty. And then I saw it. I was holding my mother's hand, and I clearly remember saying to her in Yiddish, "Now we are Americans." She smiled at me and squeezed my hand.

"Not yet," she said, "but soon."

"No," I said, pulling my hand away from hers, "now I am an American."

I had decided to be a real American on July 17, 1890, the day my mother and I arrived in New York from Europe. On that fateful day, as we stood on the deck watching the New York skyline gliding by, I resolved that, from that moment on, I would be a one hundred percent American—not a Polish-American, not a first-generation American, not even a Jewish-American.

And from that time on, I never spoke Yiddish or Polish again. I dressed American, and the only kids I hung out with were the tough kids on the Lower East Side where we lived. I taught myself to walk like them and talk like them because I believed that they were real Americans, and I had to learn to be like them.

I guess you could say that I am a self-made man in the most literal sense: starting with my name. When I arrived, I was Jacob Rubinowitz, and, as soon as I could, I became Jack Rubin. Throughout my life I have invented, reinvented, burnished, refurbished, constructed, and reconstructed myself as often as necessary in order to achieve my ultimate goal: to be a real American.

It took me nearly half a century to accomplish this, but, in the end, I can proudly and confidently say that I am finally an authentic American in the fullest and proudest sense of the title.

I learned my first American words from the sailors on the ship; the rest I learned on the street, so you can imagine what they were and how I sounded. I only spoke "American" and I only dressed "American." I rejected the "Old World" clothing and mannerisms that my mother had valued so highly in Europe, and I refused to be seen in public unless I was properly dressed in what I felt was genuine "American" style. I told my mother that I would rather stay home than look and sound like a newly arrived immigrant, a "greener," and I begged her to use the little money that she had brought with her from Poland to buy "American" clothing for me.

We had come from Minsk, a town on the Russian-Polish border, with a trunk filled with clothing and personal memories, but my father, who had gone to America two years earlier and who was supposed to meet us at the boat, never showed up. An "uncle," who may or may not have been my uncle, found us a place to live.

My mother had grown up wealthy in Warsaw. Her family owned a successful factory, and they had sent my father to America to develop a market for their products. He had sent back glowing reports of potential opportunities in the New World, and they had sent him money to get the business established. They had also encouraged my mother to join him in New York.

My mother and I had embarked from Bremen with great expectations. But once in America, and without a husband, my mother discovered that the skills that she had valued as a middle-class woman in Warsaw, such as playing the piano, doing fine needlework, and decorating a home, did not transfer well to her new situation. In the world in which she now found herself, she had no marketable skills, and she had trouble keeping a job and earning money. For a while, she sang and played the piano in a local tavern, but, eventually, she became dependent on my so-called "uncles," and the occasional gifts from her parents. She never told her family that my father had disappeared and, instead, sent glowing reports of life in America.

At first, friends and neighbors helped her, but they soon got tired of her fancy and pretentious ways. It was rumored that my father had married someone and had another family somewhere in the west. We never heard from him.

I was not a particularly good student, and we were always having money troubles at home. So when I finished the eighth grade, three years after my mother and I had arrived in New York, I had to quit school to work full-time to provide for us.

My first official job was on the back of a newspaper delivery truck delivering newspapers twice a day to newsstands, and picking up the remainders on the way back. We loaded the truck around three in the morning and finished our first route before five. We then had some breakfast, loaded the afternoon edition, and were done delivering and picking up by noon.

After lunch, I would go down to the schoolyard to wait until it was time for my friends to get out of school. This was the hardest part of the day for me. I sat in the park across the street, feeding the pigeons. Occasionally, when I got cold or bored, I would walk over to the library and look at some picture books. I was a slow reader and was embarrassed that people might notice how I struggled.

Sometimes in the afternoon, when my friends were out of school, I would jokingly look at their school books. I was curious about what they were learning and was jealous that they could go to school and that I couldn't. Although I had never liked school, I was sure that I would be more authentically American if I attended. But we were too poor, so that was impossible.

I lived in two worlds: my mother's immigrant world and the gritty world of unskilled laborers—and I was accepted in neither. The men on the truck teased me about my age and naiveté, and they never included me in their after-hours friendships. The few friends that I had made in elementary school now had new friends and new experiences in high school. I had nothing. No friends, no money, and no father. I had rejected my Polish and Jewish background, so I didn't even have that. I was the poorest kid in the neighborhood.

I liked the camaraderie on the delivery truck and the feeling that all the older men treated me like an adult, but, at the end of the shift, they went home to their families, and I had nowhere to go. I longed to be with people my own age, but I felt more and more like an outsider. I knew that my mother and I could not survive without the money that I made on the truck, and I bitterly resented my life and obligations.

I was so frustrated and angry that I began to look for other, faster ways to make money. I figured that if I couldn't go to school, at least I could make enough money to have something to show for it. I was short and slightly built, which made it difficult to find construction jobs, and I didn't want to work in a factory because I had heard frightening stories about how the workers in the sweatshops were forced to work long hours for very little pay. I had heard, however, that there were opportunities on the street for quick money, and I asked the men on the delivery truck where I could find some afternoon work. One of them told me that I could make really good money working as a kind of messenger. He gave me a paper with an address written on it and told me to go there after work.

The office that I was sent to was not far from my house. It wasn't really an office, just someone's apartment. When I got there, they told me to go into the kitchen where other young boys like me were waiting. The boss, a gruff man with yellowed fingers, asked me what I knew about being a runner. I said that I didn't know much but that I was willing to learn. The other boys looked at each other and laughed.

"That's a good boy," the man said. "Here's all you have to do: I give you an address and you go to that address and ask for the person I tell you. They will give you an envelope, and you will bring it to me. Is that clear?"

"Yes, it sounds pretty simple."

"Yeah, there are only a couple of things you gotta remember," he growled. "First, you might be carrying a lot of money in those envelopes. If I ever find out that you took any of the money, you'll be very sorry. And second, keep away from the cops. If you see one around when you are making a pickup or delivery, don't make the delivery—just walk away. If they stop you and ask what you're doing, don't tell them where you are working, or I will make sure that your family suffers. Is that clear?

"Oh yeah, one thing more. I pay you two bits every time you make a pickup or a delivery. Make both on one trip and you can make half a buck for only a few minutes' work. Any questions? No? Then go sit over there, and I'll call you when I need you."

I sat with the other boys along the wall on wooden kitchen chairs forming a line. As one boy was called, the others moved up one chair until their turn came. The line seemed to go quite fast. The phone would ring and the man with the yellow fingers would write something down on a pad in front of him, then call the next boy and tell him the address.

When it was my turn, I was told to go to an apartment on East Twenty-Seventh Street. "Take the Lex to Twenty-Third and then walk uptown. You got it? Give this to Solly. Don't give it to anyone else. If you don't know who Solly is, ask. Stick it inside your shirt, OK?"

Excitedly, I took the envelope and slipped it into my shirt. I walked over to the subway and took the uptown train. At first, at the Twenty-Third Street station, I walked the wrong way, but then I got my bearings and purposefully walked up the stairs and out onto the street. I found the address without difficulty, walked up the steps to Solly's apartment, and knocked on the door. A huge man in just an undershirt opened the door.

"Are you Solly?" I asked.

"Yeah," he answered.

So I handed him the envelope that I had been carrying in my shirt, and, in return, Solly handed me a small envelope.

"You're new, huh?"

"Yes, sir, this is my first trip."

I took the envelope that Solly held out to me and slipped it into my shirt as I had been instructed. "Good kid," Solly said, "here's a buck for you. Keep your chin up."

As I emerged from the building, two men fell into step behind me. I started to walk faster, but the men broke into a trot. When I got to the subway entrance, one of the men grabbed my arm. The other flipped open his wallet to display his badge.

"New York City Police, kid. Mind showing us what you've got inside your shirt?"

"I don't have anything in my shirt, officer."

"Mind if we take a look?"

And with one smooth movement the policeman who had been holding my arm reached inside my shirt and withdrew the envelope.

"Well, what have we here?" he asked mockingly.

"I don't know," I replied truthfully, "the man gave it to me."

"What man?"

"I don't know his name, sir."

The policeman tore the envelope open and rifled through the money that was inside. "And where are you bringing this envelope?" he asked.

"I can't tell you that, sir," I stammered.

"And why not? You know you're in really big trouble!"

"Sir, they said they would hurt my mother. If I tell you they will hurt my mother!"

"Look, kid. Don't bullshit me. I've heard that sob story before. What do I care about your mother? You wanna go to jail? Is that what you want?"

"No, sir."

"Well, if you don't tell me where you're bringing this dough then you're going to jail," he explained.

The policeman had let go of my arm, and he was standing with his arms folded across his chest.

"Where do you live, kid?"

"The East Side."

"Look, kid, we can let you off, or we can book you. It's up to you. All you gotta do is tell us who you're working for and sign a statement. You're running numbers and that's a crime, and you could end up in jail. If we book you it will go on your record for the rest of your life. You're going to have an arrest record. You won't be able to get into the army, or go to school, or find a job. Anything. So here's the deal. You tell us where you work, and we don't book you. OK?"

"Sir, I can't do that. They'll hurt my mother."

The other policeman, who had remained silent until then, turned to his partner. "He's just a kid, and he's scared." Then he turned to me, "Look, kid, I want to let you go home to your mamma, but my buddy here is kinda tough, and he's the boss. So, do me a favor, you don't have to tell us anything. I'll write the paper myself, and all you need to do is sign it. What do you say? We got a deal?"

"No, sir," I answered, starting to cry. "I need to take care of my mother, and they said they would hurt her. I promise. I never did this before today, and I'll never do it again."

"Oh yeah?" the first policeman said. "And how have you been supporting your poor mother until now?"

"I've got a regular job, but I tried to make some extra money," I sobbed.

"Where do you work?" he challenged.

"Newspaper delivery service. I do two routes in the morning."

"How old are you, kid? And why aren't you in school?"

"I'm eighteen, and I already finished school."

"I say you're about fifteen, and you quit school. Am I right?"

But I didn't answer. I was worried about what would happen to my mother and me. I figured that if I told the police where I worked, the boss would definitely hurt my mother, but if they found out that I had been arrested and didn't tell, then it would be OK. I figured that I could offer to pay them back.

The first policeman was still talking. "OK, kid, it looks like we're going to have to book you. Now, if you don't mind, put your hands behind your back, and I'm going to cuff you."

At the police station they told me to sit on a bench, and they hooked one of my handcuffs to a ring in the wall. Policemen came and went, and sometimes they brought other people that they had arrested into the room. But these people eventually were led away, and I stayed by myself. No one spoke to me, and I was too frightened to ask anyone what was going on.

Finally, at around five o'clock, the policeman who had hooked me to the bench came back into the room.

"I'm going to take you in front of the judge now," he explained. "Go into that bathroom and wash your face. You need to look good for the judge."

The policeman held me tightly by the arm and led me into an elevator and then down a long corridor. We stopped in front of a closed door. The policeman knocked and then walked in.

"This is the boy I told you about, your honor," he said to the judge.

The judge, sitting behind a massive desk, didn't look up. "I'll be with you in a moment," he said with a slight German accent.

The policeman showed me where to stand, and stood beside me.

Once he finished his task, the judge asked me my full name, date of birth, address, and where I came from.

"I was born in Europe," I answered as clearly as I could, "but I grew up in New York."

"And what about your parents?"

"My father came here first, and then my mother and I came. But something happened to my father, and we never found him."

"No father, eh? Who supports you?"

"I do, sir. I work on a newspaper delivery truck."

"This paper says that you were running numbers. Is that true?" he asked.

"Yes, sir. I was trying to make more money. I don't make enough on the truck."

"Doesn't your mother work?"

"When she can, but the bosses are mean, and she keeps getting fired."

The judge told me to tell as much as I could about my family and what life was like at home. He asked about my friends, asked again why I wasn't in school, and where I was working.

I tried to answer as completely as possible. It seemed to me that the judge wasn't just asking questions for the record but was really interested in what I had to say. I told the judge about how hard life had been when we had first come to New York, and how I hated having to ask people for help, and that I just wanted to be an American. I told the judge about my job and about waiting in the schoolyard after school and wishing I could read better.

But then the judge stopped asking questions, and the room

got very quiet. He took off his glasses and put his hand over his eyes like he was very tired. I thought that it seemed as though he was about to cry. I looked at the policeman who was standing next to me, but he just shrugged his shoulders and stood there. Then the judge thanked the policeman and told him that he could leave and that he would handle it from there.

The judge stared at me for a long time. "Do you prefer to be called Jack, or do you have another name?" he finally asked.

"Jack, sir," I answered.

"OK, Jack, I'm going to offer you a deal," the judge said. "How much money do you make on the truck?"

"I make fifty cents an hour, about fourteen dollars a week."

"And you and your mother live on that?"

"Yes, sir."

"OK," the judge said, "here's the deal. I will give you enough money for you and your mother to live on, let's say, twenty dollars a week, but you have got to go to school full-time. Not only that, but you have got to be one of the best students in your class.

"Every Thursday after school you will come into this room, and you will sit over there and wait for me. You will bring me all of the homework that you have done for the week. You will bring me your report card when you get it. You will bring me every single note that your teacher gives you, every test that you get back. Everything. I want to know exactly what you are doing in school every day. If you're doing OK that week, then I'll give you the money. But if I find out that you screwed up, even once, I stop giving you money and you go to jail. Got it?"

"Yes, sir. Only . . ."

"Only what?"

"Only I'm not so good in school. I don't read good, and everyone else is two years ahead of me." I felt as if I was about to cry, and I chewed on my lip to hold it back. "What happens if I can't keep up?"

The judge looked up at me intently, "Son," he said, "you are in America. And in America, with hard work, anything is possible."

Then the judge reached into the top drawer of his desk and took out a paper. He dipped a pen into his inkwell and wrote a brief note. "Take this to Miss Baker at the high school. If you can't find her, ask someone, but don't give it to anyone except Miss Baker. She'll tell you what to do. And here," he said reaching into his pocket, "is twenty dollars. Take it home and give it to your mother, and I'll see you here next Thursday."

The judge waved his hand, indicating that I was to leave.

As I was leaving, the judge called out to me. "Jack," he said ominously, "don't fuck up. You might not get a second chance." And he waved me out of the room.

———————◦———————

Many years later I learned that Judge Adolph Heimlich had been the ambitious child of an upwardly mobile merchant family in Berlin, Germany. He had attended the best gymnasium in Berlin and had studied law in Zürich, Switzerland. It was his parents' intention, nearly from the time of his birth, that he should study law, and that he should go to America, and that, after he established himself in America, he would bring his younger siblings over.

But, once he arrived in America, he encountered many unexpected obstacles. The first was the language barrier, which he felt he could overcome through intense study, but the second was much more difficult. Most of the best law offices were known, at that time, as "white shoe" firms, which meant that they were managed exclusively by white, Anglo-Saxon Protestants and no Jews were allowed. He was forced, by the merciless combination of snobbery, lack of credentials, and rampant anti-Semitism, to open an office of his own. He shared this office, which was on a side street off the Grand Concourse in the Bronx, with an accountant and a salesman. He had very few clients, and, of these, even fewer had enough money to pay him his full fee.

Although he had very few clients, the location of his office turned out to be fortuitous when the local Democratic Party opened an office in the adjoining store. As luck would have it, they were looking for a local candidate to run for the position of Municipal Court Judge, and, having nothing to lose, he allowed his name to be put on the ballot. It was a predominately Democrat district, and his election was a foregone conclusion. He closed his struggling law practice and became a full-time Municipal Court Judge, to which office he was regularly reelected. Although he finally had full-time employment, he did not make enough money to pay for his siblings to come to America, but he was able to help young Jewish teenagers like me. He married a local high school teacher, and they lived modestly in the apartment that he had taken above his original storefront office.

From time to time, he would encounter young boys who, he felt, had the potential to turn their lives around. He had five such boys coming to his office every week, one each afternoon. We each thought our situation was unique, and we were never aware of each other. The judge and his wife were childless, and they lived frugally so that they could afford the one hundred dollars per week that he gave us.

They were careful not to get too involved in our personal lives, they never met our parents, and they never had contact with us after we finished high school. In moments of depression, they would reassure themselves that we boys were their surrogate family, and that what they were doing would make a difference.

CHAPTER 2

It was a struggle, but I tried faithfully to keep my end of the bargain. I worked very hard in school, but learning didn't come easy to me, and it took me much longer to do my work than my more experienced classmates. When I told the judge how hard I was finding it, he spoke to the principal of my high school and arranged for me to get tutoring to help me catch up. I went to special tutoring classes after school and on the weekends, and even a special program during the summer.

Eventually, I started doing well in school, and, as my confidence grew, my grades improved. And every Thursday, as I had promised that first afternoon, I went to the judge's chambers and waited and reported, exactly as I had been instructed. The judge never failed to ask me about my mother, and he even gave me extra money to buy her a birthday present. In the summer, the judge arranged for me to work after classes as a porter in the Henry Street Settlement House so I could make a little extra money.

In the middle of my senior year of high school, the judge told me that I should apply to City College. He said that the dean was a friend of his, and that he was expecting my application.

In the end, I proudly graduated from high school in the top ten percent of my class. On the Thursday before my graduation, the last Thursday that I was obliged to come to Judge Heimlich's office, he came around from behind the desk, and, with tears in his eyes, he shook my hand.

"Good job," he said. "I am very proud of you. I knew you could do it. As I told you when we first met, this is America and anything is possible. Never forget that. Everything is possible in America, even for a Jewish kid from Eastern Europe. Now the rest is up to you."

"I wish there was a way to thank you," I stammered, "but I don't know how. You did so much for me that whatever I do or say won't be enough."

The judge took a deep breath. "Make a difference," he said softly, still holding my hand. "That's all the thanks I need, just make a difference."

That same afternoon, when I went to the Henry Street Settlement House to do my work as an evening porter, my boss called me into his office.

"I know you're graduating from high school so I'm not going to beat around the bush," he said. "You're the most reliable worker we have on our staff. I'd like you to consider staying on here full-time after your graduation."

"Thank you very much, sir," I answered stiffly, "but I am planning to go to college in the fall, so that won't be possible."

"Maybe I didn't make myself clear," my boss said with a smile. "I want you to be my assistant. You'll have that office over there, and you'll be in charge of the day to day maintenance of the complete complex. The pay is three grand a year to start."

Three grand a year and my own office! That was a level of pay and prestige that I had never even thought possible. So without hesitation, and with a broad smile and a hearty handshake, I gratefully and enthusiastically accepted.

I never did go to college.

But I loved my job. I was now making a comfortable salary and was learning every aspect of building construction and maintenance. I was the first to arrive in the morning and the last out at night. Believe me. I would have slept in my office if they had let me. I was everywhere throughout the building and took on additional responsibilities whenever I could. I treated everyone with respect, and both the senior management of the Settlement House and the workers liked me.

But, although I had a good job and was now reasonably financially secure, I was not happy about my chances to fulfill my dream of being one hundred percent American. Real Americans, I reasoned, have a family and live uptown in a nice house. I, on the other hand, was still living with my mother. I was just a glorified janitor working in a building that serviced the needs of immigrants on the Lower East Side. Even though I now had money, and an office, and even though I went to work in a suit and a tie, I was still a maintenance manager. I dreamed of being a wealthy, powerful executive somewhere near the top. A real American.

I was very well aware that I didn't have the knowledge, skills, or connections to become an executive, but ambition dogged me. Just as I had jealously, those many years ago, yearned to be among my friends who were in school, I now looked enviously at the "uptown swells" and yearned to be one.

Five years quickly passed, and I wasn't any closer to my dream of becoming a real American. When I had first started my job at the Settlement House, I had figured that I could always quit and go to college. But now, five years later, I hadn't gone to college, and I wasn't ready to restart the struggle, yet my dream still gnawed at me. Time was running out, and now

I needed to find some kind of shortcut. I simply had to get rich immediately. There was just no other way.

I had tried industriousness, and it had only taken me so far. It now became clear to me that, no matter how hard I worked in the future, I would not be able to move up the economic ladder far enough to be a real American. Only one solution remained, and it was as plain as the nose on my face: I had to marry a rich, uptown girl. The only way an immigrant guy like me with no money, no credentials, and no special skills could become instantly rich was to marry a rich girl.

This may sound presumptuous, or maybe even cocky, but I was getting desperate. My dream of being an authentic American had taken me away from my street friends, and now I was nowhere. I was afraid that I would never achieve my new goal of being an affluent, uptown American, and I was not willing to settle for anything less. In my mind, being a real American was more than language and dress; it was style, and I now aspired to have "uptown" style.

But how? I knew very well that real rich, uptown, American Jewish girls would not be interested in a poor immigrant kid from the Lower East Side like me, no matter how well I spoke and how well I dressed. I figured that I would have to find an immigrant girl whose family had recently become wealthy, and who were just entering uptown society. She would have to be a girl from my social class whose family had recently made a lot of money, but still valued their immigrant ties. Unfortunately, I didn't know anyone like that.

And to make matters worse, although I had ambition, I had very few social skills and even fewer connections. My main social outlet was the Henry Street Settlement. People took classes there, and socialized there. I had met a few girls at these events, but they were poor girls who took classes after work in order to move up the economic ladder. Plus, the circumstances at the Henry Street Settlement, with me being a staff person and they being clients, weren't right for socializing.

But once a year, the Henry Street Settlement House, in

conjunction with HIAS, the Hebrew Immigrant Aid Society, and B'nai Brith, the three most popular Jewish organizations in New York, held a dance in the Broadway-Central Hotel on Broadway and West Third Street—one of the fanciest hotels in New York. It was, for the young people in the Jewish immigrant community of the Lower East Side, the social event of the year. Parents of girls scrimped and saved for months so that they could buy their daughters a suitable dress because they hoped that their daughters would meet eligible Jewish boys. This could have been an opportunity for me to meet a rich girl, but, in point of fact, most of the girls at the dance were just as poor as I was.

Still, it was my only hope, and, I reasoned, it was a start. I practiced dancing with my mother, and bought an appropriate suit for the occasion.

The night of the big dance was really special. The hotel was nearly a block long, and there were crowds of young people standing outside waiting to show their tickets at the door. I pushed my way through the door, but, once inside, I was floored. The place was all red velvet and crystal chandeliers. To me, it was the most beautiful place I had ever been. There were girls everywhere, millions of them it seemed, and I was overwhelmed. But as I walked slowly around the room I realized that the girls were all standing in groups in the middle of the room while the boys were all standing, pretty much alone, along the wall. The orchestra was playing, but no one was dancing.

Fortunately for me, Rose happened to be at this dance. She wasn't part of a group, and, although she was standing alone, she seemed to be more confident than the other girls. I spotted her almost immediately, but I wasn't sure how to approach her, so I stood a little off to the side watching her.

But then she looked me straight in the eyes and started walking over to me.

"Are you going to ask me to dance?" she asked. "Or are you just going to stand there all night staring?"

She didn't seem to be particularly wealthy, although I wasn't sure how I would be able to tell, and she wasn't an especially good dancer, but she was very beautiful. And extremely confident and tall. Taller than me. I was smitten. She had an aura of confidence, power, and disdain which, I'm sure, must have repelled or frightened most of the boys at the dance but attracted me. I danced with her nearly the whole night, and I took her home to Brooklyn on the subway. For Rose, this was her first real romantic attachment. For me, it was love at first sight, and, when we arrived at her stoop, I told her.

"I'm going to marry you," I said as I kissed her tentatively at her front door.

"I know," she answered.

CHAPTER 3

I was surprised when he said that, and I was even more surprised by my response. But, when I had a chance to think it over, I was kind of pleased. I had been afraid throughout the evening that I had not been handling things well, and that he was dancing with me just to look sophisticated.

This was long before anyone had a telephone so there was no quick way for us to communicate. At that time, people had to communicate by mail, and he wrote me the most beautiful letter thanking me for dancing with him, telling me how much he had enjoyed the evening and repeating his desire to get married. I wrote back, and we set a date to meet and discuss it.

As far as I was concerned, he was nice, reasonably good looking, and it was time for me to get married—I didn't have the time or energy to spend on a long courtship. So I asked him when we met if he was serious about getting married. He said he was, and he didn't seem at all surprised by my question. So we set a date, and we got married. My father was there, along with his mother, and the Rabbi.

I wasn't sure, not even on our wedding day, if I really loved him, or if he loved me. Our love, I believed, would come later and didn't really matter at the moment.

Jack has always said that one of the main things that he had found attractive about me that first time we met was that I was born in the United States. It is true that I was physically born in this country, but, for all intents and purposes, I was actually an immigrant. My mother, Rivka, who had somehow managed to cross the Atlantic pregnant, gave birth to me in the hospital on Ellis Island barely hours after her arrival in the United States. Unfortunately, she never recovered from the strains of childbirth and passed away a few months later. My father, Ben-Zion Perlman, who was an intellectual and not much more, ended up with the sole responsibility of raising me.

Back in Lomza, the town in the *Pale of Settlement* that they had come from, my father had been recognized as a brilliant young scholar. He had expected to be the next Chief Rabbi of Lomza because the current Chief Rabbi had no sons, and it stood to reason that he, the most brilliant young scholar in the town, would marry the Rabbi's oldest daughter and succeed to the title. But the Rabbi's oldest daughter chose to marry the younger son of the Chief Rabbi of a neighboring community, and this "interloper" was then designated as the heir apparent. My grandmother, Ben-Zion's mother, in a face-saving effort, arranged for him to marry the daughter of a wealthy merchant instead.

This merchant arranged for my father and his new wife to travel to America. He expected that, in the "New World," my father would be welcomed as a scholar, and that his daughter would be an important person in the community. So, still in their early twenties, my father and his pregnant young wife set off for America. But his wife didn't survive the trip, and Ben-Zion, lacking credentials and ambition, was welcomed in America with less than open arms.

That was in 1884, when there had been a great exodus of Jews from Poland as a result of the Cossack rampages in the Jewish community, and the Lower East Side was filled with authentic and not so authentic Jewish scholars; all of whom were vying for the few legitimate teaching opportunities available. My father, although he looked the role with a full, dark beard and piercing eyes, was not sufficiently aggressive or persuasive. And so my father, the brilliant young scholar, eventually settled into life as a not very skilled shoemaker.

We lived, my father and I, along with a wet-nurse for as long as she was needed, in a railroad flat on the Lower East Side, and my father got a job as a factory worker for a fellow immigrant. Although he did not have much skill and even less ambition, he was able to support our family, pay rent, and put a little aside for my education. He never remarried.

When I was old enough, my father sent me to a Jewish religious school for girls. Although they said I was bright, I was not, as he had hoped and expected, a good student. I was a difficult, aggressive child who fought frequently with the teachers and the other immigrant children. I managed, one way or another, to make it through the eighth grade at the religious school, but then my teachers recommended that I be sent to a public high school, rather than continue my religious education.

My formal schooling ended two years later when I was suspended from high school for fighting. My father was desperate. Even though he had been working for the same company for more than a decade, he was barely making a living, and the idea of having to worry about his daughter being home all day in the slums and poverty of the Lower East Side was overwhelming. He appealed to his boss, who had an outlet store in Macy's, to do whatever he could to help me find a job.

Fortunately, this man was having an affair with the head of the millinery department, and he was able to get me a job there. I had always been good at sewing and had made most of my own clothing, so I had no difficulty qualifying for the job. Two years later, when Macy's moved uptown to Herald Square, my boss went out on her own, and took me with her.

For the first time in my life, I was doing something I liked. The same aggressive and challenging personality characteristics that had gotten me into trouble in school served me well in the business world. I had enormous energy, and I was both curious and creative. The world had opened for me.

One of our customers was a young and very beautiful movie star named Linda Henderson who was married to a famous movie director. She was about my age or maybe a few years older. I liked making her hats because she didn't seem to have any inhibitions, and I could just let my imagination go wild. She was very creative, and she used to like to sit at my workbench and make crazy and silly suggestions. In some ways, she was the closest thing I had ever had to a girlfriend. Of course, she wasn't Jewish so she never would have been my friend outside of the shop. But in the shop, and in the coffee shop across the street, we were like sisters.

"You're so talented," she said to me one day. "Why don't you go out on your own?"

"I wish I could," I replied, "but I don't have any savings, and I have to support my father."

"What if I loaned you the money? What then?"

"I couldn't afford a store in New York," I said as gratefully as I could, "but I probably could find a cheap store to rent in a nice section of Brooklyn."

"Why don't you figure out what it would cost you to run the store for one year, and I'll ask my husband to lend you the money."

And so, at the age of nineteen, I opened my own millinery shop in the trendy Williamsburg neighborhood of Brooklyn. Linda, of course, was my first customer, and she sent all her uptown friends to shop in my store.

I was young and tall and exotic looking, with high, prominent cheekbones, broad shoulders, and a thin waist. After all, I was still a teenager with a teenager's body, but Linda was an actress, and she taught me to walk and talk in a way that greatly impressed my customers. My hats were extravagant fantasies: very expensive and very exclusive. I personally designed each hat for each customer, and no two were ever alike. I did all the designing, all the sewing, and all the sales.

The year was 1906 and a new look in women's fashion was sweeping the country. The unnatural women's figures of the nineteenth century that had been pushed and pulled with bustles and corsets were replaced with a straight, natural figure. The waist was loosened, and a straight line was adopted. The frills and flounces were gone, and large hats with wide, face-shadowing brims were becoming the height of fashion. As skirts were narrowing, hats were becoming the major fashion statement. My hats were quite large, often exceeding the width of the shoulders. I built them with towering masses of flowers and feathers, and they were quite expensive and appealed mostly to the snobbiest of the well-to-do.

The talk about my shop and the kind of hats that I was creating traveled rapidly through wealthy New York society, and my shop was successful. Very successful. The fancy society ladies loved the idea of having their chauffeur bring them to my shop in Brooklyn, which they all claimed to have "discovered."

Within a year, my father and I were able to move from the slums of the Lower East Side to the front portion of a parlor-level apartment in a brownstone, right across the street from my store.

My father gave up his job in the shoe factory and began teaching adult classes in the local synagogue. He was now becoming the scholar he had always dreamed of becoming, and I got my own bedroom and a parlor.

Although I had had no time for social matters, I discovered that I had natural social skills and presence, and I focused these social skills intensely and exclusively on building my millinery business. I understood that the sale of my hats had as much to do with my personality as with my millinery skills, and that the greater and more exotic my reputation was, the more hats I would sell.

Because I did all the sales, designing, and manufacturing, I spent nearly all my waking hours in the shop. My only day off was the Sabbath, which I spent with my father. I always went back to the shop in the evening, at the end of the Sabbath, to prepare for the Sunday rush of customers.

My free time was limited to the hours I spent studying with my father. My business was growing, and, although my father encouraged me to "get out and meet people," I felt that I was riding the crest of a trend, and that this very lucrative time would not last forever. I simply did not have time to spend meeting men. But, as my father kept telling me, I was getting older, and I needed to think about getting married.

The young, fashionable women who frequented my shop often asked me about my family and my social life, who I was seeing and when I planned to settle down and raise a family. It was inconceivable to them that I could be so focused on success that I hadn't given much thought to family matters. One of my customers, a woman not much older than me, suggested that I consult with a marriage broker, which sounded like a good idea. But, when I mentioned this possibility to my father, he told me that everyone has a *bashert*—a soul mate who was chosen for them by the angels in heaven. He said it was possible for a matchmaker to suggest a good match, but only through intervention from heaven would I find my bashert.

"It doesn't have to take long for it to happen," he said. "After all, Rachel and Jacob fell in love after just one meeting."

My father urged me to at least try to meet a man, but I argued that I didn't have time, and that the courting process was slow and time consuming and usually unproductive. But he insisted.

So, reluctantly, I agreed to attend one dance: the city-wide Jewish dance that was soon to be held at the Broadway-Central Hotel. And that's where I met Jack.

I spotted him within seconds after he entered the hall, and I sized him up correctly. He was a dandy, although he wasn't comfortable in that role yet. I could tell that he was a hard worker, and, from the cocky way he walked, I guessed that had just been promoted. He seemed to be more concerned with how he looked than with actual achievement, but I got the feeling that he hoped that this community dance would open a new window of opportunity for him. He was young and Jewish and reasonably attractive, and, for some unknown reason, I immediately decided that this was my big chance.

I watched him swagger across the hall to where I was standing. He was obviously hoping that he appeared confident, although it was clear to me that he was very nervous. "May I have the next dance?" he asked with a slight bow.

I looked him straight in the eye—this was the do or die moment. "Why?" I asked.

"Because you are the most attractive woman in this place, and I would like to dance with you."

I looked at the girl nearest me and rolled my eyes.

"I'm not a very good dancer," I said.

"Neither am I," he replied with growing confidence, "but let's try."

We danced, and we talked, and we had a snack and some punch, and then we danced and talked some more, and, by the end of the evening, that first evening together, I knew.

(You might notice that this is somewhat different from the way my husband remembers it. Men always seem to picture themselves as more macho than they actually are.)

I felt that I was finally able to put the match making process behind me. I recognized that Jack would be a true partner with whom I could share my aspirations and anxieties, and I felt comfortable in his arms; not for what he was, but for what I knew he, and we, would be.

Jack had spent his entire young life doing whatever was necessary to survive and prosper in the new world, while I, who had equally great ambition, had spent my adult life until that fateful moment, building my business. We each needed a partner who shared our ambition and single mindedness. We both had come from immigrant roots, and we both had the dream of becoming authentic Americans.

We were married in the local synagogue; the reception was held in the synagogue basement with just our families present. Jack's mother, having, in her eyes, raised her only son successfully, returned to Poland within a month after we were married. Mercifully, she passed away before the Holocaust. Jack moved into my apartment, which created a tension with my father that dominated our relationship from that day on.

Mein Liebe Rivka,

Well, our daughter Rose is married. I don't know why she chose this man. He has no education and he works as a janitor in the Settlement House. He doesn't even speak Yiddish.

He has moved into our apartment with us, and now I have to sleep in the parlor because he is sleeping with Rose in the bedroom. I do not like him, and I will not make him welcome in our house. I hope he changes his mind and moves out.

Young people today are so foolish. I wish you were here to help me deal with this ignoramus.

May God protect you and bless you.

CHAPTER 4

As a result of my desire to be an authentic American, I was always very aware of the impression that I made on others, especially those who were on a higher social level. When I had decided, on that first day in America, to be a one hundred percent American, I had believed that being an American involved looking, behaving, and speaking like an American. As the assistant manager at the Henry Street Settlement House, for example, I always wore a suit and a tie to work. So based on my often repeated credo that "first impressions last," I encouraged Rose to improve the first impression that she and her shop made.

I quit my job at the Henry Street Settlement House and devoted all my time to Rose's business. I began by rebuilding the shop. After all, I had all those years of construction and maintenance experience, and, as a result of a lifetime of self-re-invention, I had a highly developed marketing sense. Although I had no retail experience, I knew that it was important that the shop itself make a good impression.

Rose's shop was a basic storefront that was not much changed from the way it had been when she had first rented it.

It had two display windows on either side of a glass entry door, a sales counter on one side toward the front of the store, and display shelves on the other walls. She had a couple of portable folding screens in the middle of the shop that separated her work area in the back of the store from the sales area in the front.

I decided to redesign Rose's store into what they called in those days, "a salon." I put tie-back drapes on the front windows, flocked wallpaper on the side walls, and built a new partition right across the middle of the store that separated the sales area in the front from Rose's work area in the back. I wanted the store to look like an elegant living room, so I furnished it with plush velvet easy chairs and a loveseat. I found a huge, ornate, gold, three-panel, Victorian-style mirror that I hung right in the middle of the back wall so that it was the first thing that customers saw when they entered the store. I hung original artwork by local artists on the other walls, and I laid a Persian rug on the floor. The shop was like a really beautiful living room with an unmistakable atmosphere of elegance. Rose did all her designing in the workroom in the back of the shop, but she kept a small, special work area in the front so that she could do some last minute "customizing" for her customers, right then and there.

She began wearing exotic clothing instead of her usual work clothes, and she had a maid serve tea to her customers, who we now referred to as clients, and who were encouraged to make appointments rather than just show up. Visiting Rose's shop became a total experience as compared with just buying a hat from some other millinery store.

Over the next few years, we continued to upgrade the shop, and the more we spent, the more the business thrived and grew. The salon exuded an aura of exclusivity and personal service. Eventually, as our sales volume increased, we expanded the salon to fill the entire shop, and we moved the workshop to a nearby vacant store where Rose had a team of young apprentices doing most of the sewing.

Although we had received many attractive offers, we resisted the temptation to sell the business or to open additional shops. We had completely redefined the millinery business, and, although many other copy-cat shops did eventually open, they didn't have Rose, and they didn't have her personality. Most of our customers considered them poor imitations, and, rather than drain our business, these competing shops only served to enhance our shop's reputation.

Rose handled the shop, and I handled our finances. Although I had no business management experience to speak of and had never held a professional job, I had learned the value of a buck the hard way, and I turned out to be a pretty astute and wily businessman. Rather than investing the profits from the salon in the rapidly rising stock market, I invested instead in real estate. I figured that Rose and I had worked too hard and too long to earn our money, and I was not about to risk it on any "get rich quick" scheme no matter how "sure" anyone told me it was.

The American economy, at that time, was growing like crazy, and I figured that as the economy improved, and the poor immigrants of the Lower East Side started to make money, they would want to move up the social ladder. Many of them, I figured, would move out of the slums of the Lower East Side and journey across the Brooklyn Bridge to Brooklyn.

So I decided to buy rental property in Brooklyn. I chose the Parkside area because it was near Prospect Park, and it was on the direct subway line from the Lower East Side. I don't know if it was because I was smart or just plain lucky, but I had gotten in on the Brooklyn housing boom just as it was starting to take off.

As demand for the apartments increased, rental prices increased as well, and because Rose and I lived so conservatively, I was able to use most of the rental income and the money from the store to buy more properties. The Parkside area was developing rapidly, and, within a couple of years, we owned many of the best buildings. Rose and I were on a roll and we never looked back.

We decided to start a family and had originally planned to have four children, but after I saw how my figure had changed with my first pregnancy, I decided not to have any more. Having children had been a wonderful dream in the abstract, but the actual fact of having them went sharply against my new self image.

Our daughter Ruthie was born on a snowy day in February, 1908. After she was born, I went into a steep depression from which I only emerged after I had fully recovered my figure. That's when I decided that, like Jack and me, Ruthie would be an only child.

As it turned out, that was a good decision because Ruthie was a difficult child, and, as she grew up, she became one of our most complex challenges. If, as Henry Wadsworth Longfellow wrote, "into each life some rain must fall," Ruthie's presence in our family might be likened to a monsoon. Nearly from birth it was apparent that she was going to be a dominant force in our lives. She had inherited my creativity, competitive spirit, and aggressive personality, and she had inherited Jack's single mindedness and rigidity. Her obviously strong personality led to constant contention and, from time to time, outright warfare.

Jack had no "father figure" to draw upon, and when Ruthie was born, he quickly discovered that being a father did not come naturally to him. He didn't remember his own father, and the substitute "uncles" that his mother had found were rarely around long enough to make a lasting impression. When Ruthie was born, he looked at her dispassionately in the hospital nursery. She was pretty, and he boasted that she was the best looking baby in the nursery. But when it came time for him to hold her, he said that he felt uncomfortable and quickly handed her back. During the time that I was in the hospital, Jack decided that since I was the artsy one, he should be the responsible parent. He felt that I had an artistic temperament, that I would be too emotional, and that he would try to counterbalance that with careful planning. He expected that I would be permissive, and so he intended to be the disciplinarian. Discipline, Jack said, would be his contribution. From the very start, even though I was still the primary breadwinner, the idea of being the "boss" of the household gave him satisfaction.

He had been correct in his expectation that my artistic temperament would be permissive, but he had not anticipated the impact that my father, Ben-Zion, would have.

Strange as it may sound, my father was the only adult in the family who had had a traditional two-parent upbringing, and who had experience raising a child. His parenting style was diametrically opposite to what Jack and I believed. Where we were either permissive or restrictive, my father was warm and inclusive, and he and Ruthie bonded instantly. Ruthie loved him and spent an inordinate amount of time with him. Over the years, their bond and the level of my father's influence on Ruthie was a constant source of jealousy and irritation to Jack. Whenever possible, Jack tried to compete with my father for Ruthie's affection, but he simply didn't have the background or the emotional core to give her the sort of paternal love that came so easily to my father.

After Ruthie's arrival, we expanded our apartment to include the first floor, which allowed us to have a separate bedroom for Ruthie and another for my father. Both Jack and I, having grown up in a railroad flat, were proud that our daughter would have her own room right from the start.

When Ruthie was old enough, I insisted that we send her to public school rather than a girl's religious school. I had had a terrible time in religious school and the memories were still painful. I reasoned that it would be better if my father took responsibility for Ruthie's Jewish education. Jack, who was already having problems competing with my father, reluctantly agreed to this decision.

My father enthusiastically welcomed this opportunity to

interact with and influence his granddaughter, and, during most afternoons, he studied with Ruthie in her room after school. He also taught adult classes at the synagogue. In the evenings when he was not teaching a class or working with Ruthie, he read and studied in his bedroom. Other than dinner, and the time he spent with Ruthie, he rarely participated in family affairs.

Mein Liebe Rivka,

Rose had a daughter—a beautiful, perfect girl. They named her Ruth after you. I cried when she was born because she is so beautiful, and because I wish that you had been here to see her.

Jack is a total fool. He does not even have any idea of how to hold a baby. I have to teach them everything. But now I have a reason to be in this family—I will take care of little Ruthie and raise her my way—I will make sure that she grows up to be a proper Jewish girl.

We have moved to a larger apartment, and now I have my own room. This is very good, expecially because I take care of Ruthie so much.

I have been teaching a little, and I study the rest of the time. My life has not been like I had expected, but now that Ruthie is here, I plan to dedicate myself to her upbringing. Even though she is a girl, I will teach her everything that a Jewish boy would learn, and I know that in heaven, you will watch over her.

May God protect and bless you.

Jack and I had been working without a break since we were teenagers, and our dedication was now paying off handsomely. The combined income from my salon and Jack's real estate investments had skyrocketed, and we were now very wealthy. There was a war going on in Europe, and the United States, which was exporting non-military supplies to both sides, was benefiting immensely. But then, in 1917, once the government instituted the draft, things changed. For one thing, women entered the workforce in great numbers. You would think that, with the increased employment of women, and with the increased availability of spending money, my business should have been booming, but instead, I sensed that things were starting to change. At first it was just a feeling, but then, as Jack pointed out when he did our year-end calculations, sales had actually declined.

Women were just not buying my very expensive hats like they had been. There had been a tremendous change in fashion, and it had a lot to do with the war. As the boys went over to Europe to fight, more and more women began going to work, and they wanted clothes like shirtwaists and tailored suits that were more appropriate for their new activities. And, even though they had the money, they were dressing less extravagantly because of appearances. Plus, most of the social events during the war had more to do with the war than with elaborate style. There just weren't the same number of really dressy social events where women would want to wear my hats.

"It all has to do with women joining the workforce, or at least giving the appearance of joining the workforce," I told Jack. "My hats are just too extravagant."

"Can't you make hats that would fit the new fashions?" he asked.

"Maybe," I said, "but I'm not sure." It wasn't really my taste, and it was not what I was known for. Besides, a lot of the clothing designers had started making hats that matched their clothing designs. It was a completely different kind of style, and I realized that even if I could make them, my customers probably wouldn't buy them from me. They would all go to the big name couture houses like Lanvin and Molyneux where they could buy complete outfits, hats and all.

But Jack wouldn't give up. That was not his style. "Why don't we start talking to some dress houses?" he asked. "Like they say," he went on, "'if you can't beat 'em, join 'em.'" He was certain, he said, that I could make cloche hats to match their clothing. They seemed so simple to him compared with what we had been making.

But to tell the truth, we didn't need the money, and I was so tired—really, really tired. We had been working ten or twelve hours a day since we got married, and God only knows how long before that. We had done really well, and we had made a lot of money, and I told him that we could be very proud of that. But, I also told him, we had nothing to show for it. We never had time for anything, and we were still crammed into that same little apartment across the street from the shop. We had never even taken a vacation, and I never had any time to play with Ruthie. I realized that I hadn't even read a book in three years.

"Enough," I said with unexpected passion. "Enough is enough!"

Jack didn't say anything for a long time. He looked so deflated that he seemed to have shrunk in the last few minutes. He had obviously stopped listening to me, and it was as if he was having a private internal conversation with himself. I hadn't meant to get so passionate, but we really had been working unreasonably long hours since our marriage, and, though we now were making real money, it had come at a great physical and emotional cost.

"Look," I said with a sigh. "You're almost forty, and we're finally comfortable, and the income from the houses is enough to sustain us. Look at yourself in the mirror; we're exhausted. I think it's time for us to cash in and retire."

I had been hoping that Jack would agree with me, but he stayed painfully silent. Minutes passed and now I was afraid that I had gone too far and was hoping that he would just respond.

"What would we do if we retire?" he finally asked. "What would I do? I have no skills, none at all."

"We could move uptown to New York like you always wanted. We could get an apartment on Central Park. You could be one of those fancy Jews you always wanted to be."

"Yes, we could probably afford a really nice apartment," Jack said glumly, "but I wouldn't fit in. They are all fancy and educated, and I'm just a snotty kid from the Lower East Side. What would I do there? No one would even talk to me." Tears welled up in his eyes. "What would I do?"

I put my arms around him. Even without my high heels I still towered over him and had to bend over. We stood there pressed against one another, clinging.

"Look," Jack finally said, "I'm not an uptown guy, I'm just a kid from the East Side, and here in Brooklyn is where I belong. Maybe someday."

"Maybe someday what?" I asked pulling back to look at him.

"Maybe someday Ruthie will marry some uptown swell," Jack said with a smile, "and then I'll have someone to talk to up there."

"From your mouth to God's ears," I laughed, and Jack laughed too.

"I have an idea, though," Jack said optimistically. "We could move to the Borough Park neighborhood in Brooklyn. It's just being developed and no one who lives there has been there for very long, so we would be newcomers just like everyone else. There's a nice *shul* there that we could join, and everyone will be on the same social level."

Jack's sudden enthusiasm was infectious, and we laughed with relief. It was going to be OK. We made a plan to look at houses in Borough Park and to talk to some developers.

The community of Borough Park, parts of which were still called by the original Dutch name, Blythebourne, had been a Dutch and English dairy farming community until the start of the twentieth-century when developers began carving it up into streets, avenues, and building lots. In the 1920s, when Jack and I started looking for a place to build our home, much of the area was still rural. It was being populated by what the uptown swells called *nouveau riche*, just like us. The streets and avenues were consecutively numbered in a formal grid. Thirteenth Avenue was the shopping street, the synagogue was on Fourteenth Avenue, and we bought a just-built house on Fifty-Fifth Street, near Fifteenth Avenue, in the most stylish part of town.

The house we chose was in the Victorian style, which was very popular at that time, with a wraparound porch on the first and second levels, and a turret style master bedroom. The first floor had a grand foyer, a parlor, a library, and a formal dining room. The second floor had four grand bedrooms, and there were maids' rooms on the third floor. I hired a top-notch decorator, and we decorated the house from top to bottom in the most formal and elegant fabrics and furniture I could find.

We sold our store to my largest competitor at a very good price. And then we, Ruthie, Jack, my father, and I moved from our cramped little apartment in Williamsburg to the house of our dreams in Borough Park.

We were young, attractive, and comfortable, and we now lived in the luxurious world of the wealthy. I fit in, very smoothly, to the upper class Jewish women's social network. Like the rest of the women there, I was a fashionable *nouveau riche* woman who wielded my wealth, power, beauty, and influence within the growing Jewish community. Jack, however, struggled to acquire a new persona. He wanted his personality to project authentic "American" affluence, but the transition was difficult. He had been a wily, shifty, sharp-eyed child of the slum. As he had matured, and especially after he and I were married, those same characteristics had been repurposed into his being a clever and tough business man. Now he sought to soften the tough aspects of his personality and to reinvent himself as an affluent, charitable, and civic-minded member of the Jewish community—a real American.

In all appearances, I was now a one hundred percent real American. But I didn't feel like a real American. When Rose had first suggested retirement and when I had agreed that we could afford this new level of luxury, I was sure that I would soon enter the ranks of the true Americans. After all, I spoke American, I dressed American, and I now owned a house like a real American. But as time went on, even at that elevated level, I became more and more certain that I wasn't a real American, at least not yet. I felt that there had to be something more, but I couldn't put my finger on it. It seemed to me to be a kind of unattainable dream; something that would always be just beyond my reach—a dream, rather than a definite reality. I was sure that there had to be something more. But I wasn't sure what.

My mother had gone back to Europe, and I had completely severed my ties with the Lower East Side immigrant community where I had grown up. I lived a life of cultured affluence, and I was now, I was certain, absolutely liberated from my immigrant history. I was now, I kept telling myself, able to associate and interact with real Americans on whatever level they chose. I expected that now, since my friends and acquaintances were all real Americans, they would accept me as if I was their peer. And, in fact, I was their peer, and they did accept me.

But even though they accepted me, I still didn't feel authentic. *If only,* I thought to myself, *if only.* But I couldn't finish the sentence because I didn't know what I was seeking. If only what?

CHAPTER 5

Although Rose had retired in the full sense of the word, I had only partially retired. I still managed our properties and our investments, which took an hour or two every morning. That left me with six empty hours. I was in my early forties and in good physical shape, and I was at a loss of what to do with all my spare time. Rose had been able to slide into retirement very easily because most of the women in the community had never worked, so they had established routines of leisure and community service activities that she could easily join. But for me, the path was much more difficult. Most of the men in the community went to work every day and played tennis or golf on the weekends. As a result, I had no one to play with during the week, and, having grown up in poverty on the Lower East Side, I had never learned to play tennis or golf, and I felt I was too old to start learning.

The only social activities that I could easily join revolved around Borough Park's two synagogues: the large and impressively domed Temple Beth-El, and the smaller and more intimate Congregation Shomrei Emunah. Although both synagogues were equidistant from our home, I gravitated toward the warmer Shomrei Emunah where services were less formal. Since it was an Orthodox synagogue, there was separate seating for men and women. I chose a seat on the left side of the Synagogue, and Rose, when she came, sat upstairs in the women's balcony on the right side. We were able to see one another, and we communicated by hand signals.

At first, I felt uncomfortable in the synagogue because I had very limited synagogue skills. I had grown up without a father and with only a little Hebrew school training, and I read the Hebrew prayers with difficulty. Although I attended synagogue every *Shabbos*, I lived in dread of being singled out to perform one of the ritual "honors." Fortunately, the sexton of the synagogue was sensitive to my fears and worked with me quietly to improve my prayer skills and help me feel more comfortable during the synagogue service. As my confidence grew, my enjoyment of the synagogue increased. I made some friends, and because I had the time, and also because of my relationship with the sexton, I started attending Friday evening services and Saturday night services in addition to the main Saturday morning service. The Rabbi and the regular members of the congregation made me feel welcome, and within a few months, I also began attending the daily morning and evening services. As my confidence grew, I became an increasingly active participant in the service.

While I was intent on being accepted in the synagogue, my father-in-law, Ben-Zion, who had been steeped in Jewish tradition from birth, led a small iconoclastic early morning service, and taught a daily class on the *Talmud* in the study hall of the synagogue. He and I avoided each other as much as possible.

I loved attending synagogue. I became a member of an inner coterie of worshipers who, along with the Rabbi and sexton, took responsibility for the day-to-day operation and management of the synagogue. For the first time in my life I felt that I was valued for myself.

Although I had developed the necessary synagogue skills, I was embarrassed about my lack of a religious education, and

I was constantly worried that my ignorance would be discovered. I was afraid to hire a teacher within the community, and I would be damned if I would ask Ben-Zion for help, so I decided to study on my own. I created a home office in the house's library, and I outfitted it with an enormous roll-top desk, leather chairs, and an impressive bookcase. To my mind, having an office with a roll-top desk and bookcases was a concrete indicator that I had "arrived." The room also had oak pocket doors which I always kept closed.

That office became my sanctuary. No one was permitted to cross the threshold without permission. I entered my office every weekday morning as soon as I returned from the synagogue, came out for lunch at precisely one o'clock in the afternoon and again for a cup of tea at three o'clock. And then, I stayed in my study until it was either time for dinner or time for me to return to the synagogue for evening services. Whenever I emerged from my office, I securely closed and locked the doors behind me. My daily routine was accepted and respected by everyone in the house.

Mostly, I wanted to learn how to perform proper Jewish rituals, and I was especially interested in their effect on family dynamics. More than the actual rules, I wanted to learn the rationale of the behavior that was required for a traditional Jewish lifestyle. Remember, I had no father to teach me, and my mother was far from being a scholar. Although I had attended a Jewish after school program until my *bar mitzvah,* I had learned very little. And because I had no father, I had had minimal personal connection with Jewish tradition. My mother, whose family had not been particularly religious in Poland, was more concerned with survival than with Jewish tradition. Now I was trying to catch up.

During the hours that I secluded myself in my office, I managed our properties and investments for an hour or two in the morning, and then I studied Jewish subjects for the rest of the day. This study was not easy for me because I had no background to measure it against, so I was literally starting from square one. Unfortunately, most of the books at square one were written on a juvenile level, so I was forced to go directly to the sources. This was, to put it mildly, torture. But it was also, in the final analysis, rewarding, because the material had not been filtered through an author. I labored over an English translation of the *Torah*, then I read an English translation of the *Mishnah*, and then some sections of the *Talmud*. Finally, I read an English translation of excerpts from the writings of Maimonides. The English was often oblique and obscure, and I struggled to make progress, rereading some passages over and over until their meaning became clear to me. I felt confident, though, that once I had acquired even some minimal knowledge, I would be able to participate more intelligently in discussions in the synagogue.

Because I wasn't always familiar with the authors or their sources, I also read whatever background information and commentaries that I could find on all of the books that I had been studying. I didn't understand everything, but I reassured myself that after I had achieved a deep enough general background I could go back to the books and reread them.

I was especially interested in learning about Jewish traditions and ritual, of which I had very limited knowledge. My mother had selectively followed as much of the Jewish ritual as she could remember from her youth in Europe, but she had never explained its meaning except to provide a never-ending list of things that I was not permitted to do. Now I had an opportunity to learn the rationale and history of Jewish ritual, as well as the proper ways of observing it. As my knowledge increased, I insisted on the incorporation of traditional ritual into our family's daily life, and pretty soon we became a thoroughly observant Jewish family.

My studies took two distinct routes. On one hand, I was learning basic information about Jewish history and ritual—the sort of information that most of my contemporaries in the synagogue knew from their childhood schooling and upbringing. And on the other hand, I was learning about Judaism's place in history and especially its influence on, and response to, modern *mores*. This interested me enormously. I was impressed by the idea of Jews having been selected by God as the "chosen people," even though this "chosenness" had resulted in their frequent persecution. This separation and persecution, I believed, had brought about Jewish compassion for the sufferings of others, along with Jewish philanthropy, chastity, and faith. The more I read, the prouder I became of Judaism in general, and of Jewish Orthodoxy in particular.

I now felt confident enough to express my own opinions on a variety of religious subjects, and I eagerly sought opportunities to demonstrate my newly-acquired knowledge in order to shore up my credentials as an educated member of the congregation and the community.

My knowledge and my dedication to the physical well-being of the synagogue, not to mention my financial openhand-edness, helped me to quickly move up the Jewish social ladder, and, in a relatively short time, I was made a vice-president of the synagogue. This position carried with it substantial prestige both within the synagogue and within the larger Jewish community. In Borough Park, in those years, the presidents and vice-presidents of the various synagogues wore a top hat and morning coat at Sabbath morning services. I loved to slowly walk the streets of Borough Park every Saturday morning in my high hat and tails, greeting my neighbors on my way to services.

I assumed an imperious attitude in the house as well, which set me somewhat apart from the rest of the family. At dinner, I sat at the head of the table and insisted that no conversation be held until I said the blessing over the bread. This superior attitude, I felt, enabled me to counter Ben-Zion's growing influence over Ruthie.

Unfortunately, although Ben-Zion always accepted my decisions on family matters, this deference only added to my insecurity, and the tension between us was palpable. When we had first moved to Borough Park, Ben-Zion had been invited to apply for a full-time teaching job in the local *yeshiva*. But teaching in the yeshiva required certification, and Ben-Zion believed that he had sufficient knowledge to teach in the yeshiva, but resented what he perceived as an implied slight by the requirement for certification. He chose, instead, to teach a free, daily adult *Talmud* class in the synagogue. Since he didn't have to worry about his financial security, he spent most of his time studying in the synagogue or at home by himself.

I have to admit that Ben-Zion had two sterling qualities: he was a brilliant Jewish scholar, and he was, for the most part, a positive influence in Ruthie's upbringing. But he was also an intentionally troublesome presence in our household, and this disruptiveness had begun the moment that Rose and I were married.

In the beginning, it was just the usual competition between a father and a husband for the love of a daughter or wife. After all, Rose was Ben-Zion's only child and his only connection to his late wife. His resentment and jealousy of my relationship with Rose, although it was immature, was understandable. It is also easy to understand our competition for the love of Ruthie, the only child in the family. What is more difficult to understand, was our vitriolic and, as it turned out, nearly fatal personal animosity.

From the start, we were in a highly volatile situation: Ben-Zion was a meddling, non-contributing permanent guest in our home, and I resented his presence enormously. I seized every opportunity to make him feel uncomfortable and unwelcome in the hope that he would voluntarily move out. But he had almost no domestic skills and no viable source of income. And so, as Rose often pointed out, we had a responsibility to shelter him because he could never afford to live on his own. Plus, he was a recognized scholar in our Jewish community, and his presence was welcomed with pride. It was therefore socially unacceptable for me to force him out or to even confront him in public.

The fact is that Ben-Zion really was a misplaced scholar. Had he remained in Poland, he would have been highly respected locally and perhaps even nationally for his monumental knowledge. But in Brooklyn, in our house, he was just the father-in-law of someone he considered to be an ignoramus.

So, in order to punish me for the way I treated him, he struck at what he assumed was my greatest vulnerability: my refusal to speak Yiddish. From the minute I moved in with them, he only spoke Yiddish, hoping to force me, who had sworn to only speak American, to speak Yiddish with him. He also filled Ruthie with traditional European Jewish folk tales, which, in my mind, were "Old World *bubbe-meises*" and were definitely not American.

I was sure that over the years that he had lived in the United States he must have, out of necessity, learned to speak English. But all the while in our house, he continued to choose to speak only Yiddish and to pretend not to understand us when we spoke English. This artificial obstinacy created perpetual tension. It was as if a wall had been erected through the house with Ben-Zion on one side, and me on the other—with Rose and Ruth who were, of necessity, bilingual, shuttling back and forth across the border.

To the outside world, our household was a model of peaceful generational transition. Inside, it was as if the Civil War's Battle of Gettysburg was being fought every day.

CHAPTER 6

For me, the move to Borough Park was transformational. It meant a break with my past and an unclear idea of the future without any sort of a support system. In Williamsburg, where I was born, the streets were familiar, and the noise of the trolley car was familiar, and my friends were familiar, and I walked to school every day. Now, I would be attending New Utrecht High School along with more than 3,600 other teenagers, and I would have to travel on the elevated train to get there.

In Williamsburg, although my parents were not always around, the store was located directly across the street from where we lived—I felt reassured that my parents were nearby, but I also enjoyed the feeling of being alone when I wanted to be. Now, even though my parents were present all the time, they seemed much less accessible because of their social engagements. Of course, as teenagers often do, I rejected my parents' new social values, and I considered myself a rebellious bohemian.

My mother, however, had a different image of how the daughter of a socially prominent Jewish family should look and behave. She carefully supervised my wardrobe; unless my skirts were more than two inches below my knees, they were strictly prohibited. My mother carefully inspected me every morning on my way out the door, and her rulings were absolute—no negotiations were tolerated.

But the rebelliousness of teenage girls cannot be denied, and, if suppressed in one direction, it often breaks through in another, usually unexpected, direction. In my case, I made my defiant stand at the local library.

The Borough Park Public Library was located in two adjacent store fronts on Thirteenth Avenue, the main shopping street. The store on the left contained the adult section, and the store on the right contained the children's and teens' sections. The librarians' desk was in the center, between the two store fronts. Adults were issued white library cards, teens, green cards, and children, yellow cards. The age limitations were: children, seven to eleven years of age, teens, twelve to seventeen, and adults, eighteen and older. Under certain circumstances, a child might be permitted to take out a book from the teen section, but a teen was never permitted to take out an adult book. These restrictions were aggressively enforced by the librarians. There was also a gated area in the corner of the adult section for books like *Candide*, *The Canterbury Tales*, and *Fanny Hill*, which were especially restricted. This section required a special key that had to be obtained from the librarian.

I was a voracious reader and by the time my family and I moved to Borough Park, I had read all of the books that were in the children's section, and nearly all of the books in the teen section. So I asked the librarian for permission to take books out of the adult section. This permission was instantly and firmly denied.

"What is your name?" she asked.

"Ruthie Rubin."

"How old are you?" she continued.

"Thirteen," I replied.

"I'm sorry young lady," she said with a snooty look, "the adult section is restricted to people over eighteen. You are very far from that age. I'm sure you can find a nice book in the teen section."

"But I've read all the books in the teen section." I said quietly.

"I'm sure that is an exaggeration," she said, obviously annoyed. "I would be glad to help you find a book that you haven't read."

I sensed that even though the words were polite, the librarian's tone was hostile, but I dutifully went along with her and told her what each of the books that she pulled from the shelf were about.

"Have you read the books in the boy's section?" the librarian asked.

"Yes, ma'am," I replied, "at least the ones that weren't about sports. I'm not really interested in sports."

"Then I think you should go back and reread some of the books you liked the most," she said, walking back to her desk.

"But that would be a waste of time since I already read them," I said right behind her. "Can't I just go into the adult section and read one book at a time?"

The librarian spun around and looked sternly at me. "Absolutely not," she said with finality, and she went back to her place behind the desk.

This, to my teenager's mind, was a declaration of war, and I was ready for battle.

I followed her and stood at the desk waiting for her to look up so I could continue to press my case, but she didn't, so I went into the adult section.

I looked around for a minute or two, and then I took a book down from the shelf. But before I had a chance to open it, I felt a strong hand on my arm. This time, it was a policeman.

"I'm sorry miss," the policeman said, "but I have to ask you to leave the library."

And with that, he forcefully pulled and dragged me out onto the street.

"Rules are rules," the policeman said when we were outside.

"And you people have got to obey them just like everyone else."

<hr />

The following day, and every day for the next three days, I went directly into the adult section of the library, only to be evicted by the same policeman. I never mentioned this confrontation to my parents. This, I felt, was my private battle, and I intended to win it.

On the fourth day, I walked into the adult section, quickly selected a book and sat down on the floor to read it. When the policeman arrived he asked me to stand up and I refused. The policeman stood over me menacingly, but I continued to sit on the floor reading my book.

Soon, two other policemen arrived. They stood in a circle looking down at me while I kept my nose in the book as if I were totally engrossed. I did not look up when they spoke to me and eventually, after an animated discussion, the three policemen left. I remained seated on the floor, reading my book for the next hour, after which I stood up, put the book back on the shelf, smoothed my skirt, and left. I repeated this disobedience every day until the head librarian came over and sat down on the floor next to me.

"You're an obstinate young woman," she said, "and you're getting to be a real pain in my neck, but I admire your courage. I'll tell you what I'm going to do. I will make a list of books from the adult section that I think would be appropriate for you, and you can select one book at a time to take home and read. When you finish that book, I'll give you another. When you finish all the books on the list, I'll make a new list. But I do not want you coming into the adult section—it sets a bad example. You will come directly to me at the desk, and I'll give you the books. Will you agree to that?"

I instinctively knew that it would be a mistake to smile in victory, so I just nodded yes, and stood up, and for the next four years the head librarian and I traded books. I would return the book I had read, and the librarian handed me the next book on the list. We never discussed the books, although I'm sure the librarian labored long and hard over the preparation of the ongoing list.

In 1920, when I entered high school, the US was still adjusting to the sudden drop in economic activity following the end of the war. Over two-million soldiers had returned from Europe, and they wanted their old jobs back, but there were new workers in those positions, and they didn't want to quit. Chaos took over much of the country. There had been major strikes in the meatpacking and steel industries, and large-scale race riots in Chicago and other cities. Anarchist attacks on Wall Street produced fears of radicals and terrorists. By the end of the year, two years after the end of the war, the economy had started to grow, though it still had not completely shifted from wartime to peacetime footing.

The election that year was the first in which women had the right to vote in all forty-eight states. There was new and revolutionary thinking in almost every sphere of human activity. The national feeling of relief that had swept the country at the end of the Great War had dipped but was now about to evolve into unbridled optimism. The stock market was poised to soar, and despite the strife, there was a growing sense of confidence in the country. The restraints of Victorian morality that had dominated the country for the previous century had been relaxed, and as women entered the workforce and earned the right to vote, fashion trends became more accessible, masculine, and practical.

Many women believed that since they were now the political equals of men, they now had the right to pursue more personal freedoms. They began engaging publicly in typical "male" activities like smoking and drinking (which was still ostensibly prohibited). They worked toward attaining sexual freedom by trying to combat the historic double-standard, which treated men who had taken many lovers as healthy, but women who had many as evil or flawed.

Skirt hemlines rose and were less constraining of women's movements. For the first time in centuries, a woman's natural body shape was now exposed as dresses became more fitted and revealing, and the constrictive corset, which had been an essential undergarment to make the waist thinner and the breasts and hips more pronounced, became a thing of the past. A more masculine look became popular—including shirtwaist dresses, short hairstyles, flat breasts, and natural hips. "Bobbed" hair and exposed legs became the new symbol of freedom.

Although society matrons of a certain age continued to wear conservative dresses, the most impressive social trend of the "Roaring Twenties" was undoubtedly "the flapper." Flappers were a "new breed" of young women who wore short skirts, bobbed their hair, listened to jazz, and flaunted their disdain for what was then considered acceptable behavior. Flappers were seen as brash for wearing excessive makeup, drinking, smoking, driving automobiles, treating sex in a casual manner, and otherwise flouting social and sexual norms.

This new freedom spilled over into the world of art and home décor, where surrealism and art deco forced a transition from the lush, curvilinear abstractions of Victoriana and art nouveau decoration to more mechanized, smooth, and geometric forms.

Jazz became the most popular music in America, and orchestras led by Fletcher Henderson, Paul Whiteman, and Duke Ellington, among others, played in the most fashionable cafes and concert halls.

To me, it was as if sex had just been invented. There was a freedom in the air that boasted new colors, new styles, new music, and new literature, and as an adventurous, post-pubescent girl, I was not about to miss any of it. My friends from the neighborhood were too timid, so I sought out new, more adventurous friends, but my parents were cautiously restrictive about whom I spent my free time with. I was bright and breezed through my schoolwork. I read constantly, insatiably, and I was bored . . . all the time.

Sundays were especially painful for me. My parents tried to schedule appropriate outings for the family, but they were always too juvenile or too old-fashioned. They were reluctant to leave me alone at home, but when they dragged me along, I hated it. So they encouraged me to take along a book to read, which was what I enjoyed most. And so, at nearly every outing, while the rest of the group would participate in an activity, I would sit by myself and read. In all fairness, my mother did try to find activities that would interest me, but, as a rule, whatever we did as a family, I hated.

I thought of myself as a "liberated" woman. I yearned to live a liberated, bohemian life, and I felt trapped in the stifling Jewish "upper" (as my mother frequently reminded me) class. I wanted to go to jazz concerts, art openings, "meet-the-authors" cocktail parties, and poetry readings. But I was only permitted the vicarious experience of reading about them in the gossip pages. I longed to sit in some exotic, little-known downtown coffee shop or café and absorb the atmosphere, but my parents kept reminding me that I was just a child—and a Jewish child at that—and that proper Jewish children did not hang around in cafes.

I *hated* being a proper Jewish child, but what could I do?

Consequently, my bohemian experiences were all second-hand. I read about them in the gossip columns of the news-papers and magazines, but I was not permitted to go to any of them, and I bitterly fought the restrictions. I devoured the art section of the newspaper, studied every literary magazine, and read every avant-garde book as soon as I could get my hands on it. I yearned to be an adult and free of restrictions, but all I ever heard from my parents was a long list of things that proper Jewish girls didn't do. I didn't want to be a proper Jewish girl, but I had no choice.

In those years, at the start of the Roaring Twenties, New York City was alive with stimulation and a pretty, young girl could get anything she wanted—I was a pretty, young girl, and I wanted to breathe and taste and hear and experience everything. I hated my parents' Victorian house with its formal rooms and its dark furniture and drapes. I wanted to *live*.

As if it was a source of life giving oxygen, I read. In fact, all of my experiences, social, intellectual, sexual, and emotional came through my reading. I was a fast and insatiable reader, and I read an eclectic variety of material ranging from the literary masterpieces that I got from the library, to the pulp magazines which I bought on a daily basis on my way home from school.

I had one reliable ally in the family: my grandfather, Ben-Zion. And we had one common enemy: my father. In the same way that I felt restricted by my situation, my grandfather resented everything about his state of affairs. He was, he felt, an underappreciated scholar—underappreciated both in the community and at home. He, too, hated the opulence of my mother's home; he felt confined and denigrated, and he felt helpless in the face of my parents' juggernaut of social achievement. We recognized in each other a kindred spirit: we were both stifled by my parents' social ambition.

As a result, my grandfather and I spent a disproportionate amount time together. He was my favorite teacher, and I was his best student. I got all of my Jewish education from him. He taught me to read Hebrew and Yiddish, and I read the *Torah* and the Prophets with him in the original Hebrew. His method of teaching was to tell me stories about how the great Rabbis of the *Talmud* and the *Diaspora* debated the laws, and he practiced debating with me. I learned Jewish history and philosophy and religion in the form of stories. And through the stories that my grandfather taught me, I absorbed, rather than merely understood, the rationale and beauty of Judaism and the history and logic of its rules and customs.

Slowly, timidly at first, but with the enthusiastic encouragement of my grandfather, I began to make up my own stories. I enjoyed this very much, and I discovered that I was quite good at channeling my imagination into literary creativity. Eventually, under my grandfather's urging, I started to write these stories down. I told my stories to my grandfather in Yiddish, but I wrote them in English. Eventually, in addition to the Jewish subjects that my grandfather had encouraged me to write about, I began to write stories that were similar to the stories that I read in the pulp magazines that I avidly devoured. I had a fertile imagination and a rich fantasy life, and I wrote freely and well. My stories were always about some sort of threat to a young girl and about heroes arriving just in time to save the "damsel in distress." There was a lot of implied sex, a lot of fainting, and a lot of intrigue. My stories weren't very creative, but I had a certain amount of skill and a large amount of pent up sexual energy. Although he was not aware of the content, my grandfather encouraged my creativity. Perhaps he recognized my abilities, or perhaps he derived perverse pleasure from encouraging my father's "perfect" daughter to do something that was outside the accepted norm—something that he suspected my father would not approve of.

I loved writing. It was my fantasy world. The stories poured out of me like water from the tap. There were dozens of them—each one a little better than its predecessor—and my grandfather encouraged me tirelessly.

The stories came easily to me, and I was proud of them. Writing them was, in my mind, my first real accomplishment, my first really independent activity, my first rebellion. In the privacy of my room and in my discussions with my grandfather, I thought of myself as a bohemian—a free thinker. My grandfather told me that I could be like Alma Mahler who wrote her own music and was married to the great Jewish composer Gustav Mahler, or Fanny Mendelssohn, who was a great female Jewish composer and pianist and was the sister of Felix Mendelssohn. I, however, dreamed of being like the society author, Zelda Fitzgerald, who was the darling of all the gossip magazines. In my fantasies, I was a famous author with a secret identity. Someday, the world would discover my treasured talent. Someday—who knows?

"What's the point of writing stories if no one reads them?" my grandfather asked me one day. "You don't even read them to me!"

"They're not the sort of stories you would like. Besides, who could I show them to?"

"How about those magazines that you're always reading? The ones you hide when I come into your room? See if there is a way to submit stories to them."

Blushing and embarrassed, I took one of the magazines out of my desk drawer and looked through it to see if there was an address for inexperienced writers to send stories. And there it was, on the back page just inside the cover: "Have a good story to tell?" it read. "Send it to our editors, and if it is published we'll send you five dollars!" There was an address to send the stories and a special form to fill out. So I sent what I thought were the best of my stories to the magazine. They published one! And they sent me five dollars!

And then I sent more stories to different magazines, and they, too, published some. And suddenly, I, Ruthie Rubin, was an author. Wisely, I had submitted all my stories under the pen name Zelda Mahler and no one ever suspected that I might be the actual author.

My stories became my life, my escape. Every day after school, I would sit at my typewriter writing and editing and rewriting and pretending and dreaming that I was a great writer.

When I wrote I was Ruthie Rubin, but I dreamed I was Zelda Mahler. In my mind I was sophisticated, suave, and urbane. I was Zelda Mahler, the famous writer wearing her cloche hat with her long cigarette holder, and her slinky dress. Zelda Mahler. People stopped at her table in the Algonquin Club just to be seen with her. Zelda Mahler, daring, risqué, and so sophisticated.

I told my grandfather that I had sold some stories, but I never showed any of them to him. They were just not appropriate.

By the time I was fifteen years old, and a high school sophomore, I, or rather Zelda Mahler, had sold seven stories. And, in return for an exclusivity agreement and with the encouragement of my grandfather, I was listed on one magazine's masthead as a contributing editor. I was now getting paid ten dollars for every story!

Of course, my parents had no idea what I was doing. It was a deep, dark secret between my grandfather and me, but I was too young and naïve, and my grandfather was too sheltered and traditional, to have anticipated the consequences.

CHAPTER 7

The maid tapped lightly on the library door. "There's a Mr. Jacobson on the phone for you, Mr. Rubin," she said through the closed door.

I opened the door a crack. "I don't know any Jacobson," I said. "Did he say what he wants?"

"He asked to speak to Miss Ruthie, but I told him that she was in school, so he asked to speak to you."

"Did he say what it was about?"

"No, sir."

I slid the door closed and went to my desk and picked up the phone.

"This is Jack Rubin," I said in my most officious tone into the phone. "How can I help you?"

"My name is Jacobson. Herman Jacobson," the man answered. "I am the publisher of a number of magazines. Among them is a magazine called *The Love Book*."

"Why are you telling me this?" I interrupted irritably.

"I'm sorry, I thought you would know."

"Know what?" I asked, suddenly worried.

"Mr. Rubin, is Ruth Rubin your daughter?"

"Yes," I said. "Did something happen to her?"

"No, sir, at least nothing bad," he said quickly. "Please hear me out, and then I'm sure you'll understand the purpose of my call. As I was saying, I publish a magazine called *The Love Book*. You probably are not familiar with it, so I will tell you that it is a book of short stories that appeal to young women. One of our most popular authors is a woman named Zelda Mahler, and she lives at your address."

"There's no one here by that name," I snapped.

"Yes, I realize that. Please let me go on. Zelda Mahler has been writing stories for us for about a year. We send her a check for each story that we publish. Because she is so popular, we would like to offer her a long term contract. I realized that Zelda Mahler is a pen name, and so I looked at the way she endorsed her checks, and I saw the name Ruth Rubin. I believe that Ruth Rubin must be your daughter."

I sat for a moment, shocked. "Yes," I finally managed to say. "Ruth Rubin is my daughter, but she is not a writer, she is a fifteen-year-old high school girl."

"That surprises me," Mr. Jacobson said. "Her stories are well-written and quite sophisticated. I thought that she was at least in her twenties. But it doesn't matter. I still would like to offer her a contract. Would you please ask her to call me when she gets home from school? I would like to speak with her."

I ended the conversation and stared at the phone, amazed. *Ruthie, a writer, stories? And didn't he say that the name of the magazine was* The Love Book? *What kind of magazine could that be?* I didn't doubt that what Mr. Jacobson said was true, what I felt bad about was that I didn't know that Ruthie had been writing stories. *Wouldn't she have told me about them; especially if they had been published and she was getting paid for them?* It was true that I wasn't especially close with Ruthie, but still, I was her father, and I should have been aware of what she was doing.

She spent so much time by herself in her room and so much time with Ben-Zion. "He probably had something to do with it," I said aloud. Then I thought, *It was an English language magazine, and Ben-Zion doesn't read anything in English. Maybe she did it in school or in the library—she spends a lot of time in the library. Mr. Jacobson said that she had written many stories. When could she have done that? At least he said that they were good stories.*

I had not paid attention when Mr. Jacobson said the name of the magazine and now I wasn't sure that I had gotten the name right. *What kind of a name could that be for a magazine? I must have misheard. Maybe,* I thought, *it had something to do with a school project.* But then I thought that it couldn't have been because Ruthie would have shown it to me if it was for school. She always boasted about how well she was doing in school. I read a lot of books, but I didn't waste my time on magazines. Magazines were too light and full of nonsense. I kept wondering what sort of a magazine Mr. Jacobson was talking about. Maybe it was some sort of news magazine. Even though Rose subscribed to a whole bunch of news magazines, I never read them because I believed that they were just for lazy people who don't read the newspaper. If you want to get the news you read the newspaper. That's why it's called the newspaper. If you want to learn stuff, you read books. Period. Magazines are for people who don't know how to think.

But, I thought to myself, *he said that she had written many stories and that he had paid her by check.* I knew that she had her own savings account at the bank, but I didn't think that she ever went there. And besides, I always went with her to the bank. But obviously, she must have been going there by herself, without me. *Why didn't they say something at the bank? She was only a teenager. Why didn't they tell me that my daughter was depositing checks at the bank?*

Why would they?

I could feel anger and frustration building inside me. I took out a cigar and bit off the end and spat it into the waste can. I leaned back in my chair and carefully lit the cigar and puffed deeply on it. It didn't make me feel any better.

I sat there exploring my options, but I felt bewildered, unsure of what to do. At first I thought that I should talk to

Rose about this but that would be avoiding responsibility. This was my problem, plain and simple. I decided that I would have a talk with Ruthie, ask her about it, look at what she wrote, and compliment her on it. *But why,* I wondered, *had she hidden it from me? There was something wrong. Very wrong.*

Somewhere, deep inside me, that same old familiar feeling was bubbling. I knew what it was, and I tried to suppress it. But I knew it was there. *This would never happen in the home of an authentic American.* Irrational, but, nevertheless, it was there, and it felt uncomfortable. Once again I felt like a foreigner. It was them against me, and I was still the outsider. Even in my own home.

I would just have to wait.

———————

When I came home, my father stopped me on my way to my room and led me into his office. He seated himself in his oak office chair, tilted it back, and motioned to me to sit in the side chair. This, in itself, was unusual, and I was uncomfortable and suspicious. I had surreptitiously peeked into the room many times in the past, but I had never sat in it.

"I received a call today," my father began in his self-important voice, "from a man named Jacobson. Herman Jacobson." At this point my father picked up a paper from his desk and studied it for a long time.

I had no idea who this Herman Jacobson was or why my father was being so obnoxious.

"This Mr. Jacobson," my father went on, "said he wanted to speak to Zelda Mahler, the writer." I caught my breath, and my heart stopped beating. My father was speaking so slowly.

"I told him," he said, intently watching my face, "that there was no one here by that name, and that there are no writers here, but he insisted. We had a long talk during which he told me that Zelda Mahler was obviously a pen name and that he suspected that it might be you."

He leaned back in his chair and took time to relight his cigar. Only then, after the cigar lighting ritual had ended, did he focus his attention, once again, on me.

"So?" he asked with a faint smile.

I didn't know what to say, to deny it would be a lie and besides, they would find out eventually, so I admitted it hoping that it would end there. But just as I had feared, my father asked to see the magazine and to show him some of my stories. He said he was so proud that his daughter was an author, and he wanted to show the stories off to his friends. But he sounded belligerent and a little angry.

"You wouldn't like them," I said quietly, "and besides, they're not very good."

"Don't be so modest," he said with a strange smile. "They must be good if they were published in a magazine. Go on, get one. I want to read it and show it to your mother and to my friends."

I knew that if he ever read any of my stories with all the sex that was in them, he would get very angry. But what could I do? He was my father, and I had to obey.

Reluctantly, I went into my room and got one of the magazines that had published my stories out of my desk. Even to this day I remember the cover. It showed a woman, with long blond hair, tied to a tree, her dress torn with one strap falling over her shoulder, her breast nearly exposed, with terror in her eyes. In the lower left hand corner of the cover, in big bold letters was written: "Zelda Mahler's Latest Story."

My father never read the story. He glanced at the cover and handed the magazine back to me, obviously shocked and embarrassed. He was quiet for a very long time, and I was prepared for the expected storm to break. But instead, he sat back down at his desk and motioned for me to sit back down in the chair.

He sat there, chewing on a nail, staring off into the distance. Quietly, sadly, and without looking at me, he said, more to himself it seemed than to me, "It's a new world, this America, and I still don't know how to live in it. Is this normal? Is this what modern times are all about? I wish I knew. I wish I knew."

I didn't know what to say. He spoke so softly that I wasn't even sure that he was talking to me so I just sat there foolishly, waiting to be excused.

Finally, he looked up at me. "Ruthie," he said quietly, "I have not been a proper father for you. I work too much. How could this be? My daughter writing trash like this! I feel so terrible. I work too many hours. I don't spend enough time with you. I don't watch you; I don't tell you what to do. I have not been a proper father. Now I have to make a change. Now I must be a father. Now I have to take control. Ruthie, from this time on, I will be your father. I will make a change right now. This will not go on."

He stood in front of me, staring down. I had never seen him so angry. "I cannot have my daughter writing such stories in my house!' he shouted. "Is this what they teach you in school? Is this why I work so hard to give you everything you want?

"Don't you worry," he snarled, now only inches from my face, "I will tell your Mr. Jacobson a thing or two. Paying a young, innocent girl to do this? What kind of a man is he? Are there no longer morals in this world? Modern times, HA!

"And you, Ruthie," he continued as he ripped off his glasses, "you will never write another story. NEVER! You will study and learn a skill and get a job and be someone, but you will not write another story! Not good stories, not bad stories, not any stories. I will watch you very closely. Listen to me, Ruthie. You will not write any more stories. Promise me that!"

I sat silently, cowering, not sure what to say. "Promise me!" he shouted, slamming his hand on his desk.

"I promise," I said meekly.

"What?" he shouted, "I didn't hear you. What do you promise?"

"I promise I won't write any more stories."

"Now go to your room!"

I sat at my desk shaking, my heart pounding rapidly. I had never spoken to Ruthie like that. I had lost control. They had told me when she was born and I was so frightened, that being a father would come naturally. But it hadn't been natural for me. Was I justified? Had I been too harsh? I was her father, after all, and a father must speak up when it is necessary.

But how could I know how a father should behave when I had no father to learn from? My father had disappeared. Disappeared. I don't even remember him. Nothing. And my mother? She had hardly been able to keep her head above water. She certainly had never spoken to me like that; she had never prohibited me from doing anything. And believe me, I did many things that I'm sure were not acceptable to her.

"A father," I said out loud to myself. "A father. Everyone had a father. Everyone! But not me."

Sure, there had been Judge Heimlich—he was the closest thing I ever had to a father, but he wasn't my father, and it's not the same thing.

I sat there for some time thinking about how Judge Heimlich had saved me. *What was that all about?* I wondered. *Why had the judge been so nice? Why had he saved my ass? And, more to the point, what's my end of the deal?*

The judge had told me that first day, "Don't fuck up, you might not get a second chance." But I had fucked up, lots of times, and I had always gotten a second chance and sometimes even a third.

"This is America," I said to myself, "getting a second chance is what it's all about.

"Second chances," I snarled at myself, "the judge gave me a second chance, but I didn't give Ruthie a second chance.

"I gave her everything a girl could want," I said aloud to the empty room. "A nice home, a warm bed, beautiful clothing, whatever she wanted I gave her—I never said no to anything. And yet, when push came to shove, when it really mattered, I didn't give her a second chance."

The gnawing insecurity that had been a part of my life for so long, and that I had been able to bury somewhere deep in my unconscious, returned. I had thought—hoped—that it was gone, that I was finally free of it, but now it was back. I knew who I wanted to be, but I wasn't sure who I was. Once again, one step forward, two steps back.

I had done the wrong thing: acted impulsively. Now I would have to find a way to undo the damage. "Don't fuck up," the judge had said.

But I had.

CHAPTER 8

My grandfather was waiting for me in the hallway as I ran to my bedroom.

"Not now, *Zayde*," I said through my tears, "leave me alone."

"You remember what Hillel said?" he asked as he caught me by the arm. "'If not now, when?'"

I tried to spin out of his grasp, but he was holding me tight—forcefully, perhaps too forcefully—it hurt. Reluctantly, I followed him into his room.

"Sit," he commanded.

I sat, tentatively, on the edge of the chair that I had sat on so many times, listening to my grandfather's stories. This time it didn't feel the same. I was no longer a child; my father had taken care of that with his punishment. My fantasies were gone. Instantly. But now I sensed a new urgency in my grandfather's voice. He must have heard what my father had said.

He went to his usual chair, took off his glasses, cleaned them, and squinted through them at me. "I want to tell you about Rabbi Nachman of Bratislava," he began. "He was the grandson, you know, of the *Baal Shem Tov*, the founder of *Chasidism*."

I sighed a sad, lonely sigh. "I'm very upset now, *Zayde*," I said, hoping he'd understand, "I can't talk or even listen. My father said that I am not allowed to write any more stories, and, if I don't write my stories, I will just go crazy!"

"Yes, I heard," he said gravely. "That is both unfortunate and unfair, but you are his daughter, and you must obey. That's why what I am about to tell you about Rabbi Nachman is so important. So take a deep breath, wipe your eyes, and listen."

"Rabbi Nachman of Bratislava," he continued, "preached a religious philosophy called *Hisbodedus* which encouraged people to speak to God in normal conversation. He said that you could speak with God in an intimate, informal manner as you would with a best friend, and that you should do it while you're in a private setting like a closed room.

"The thing about hisbodedus, is that you can pour out your heart to God in your own language, in your own words. You can tell Him all your thoughts, feelings, problems, and frustrations. Nothing, according to Rabbi Nachman, is too mundane or unacceptable for discussion, so you, Ruthie, can definitely tell God about your stories, and you don't have to promise anything in return. And if you are angry, you can use Rabbi Nachman's silent scream. You shout loudly in a 'small, still voice.' Anyone can do this. Just imagine the sound of such a scream in your mind. Depict the shout in your imagination exactly as it would sound. Keep this up until you are literally screaming with this soundless 'small, still voice.' This is actually a scream and not mere imagination. Rabbi Nachman said that just as your lungs bring the sound to your lips, your emotions bring it to the brain. When you do this, you are actually shouting inside your brain.

"So now, right here, while you feel so strongly about your situation, you should talk to God. Shout, scream, curse, whatever you need to do. I'm going to go for my walk before dinner. You sit here and talk to God."

"But I feel stupid talking to God," I replied.

"You know, that's exactly what Rabbi Nachman's students said too, so he told them a story."

Ruthie smiled to herself in spite of her sadness. With her grandfather, there was always a story.

"Once there was a prince who imagined that he was a turkey. He undressed, sat naked under the table, and refused all food, allowing nothing to pass his lips except a few oats. His father, the king, brought all the physicians to cure him, but they were of no use.

"Finally, a wise man came to the king and said, 'I pledge to cure him.' The wise man promptly proceeded to undress and sat under the table next to the prince, pecking at oats, which he gobbled up. The prince asked him, 'Who are you and what are you doing here?' The wise man said, 'Who are YOU and what are YOU doing here?' The prince replied, 'I am a turkey.' To which the wise man responded, 'I am a turkey, too.' So the two turkeys sat together until they became accustomed to one another.

"Seeing this, the wise man signaled to the king to fetch him a shirt. Putting on the shirt, he said to the prince, 'Do you really think that a turkey may not wear a shirt? Indeed, he may, and that does not make him any less of a turkey.' The prince was much taken by these words and also agreed to wear a shirt. At length, the wise man signaled to be brought a pair of trousers. Putting them on, he said to the prince, 'Do you really think that a turkey is forbidden to wear trousers? Even with his trousers on, he is perfectly capable of being a proper turkey.' The prince acknowledged this as well, and he too put on a pair of trousers, and it was not long before he had put on the rest of his clothes at the wise man's direction.

"Following this, the wise man asked to be served human food from the table. He took and ate, and said to the prince, 'Do you really think that a turkey is forbidden to eat good food? One may eat all manner of good things and still be a proper turkey.' The prince listened to him on this too, and began eating like a human being.

"Seeing this, the wise man addressed the prince, 'Do you really think that a turkey is condemned to sit under the table?

That isn't necessarily so—a turkey also walks around any place it wants and no one objects.' And the prince thought this through and accepted the wise man's opinion. Once he got up and walked about like a human being, he also began behaving like a complete human being."

My grandfather looked over the top of his glasses at me. "That's the end of the story," he said gently. "See, it wasn't that long. So now, Ruthie, let me ask you a question. Do you think the prince really thought that he was a turkey?"

I looked blankly at him. "I, I think so."

"What if being different wasn't so bad and that the problem wasn't with the prince, but it was with the father instead? Look at the story like this: the prince was doing things that his father didn't understand. In order to convince the father that his son wasn't crazy, the wise man had to behave just like the son. And once the father was convinced that his son was indeed a complete human being, just like the wise man, he was able to accept his son's unusual behavior. The wise man had to convince the father that his son wasn't so crazy, not the other way around."

We sat quietly for a moment longer, as my grandfather hoped that his oblique message would sink in.

"It's OK to be different," he said gently, "just like the turkey prince and just like Rabbi Nachman's disciples who spoke to God. So now, as I said, you speak to God, and I'm going for my walk. Talk to Him. He'll give you good advice, or maybe He won't. But you will feel better. When I come back, we'll see what we should do."

I sat in the semi-dark of my grandfather's room reasoning about what had just happened. It wasn't the fact that I was being punished that bothered me; I had been punished lots of times. But this was worse, much worse. My stories were my life, and my father had made me promise him that I would never, ever write another story.

I felt that I had reached the end of my world—the end of my dreams. I was not yet sixteen. I had been filled with ebullient optimism only an hour earlier, and now I was stopped, and I was angry. But what could I do? There was only darkness ahead; my dreams were dead. I took a deep breath, and in my head I screamed the loudest, angriest, brightest-red scream I could imagine. And then I did it again.

And then there was quiet.

And then I knew, somewhere deep in my psyche, that my life wasn't over, and that there would be new and even better opportunities. *Was that God talking to me? Or my own rationality?* I now knew that I would find a way to continue writing my stories. It wasn't just faith, it was confidence. We would find a way, God and me. The future wasn't as dark as it had seemed just a few moments earlier. We would find a way!

And I knew that my stories would get better and better, and eventually they and I would make my father proud. If only I had a place to start—some sort of opening. Suddenly I understood the challenge: I had to write better stories. Stories that would not just entertain but would actually change people's lives. *Was that God still talking to me?*

And then I knew: this wasn't the end of my world at all—it was the dawn of maturity. A gift from God?

Who knows.

———————————————

Mein Liebe Rivka,

Ruthie was asleep in the chair when I returned. I stood for some time, in the stillness of my room, looking at her, reluctant to disturb her. I was reminded once again how much she looks like you. I had loved to look at you while you were asleep. Sometimes, I would wake in the night and light the lamp and just watch you breathe. She smiles in her sleep, just like you.

In those days we never spoke about love, but I loved you, and I am sorry now that I never told you, even when you were dying.

I wish you were here to help me, but now I am here alone, and now I must do what must be done. That Jack is no better than I am.

If Rose hadn't married him she would have found someone else—
someone with some brains, someone with some sense of Yiddishkeit.
But he is like Napoleon, and I have to live in his house and obey his
rules, and listen to his childish attempts at pretending to be a scholar.
   This is now my chance to show them. This is my chance to help
Ruthie separate herself from Jack's pretentious, smothering materi-
alism. Rivka, I promise you now, just like I promised your father, I
am going to make Ruthie into a scholar, just like me. She is going
to be my scholar—trained by me, and filled with my knowledge. So
what if she is a woman? The world will soon recognize her contribu-
tion to Jewish learning, and all the students in all the yeshivas will
study her books, her pronouncements, and her treatises. And they will
say that she is the granddaughter of Rivka and Ben-Zion Perlman.
   May God protect you and bless you.

━━━━━━━━━━━━━━━━━━━━━━━━

They had lived an enchanted life in Lomza. My grandfather,
Ben-Zion's father, had been an estate manager with enough
money to send my father to the *High Yeshiva*. If my father
had been chosen to be the next Chief Rabbi they would have
happily stayed in Lomza. But he hadn't, and they had to leave
because other than studying *Torah*, my father had no marketable
skills. His older brother had been trained almost from birth to
take over their family business, but my father had been trained
to be the next Chief Rabbi. And he would have been, if things
had worked out the way they had planned. But they hadn't.

He could have stayed and become a teacher in the local
yeshiva, but there was no prestige in that, and it was too much
of a letdown after having been the heir apparent to the Chief
Rabbi. There just was no place in that small community for
another scholar, and so, his parents gave them enough money to
travel across Germany to The Baltic Sea and then to America.

They made their way slowly across Germany, going from
one family friend to another, and then they traveled in Cabin
Class across the Atlantic. They were both very young and not

very sophisticated, and they didn't realize that my mother was pregnant when they boarded the steamer in Bremen. But she was terribly sick when they arrived in New York. My father bribed the customs inspectors to allow her to enter the country, but even American medical know-how couldn't save her life.

Not one person in New York had been aware of, or even cared about, my father's reputation as a scholar. The streets of the Lower East Side were filled with newly arrived, bearded Polish Jews who claimed to be brilliant scholars. And even though they all were self-proclaimed scholars, they still worked in the "trades."

In spite of his shortcomings, and with no help, little skill, and even less ambition, my father, the often unemployed single parent, had managed to somehow raise me. It couldn't have been easy.

And now he was dependent on Jack and me, and he had to live in our house and eat our food. He had no choice. And he was obviously very unhappy.

If only he had become the Chief Rabbi, if only he had stayed in Lomza. Even if he didn't become the Chief Rabbi, he might have been the head of the yeshiva by now, and rather than living off the generosity of his daughter and her husband, he could have had prestige. A name.

But then, I would have been a Polish peasant girl rather than an important part of the Borough Park Jewish community.

CHAPTER 9

I watched my cigar turn to ash in the ashtray. I hadn't moved since my confrontation with Ruthie, and I felt the weight of that confrontation in my entire body. My initial feeling of righteous indignation had quickly turned to guilt. I had certainly gone too far. I had overreacted again. I could have—should have—talked to her about the moral issues of writing trash like that, but I had foolishly focused on the act and not on the material. She was doing something artistic. She was an author. I should have been proud, but now I couldn't go back on my word. In this world, a gentleman's word is his bond. *Shit!* Waves of regret anchored me blindly to the security of my desk.

Rose finally brought me out of my remorseful reverie by reminding me that it was Friday evening, and that we would be having a late Shabbos dinner after I returned from the synagogue, and did I want a snack to tide me over until dinner?

Friday evening—Shabbos dinner. I had forgotten. All the family would be together, and I would be at the head of the table. I could say something then—something to undo the damage that I had done.

I was so depressed about the way I had behaved with Ruthie that even walking to the synagogue with my high hat and tails didn't make me feel better. Throughout services, I was lost in thought trying to find a way to introduce the subject and to hopefully undo some of the harm that I had done. I desperately searched the Friday night prayer book hoping to find an inspiration, but none came. But then on my way home, I began thinking about judge Heimlich. *What was the message that the judge had told me?* I couldn't remember at first, and then it came to me clearly, and I remembered what the judge had said. I had asked the judge how I could ever repay him for his kindness, and the judge had replied, "Make a difference." By the time I got home I knew exactly what I would say, and, more importantly, how I would say it.

───────────────────

"This past week I was reading the book of Jonah," I began. "It's a pretty funny book. You all know the story of Jonah, and how he was gobbled up by the whale and lived inside the whale for three days and then was belched out onto dry land. I've always thought of it as an allegory about God's generosity. But this week I was rereading it, and it seemed pretty silly, and I was wondering why it is considered such an important book.

"Today I realized that the story isn't about the whale at all, it's about second chances. The book is really in three parts. In the first part God tells Jonah, who is some sort of prophet, to go to the evil city of Nineveh and warn them that God is going to destroy their city if they don't change their evil ways. Jonah decides that this is just a waste of time, but he's afraid of God. So he gets on a boat hoping to run away from Him.

"But God sends a big storm, and the boat is about to be destroyed, and Jonah tells the sailors on the boat to throw him overboard because the storm is all his fault. So they reluctantly throw him overboard, and he is gobbled up by a whale. Inside the whale, Jonah prays for God to help him, and God makes the whale vomit up Jonah on the shore.

"The second part of the story is how Jonah and God interact after Jonah is back on dry land. Here's the point of this part of the story: God could have just punished Jonah and gotten another prophet to go to Nineveh, but He didn't because He wanted to teach Jonah a lesson. That lesson was that God had faith in him and in his ability to make mature decisions. And so God gave Jonah a second chance.

"This time Jonah did go and preach in Nineveh, and the people of Nineveh repented! Just think about it: God could have destroyed their city or even compelled them to repent by punishing only a few of them, but God gave them a second chance, and they took it. The story might have ended there, but it still hasn't driven home its moral lesson.

"Now here's the third part: Jonah gets angry at God. 'I knew you'd forgive them!' he shouts at God, 'that's why I didn't want to go there in the first place! It's just a waste of time!'

"So God tells Jonah to calm down and go into the desert and take a rest. Jonah puts up a tent and settles down, and God causes a big shade tree to grow over where Jonah is resting, and Jonah is very happy. But then the tree wilts and dies, and the heat of the desert is unbearable and Jonah cries out to God.

"This time God says to Jonah, 'You really liked that tree didn't you?' And Jonah nods yes. And God tells Jonah that this is the lesson, 'You have to have faith in people that they will do the right thing. In the same way that that tree was important to you, the people of Nineveh are important to me. You must trust that, given the chance, people who have been pushed in the right direction will do the right thing.'

"The lesson for us is that we have to encourage people to make the right decision, but it is not always clear to us what that decision should be. So we can nudge them in what we think is the right direction, but we must not deny them the right to make their own decisions. The only thing we can encourage them to do is to make a difference in the world.

"Today I was like Jonah, and I assumed the worst. I was

upset about the magazine and the stories that Ruthie was writing for that magazine, and I told her that she would not be permitted to write any stories. I was wrong. I should have tried to push Ruthie into a more acceptable path. I now know that I should not have gotten angry about her writing stories. I should have been proud of that. It isn't the act of writing the stories, it's what they were about that I should have been concerned with."

I then looked directly at Ruthie. "I'm not a literary critic," I said, "but I am your father, and I have a certain responsibility to try to direct you along the right path. So now I want to encourage you to continue to develop your talent as a writer and to continue to write stories. But I would like you to write a different kind of story—stories about Jewish subjects. Stories that will teach Jewish values. Stories that will show the right way. Stories that will make a difference in peoples' lives. Ruthie, your grandfather has told you many stories about the *Bible*, and the prophets, and the scholars who wrote the *Mishnah* and the *Talmud*. I would like you to write stories about those Jewish heroes. I give you permission. No, I encourage you to write those stories."

I was not at all satisfied with the context that I had chosen or the way I had ended it. I was upset with myself that I had chosen to hide behind a story. I could have been more direct, found a more relevant context. Ben-Zion, I knew, always told Ruthie stories, and she listened because they were interesting and original. But this story about Jonah was neither interesting nor original. I looked at Ruthie, trying to gauge her reaction, but she had her head down and was absentmindedly turning her plate.

I should have told her about Judge Heimlich, but that would have been just talking about myself, and no one was interested in that. Rose, who was sitting next to me, took my hand. I tried to sip some wine, but my hands were shaking. *Had I embarrassed myself? Should I say something more?* I glanced sideways again at Ruthie, but she refused to look up. Everyone was quiet, and there wasn't the usual, animated, Friday night conversation.

And then, as if from heaven, Ben-Zion began to sing a Shabbos song. The melody repeated, and the rhythm was reassuring and upbeat. Rose joined her father, and then Ruthie, and then finally I was able to join in. It was going to be OK.

CHAPTER 10

I knew that what my father had said at the Shabbos dinner came from God. It was the answer to my prayers, and I went into my room after dinner and closed the door and thanked Him.

Over the next few weeks I tried to write Jewish stories as my father had instructed, but outside of my immediate family, I had very little first-hand experience. I really didn't know any Jewish stories, and to retell the stories that my grandfather had told me would be boring and repetitious. The stories I had written that the magazines had published were about sex and violence, and they were basically imitations of other stories in the magazines. But now I had no stories to imitate. Most of the famous Jewish writers had written about their own personal experiences, and I felt that if I made up stories they would be lies. I had to find something "authentic" to write about.

In those days, the *Jewish Daily Forward*, the Yiddish language newspaper, printed a column once a week called "Bintel Briefs." These were mostly letters written by recent Jewish immigrants who were seeking advice about living in the United States. I studied them hoping to get some idea of what their lives had been. Some of them wrote about the "old country," and I hoped to find a kernel of a story, but the only stories I found were people's reminiscences of their lives in Europe which were too uniquely personal to be turned into a story. I had no personal "old country" experience to draw upon, so I really couldn't relate to their stories, and I had no one to ask, except my grandfather, and he refused to speak about his life in The Pale. He said it was too painful for him to remember. He said that he missed his family terribly, and he just didn't want to talk about it.

I tried. For months I wrote story after story, only to throw them away. They were too obvious, too artificial. I was sure that Zelda Mahler, the famous writer, would never write such boring stories. My "famous writer" fantasy was now nothing more than an improbable dream as I realized that I didn't have anything inside me that people would want to read. And, as my grandfather had said, "What was the purpose of writing stories if no one reads them?"

But writing stories was my life, and I felt that without my stories I was just another teenage girl, and I didn't want to be just another anything. I became absentminded, distracted, and depressed. I stopped studying with my grandfather; I no longer read books or magazines, and I no longer even argued with my mother. I just didn't care. If I couldn't write, I was just a nobody. My schoolwork suffered and my grades plummeted. My teachers said that I was daydreaming in class, and I was. I didn't do any of the assignments. What was the point? The principal actually threatened to have me left back. And I didn't care. Zelda Mahler was dead.

I was concerned about Ruthie. I had only one daughter, and I had been so proud of her. She was one of the brightest in her class, and she was beautiful. People stopped me on the street to tell me how impressed they were with her. To tell the truth, I had an enormous amount of pride vested in her. Appearances were everything in those days, and Ruthie, with her bright eyes and quick wit, was at the top. But now, the possibility that my daughter might be left back in school would be an embarrassment that I absolutely could not tolerate. I demanded, in no uncertain terms, that Jack, who had caused the problem to start with, do something to wake Ruthie up and make her more interested in life.

"This is America," Jack responded to my demand, "it's not some little *shtetle* where everyone takes care of everyone else. Ruthie's got to learn to be tough. In America, people are tough. Look at you and me. We didn't let our weaknesses show, we fought for what we have. All the time. We fought. That's what Americans do. That's why this country is so great!"

"Jack!" I screamed. "We're not talking about the country, we're talking about Ruthie. She is our daughter, our only child. We have to find a way to help her."

"You're right, as usual," Jack replied wistfully. "But I just don't know what to do."

"Maybe you should spend more time with her. Ask her about her writing, talk about some of the books you're always reading. Maybe lend her some of the books so that she can read them too."

To be fair, my father did make an effort at showing interest in my writing. He encouraged me to write, and he discussed what I had written with me. But I knew that his interest wasn't sincere, and also, more importantly, I knew that what I had written, despite his flattery, wasn't good. I knew it, but I couldn't understand why. Writing romantic stories had been so smooth and easy; they just flowed. But writing these stories only frustrated me because they were so strained and poorly written. My father's efforts at showing interest, while well intentioned, only increased my anxiety and frustration.

I no longer knew where to turn. My father and my grandfather had been competing for my affection, or at least my attention, since I was a child, and I had kind of enjoyed playing one against the other. But now the competition was intensifying, and I could feel the strain. In the past, my grandfather had used his powers as a compelling teacher and storyteller to attract me, and my father had used his position as the head of the household to dominate conversation. But now I felt like I was David fighting two Goliaths because they were each using me as a weapon against the other.

And then, at a Friday night Shabbat dinner, my mother intervened. It wasn't common for my mother to speak much at our Shabbat dinners. My father usually led all the prayers and my grandfather gave a brief lesson, and I said what I had done that week. But this Shabbat, before she had even served the chicken soup, my mother stood at the table and stormed at my grandfather.

"Papa!" she shouted. "Tell Ruthie a story that she can write! This has gone too far!"

My grandfather looked up from his plate, obviously shocked at her aggressive tone. She had never spoken to him like that before. "I don't know one," he mumbled.

"Papa," she hissed, now only inches from his face, "I have taken care of you for twenty years, now it's time for you to pay me back. Tell her a story!"

Ashen, and suddenly subservient, my grandfather replied meekly, mumbling into his graying beard. "Yes, there is a story. I have been thinking about it." Then he paused, obviously upset. "There is a story that I can tell her. But—"

"No buts!" my mother snapped. "Don't delay. Her life is at risk. Jack and I have done all we can. Now I am turning to you for help."

That night, after we finished our Shabbat dinner, my grandfather asked me to take a walk with him. It was a moonlit night, and we walked slowly up Fifty-Fifth Street toward New Utrecht Avenue where the trains ran. The white stucco houses glowed in the moonlight, and the trees, with their spring leaves, rustled gently.

I liked walking with my grandfather. He didn't talk a lot when we walked so I didn't have to think of things to say. He didn't seem to mind that I was quiet, as he also stayed within himself. But we were within ourselves together. From the time I was a child, I always felt comfortable with him. This time, though, I had a feeling that something special was going to happen.

We walked toward the big, new Jewish hospital on the other side of Tenth Avenue. My grandfather liked it there because there was a little park in front of the hospital where he could sit. A train rattled overhead dropping sparks onto the roadway below. Savarese, the Italian Ices store where they sold the real fruit ices that I bought every day on my way home from school, was crowded as usual.

When we finally came to the park, my grandfather eased himself gently onto a bench and patted the bench next to him.

"Ruthie," he began, "do you remember when I told you about my sister Miriam? How she stayed in Minsk after your *Bubba* and I left?"

I nodded.

"Well, I didn't tell you the whole story. Now I will tell."

He heaved a sigh and looked at me strangely, as if he was trying to decide how to begin or whether to begin at all. Finally, he turned to face me and took my hand.

"A year after she was married," he began, "my sister Miriam had a baby, a boy. He was the most unusual baby: very beautiful, very smart, very strong. He walked and talked before he was one-year-old. He learned to read before his second birthday, and he could hold regular conversations with adults. He learned how to say the *Shema* when he was only a year old, and could recite whole sections of the *Torah* from memory by the time he was three. People came from all over to see him. Miriam was so proud.

"Then one day, not long after his third birthday, he died.

He hadn't been sick in any way, and the doctors could find no reason for his death. Miriam was shattered. After the seven days of mourning and the thirty days of restriction, she went to see the Rabbi. Now, you have to understand that at that time you just didn't barge in to see the Rabbi, especially if you were a woman. But this time, because it was such a terribly sad thing, the Rabbi agreed to see her. Usually, when a woman came to meet with the Rabbi, he always insisted that his wife be in the room with them, but this time, he sent his wife out of the room and met with Miriam alone.

"She didn't cry. She didn't say anything. In those days, you didn't speak to the Rabbi until he spoke to you. So, they sat like that, he behind his big desk and she in the chair in front. Of course, the Rabbi knew why she was there, but what could he say? Could he tell her the old phrase *'Hashem nosain, v'Hashem lokayach'*, 'God gives and God takes, blessed is the name of God'? No, not this time. Miriam was well educated—she had studied *Torah* and even *Talmud*. And the little boy was special, so smart, so beautiful, and so strong. Miriam was angry, and she wanted answers from the Rabbi and from God. There was no reason for her son's death—none whatsoever. Miriam and her husband were good Jews—they tried to observe all the commandments. And the child was so healthy. There was just no reason.

"Finally the Rabbi spoke. His voice so low, it was nearly a whisper. So low, that only Miriam could hear. 'Many, many years ago in ancient Persia,' the Rabbi began, 'there was a Sultan who had no sons. All the doctors and all the wise men in the kingdom were unable to assist him to have a son. The Sultan was very upset because, if he did not have a son, then the rule of the kingdom would pass to another family. He had an advisor whom he trusted more than any of his other advisors. This advisor told him that the reason that he had no sons was because the Jews in the kingdom had put a curse on him. He said that the only way he would ever have a son was if he expelled all of the Jews from the kingdom.

"'Although the Sultan trusted this advisor very much, he also had many business dealings with the Jews, and he was reluctant to expel them. So he said that he would wait one more year, and if he didn't have a son by then, he would expel all the Jews, and those Jews who refused to go would be killed.

"'When the Jews heard of this edict they were very upset. They tore their clothing and fasted and prayed. In heaven, the angels heard their prayers. The angels went to the souls that were in heaven and asked for a volunteer to go down to earth and be born a son to the Sultan. One soul volunteered, and a little while later, a son was born to the Sultan. The whole kingdom rejoiced, especially the Jews.

"'Because this young prince was so important, the Sultan wanted only the best for him. So, when the child was old enough to begin his education, they searched for the best teacher in the kingdom. The man they selected to be the prince's tutor said that he would agree only if he had half an hour of privacy every morning. He would be given a room, and no one would be allowed into that room for half an hour every morning.

"'The Sultan agreed, and the child's education began. The young prince learned mathematics and philosophy and spoke many languages. He and the tutor lived together and studied together every day. But every morning, for a half-hour, the tutor had total privacy.

"'One day, the young prince hid himself in the room and watched to see what the tutor was doing during that half-hour. He saw the tutor carefully lock the door, then remove a prayer shawl, *tefillin*, and a prayer book from a velvet bag. He watched silently while the tutor wrapped himself in the prayer shawl, and then put on his teffilin, first on his left arm, then on his head, and then back again to his left hand. He was amazed at how the tutor concentrated on the prayer book, how his whole body seemed to express the prayers.

"'He waited until after the tutor had removed the tefillin and carefully wrapped them, kissed them, and inserted them, along with the prayer shawl, back into the velvet bag. He waited until the tutor went to open the door before he revealed his presence and confronted him.

"'Obviously surprised and upset that he had been discovered, the tutor admitted that he was Jewish and that he was praying to God. The prince threatened to expose the tutor to the Sultan's advisor, who hated Jews and would surely have him killed, unless the tutor would teach the prince to pray to God. So, every morning the tutor and the prince would pray to God together inside the tutor's locked room.

"'When the prince came of age, the Sultan sent him to England to attend the university there. He became a teacher, and was one of the scholars who was chosen to translate the *Torah* into English. This was a very important thing because he was able to make sure that the *Torah* was translated accurately. That translation made it possible for anyone, even if they didn't read Hebrew, to fulfill the commandment to study *Torah*.

"'The prince converted to Judaism and became a great scholar and the head of a famous yeshiva. When he died, the angels in heaven welcomed his soul with great rejoicing. They wanted to place his soul in the vessel that contains completely perfect souls, but there was one problem. He had not been raised on a Jewish mother's milk. You remember that even our great teacher Moses, although he was raised by a Gentile, was given milk from his Jewish mother.

"'So it was determined that this soul had to go back for a short time so that its perfection could be completed. But such a nearly perfect soul could not be sent to just any family. It had to go to a family that had as deep a love of *Torah* and learning as the soul needed. They waited centuries until the right combination of husband and wife came along.'

"The Rabbi stopped talking, took out his handkerchief, and wiped his eyes. He looked down at the open book on his desk, then back at Miriam.

"'I believe that you were that special family. I believe that you were chosen by the angels, and maybe even by God himself, to help that soul reach eternal peace.'"

I started to cry, and my grandfather held my hand and put his arm around me. He began to cry as well, silently, with huge gulps of air. Quietly we rocked together, and slowly we stopped crying, I first. We sat huddled together a while longer.

"I never told that story to anyone, not anyone, ever," my grandfather said, wiping his eyes. "I promised my sister, I promised. But you needed a story, and it was an emergency, a matter of life and death, I had to do it."

We sat a while longer.

I finally stood up and helped my grandfather to his feet. He seemed suddenly old, and I was grateful for the great sacrifice that he had made for me. I believed that there are certain rules of life that must never be broken. A sister's secret, the intimacy between her and God, these things must never be told. They are too private.

I was overwhelmed. For my grandfather to have carried that story for so many years, and to have felt his sister's pain—for him to have missed his sister so much and to not have been able to go to her and hold her hand, and cry with her, and kiss her, and tell her how much he loves her—was overwhelming. But he was here in America, and she was still in Lomza, so far away. He would never see her again. Never.

And I finally had my story. I knew, from the moment I heard the story, that this would be my opportunity to revive my dream of becoming a famous author. For days, after I heard the story, I kneaded it in my mind. I was so moved by it that I waited nearly a month before I tried to put it down on paper. And then I began. An hour or two every night, then three or four hours a night, then deep into dawn. It was all I could think about. I couldn't wait to get home from school to work on my story. I didn't want to leave it in the morning. It had to be perfect. Every word.

I wrote it in pencil, in longhand, in my school notebook because I wanted to feel the energy of writing. I wanted to feel the pencil and the paper because I believed that my soul and the soul of my grandfather and his sister were in it.

To me, this was much more than just a story—this was the very essence of my being. *Who am I to write such a story?* I thought to myself. *I'm just a teenager.* And yet, I did it. And word by word, day by day, it grew.

The stories that my grandfather had told me about the Baal Shem Tov in the forest, and the esoteric teachings of *Kabbalah*, and all the folk tales, and all of the imaginings and dreams that I had absorbed, and all the tales that he had told me since I was a child, became a dark, deep pool from which I drew the background for my story. And his sister Miriam, and her baby, and their tragic story, were like a white foaming geyser of water soaring from the darkness into the heavens, carrying with it all of the characters. The story churned inside me and tumbled out through my hand and pencil onto the paper.

Emotional memories, things that I had heard, or read, or just imagined, took their place in my story. My grandfather's tales of demons, and *dybbuks*, paraded through my mind, and these too found their way into my story. The seven heavens and their archangels that I had read about in the library formed the heavenly structure. These magical elements of my story bubbled out from my unconscious. They were not merely memories or things learned—they were more than that. They carried the energy, electricity, and sensations of events that I had never experienced, but that had somehow colored my life. Some internal force, that I had never previously known, shaped my thoughts and guided my hand. These memories, if one can call them that, which cannot be explained by science or by circumstances, had now become part of my very being.

Sometimes, late at night, I heard the voices of my characters. They talked to me. They told me that there is a history that I never knew—one that I can only imagine. One that must be told.

Should I tell the story as a dream? Or maybe an analogy or an allegory or a parable? Did it really happen? Would the Rabbi have made up such a preposterous story just to placate my grandfa-

ther's sister? Rationality and irrationality competed with each other. At that moment, my passions had replaced practicality. They carried me beyond normal behavior into the world of the possible. "Dream!" they told me. "Go beyond rationality. Everything is possible." The world was as nothing for me. I went to school, talked with my friends, ate dinner with my parents, rested on the Sabbath, and all the time the story was forming within me, within my soul.

The story came slowly, painfully, every word a struggle. I had to get it exactly right. I knew that it would be my only chance.

In the end, it was the longest story I had ever written. I tried to edit it but none of the words would leave the page. I tried to read it to my grandfather, but he wouldn't let me, and my father, although he said he was interested, never had time to listen. So I sent it to a major literary magazine, one that I had never dared to approach before.

I knew that they would accept it, and I knew that they would agree to publish it exactly as I had written it with no editing. I had no doubt about it.

And so it was.

In the end, after it was published, I felt no special elation. I didn't even feel relief. I kept waiting for some reaction, but none came. I got up in the morning, and I went to school as usual, and I came home as usual, and I ate dinner as usual, and I did my homework as usual, and I went to bed as usual.

I no longer had a burning desire to write.

The magazine with my story in it remained unopened on my desk. My parents never asked to see it—never even mentioned it. My story-writing notebooks and typewriter remained unused. Whatever had happened to me was gone; my crisis had passed and was nearly forgotten. I was seventeen—a high school senior on my way to college. There were no confrontations. My father's real estate investments were doing well, my mother enjoyed retirement, and life at home was finally peaceful.

CHAPTER 11

Two weeks later, my father received a telephone call from Jerome Davis, the head of the giant book publishing company Davis and Hart. He told my father that he had read my story, and that he would like to speak to me about expanding it into a book.

My father was impressed. Although he hadn't read my story, nor had he ever heard of Mr. Davis or Davis and Hart, he was certain that having a daughter who was writing a book would give him the highest level of prestige. Stories were nothing in his mind, but a book was a book.

"You're writing a book!" he greeted me excitedly when I came home from school.

"Who says?"

"Jerome Davis, from Davis and Hart. He called today, and he wants you to make your story into a book. They're a big time publisher, you know. This is a real opportunity."

"I can't write a book; I don't know how. And besides, writing a book can take years, and I don't have the time. I'm going to college in the fall, in case you forgot."

"Look, Ruthie, this is a great opportunity. You can write a

book, and you can go to college, too. I have a lot of confidence in you. Besides, a book is just a very long story, and you've already written the story."

"I just can't. Look, I never wrote a book. I don't know how."

"Ruthie, listen to me," my father said, a little too harshly. "You will call Mr. Davis tomorrow and talk to him. Maybe he has an idea. But Ruthie, this is a big chance, don't let it get away."

Life had changed sharply for me. My writing had gone from being an anathema for my father to being tolerated, and now I was being encouraged, even pressured.

***

I now had the opportunity to be the father of a famous author. It would be my next transformation—my latest step along the path to being a real American. I could already imagine myself in literary circles, hosting grand salons, boasting to our neighbors. All that was necessary was for Ruthie to contact this Jerome Davis. It wasn't that hard. I absolutely could not understand her reluctance.

One minute she wants to be a writer, and then, when the opportunity actually comes, she doesn't want to do it, I thought to myself. *Well I'll push her into it. After all,* I reasoned, *it's for her own good.* Now that I had seen the chance to be the father of an author, I wasn't going to give up.

Ruthie called Mr. Davis the next day from my office. Obviously, she was hoping to dissuade him. She explained that although she was flattered by his interest, she was only seventeen-years-old, and had never written a book. He said he understood, and that she shouldn't worry. He said that he would help her. He explained to her the concept of an editor/ghost writer—who he called a "coach"—and he said that he would send her an editor who would work with her for as long as it took to help her write the book.

Ruthie told him that she was in high school, and that

she had a lot of homework, and that she and her family were Sabbath observers, and that she had a busy social life, and that she would soon be going to college, and that she couldn't possibly have time to work on a book, and that he would be just wasting his time and money. In fact, she did everything she could to dissuade him.

But Mr. Davis said he understood Ruthie's reluctance, and he offered to send the coach, just once, to meet with her at our house on a Sunday to discuss it. He told her that if she decided that she didn't want to go any further, he would understand. He was so smooth and convincing that she felt she had no choice.

Mr. Davis then spoke to me. He reviewed the conversation that he had had with Ruthie and explained the offer of an editor that he had made. He was very careful to make clear that he already had a highly-skilled, Jewish editor in mind, and that he was confident that this editor would be able to work amicably with Ruthie. He said that he thought that there was great potential in this partnership.

"Partnership?" I interrupted. "My daughter is the author of this book, and she will not have any partners."

"Yes," Mr. Davis replied smoothly. "I only used the term partner to imply that he will be supporting her in her efforts. Of course hers will be the only name on the book."

"What happens if this partnership doesn't work out?" I asked. "Who pays this editor?"

"The cost of the editor is all mine," Mr. Davis replied. "You will have no obligation. But I want you to understand that this is a great opportunity for your daughter. Don't let her miss it."

I must admit that I was very proud that Mr. Davis had sought my support and approval, and I promised to encourage Ruthie to agree.

That Sunday, at ten o'clock sharp, the editor, Harry Berger, appeared at our door. He was very tall, and very good-looking.

When he came into the parlor he filled the entire room with his personality. He went directly to my father and introduced himself. His powerful grip and presence implied an athletic background, and I immediately thought that he must be a graduate of an Ivy League School. My father then introduced him to my mother, and he bowed to her and took her hand.

We sat uncomfortably in the living room, my father and Harry on the sofa, my mother on the easy chair, and I, trying to maintain a separation, on a dining room chair which I had turned around. My mother served tea and little cookies.

"So," my father said a little too loudly, "you are an editor. That's an interesting profession. What exactly do you do?"

"I work with authors to help them develop their work," Harry replied deferentially.

"And did you go to school to learn how to do this?" my father probed.

"Well, not exactly. I went to the University of Pennsylvania, and I majored in journalism. But after I graduated from Penn, I became an editor rather than a writer."

"And how long have you been doing this editing?"

"Not very long. When I started college I had planned to be a journalist, and then, eventually, an author, like your daughter. So while I was in school, I worked as a cub reporter for a newspaper in Philadelphia. But then, although I was studying to be a writer, I got involved with a group of artists who called themselves the Ashcan School. Perhaps you've heard of them."

My father shook his head no.

"They were a group of newspaper illustrators who believed that when you draw a picture for a news article in a newspaper, it should show life as it really is rather than how a newspaper editor would like it to be. So their news illustrations showed all the bad parts of what they were illustrating as well as the good. Metaphorically, they showed the ash cans when they drew pictures of streets."

"But I thought you said you're a writer, not an illustrator."

"Yes, that's right. One of the artists was a friend of mine, and what they were doing at the time was very controversial. A lot of the newspaper publishers were fighting it because they didn't want their papers to show anything that looked too bad. I started writing news articles defending and promoting what they were doing. It turned out that I was pretty good at it, and they gave me more and more responsibility. But nothing that I wrote was original, it was just reporting.

"Mr. Davis's son had been in some of my classes, and we became friends. He recommended me to his father. He thought that I should write a book about the Ashcan School, and Mr. Davis asked me to send him a synopsis and the first few chapters. Unfortunately, or maybe fortunately, when Mr. Davis read what I had written, he offered me a job as an editor instead. I took the job and I've been editing for two years now. I like doing it very much."

"So what do you edit?"

"Usually books that someone else has written. I help them rewrite it to make it more interesting."

My father was nodding enthusiastically. "What exactly can you do with Ruthie?" he asked, nodding at me and hoping that I would join the conversation.

"Well, I read her story, and I have to tell you that what she has written is much better than anything I could have written. I can help her expand it into a full-length novel. But she will do all the writing—I will just be like a coach. I'll make suggestions and encourage her."

My father now gestured openly to me to join in the conversation, but I held back, still sitting outside the conversational circle.

"So," my father said, as he stood and walked over to me and put his hand on my shoulder, subtly nudging me into the conversation, "what do you say Ruthie?"

I felt trapped, there didn't seem to be much of an alternative. "I guess we could give it a try next week, if that's OK with Mr. Berger."

"There's no time like the present," my father said heartily, "if that's OK with Mr. Berger."

"You can use the dining room table," my mother said, rising from the easy chair. "Is that OK?"

I felt trapped, and I looked helplessly at Harry Berger. "I'm sure Mr. Berger has other appointments today," I said a little too quietly. "Maybe we should wait until Mr. Berger has more free time."

But my father and mother had already begun removing the lace cloth from the dining room table. And then, as if orchestrated by some unseen stage director, they walked into the kitchen, leaving Harry and me alone.

Harry was obviously uncomfortable, and he remained on the sofa. I sat where I was, facing him with my back to the dining room table.

"I think I should tell you a little about myself and the reason why Mr. Davis is interested in your story," he began. "First of all, other than Mr. Davis, I'm the only Jew at Davis and Hart. And actually, although Mr. Davis was born Jewish, he is married to a non-Jew. His family, which is quite wealthy and influential, has been pushing him to publish a book on a Jewish subject. So when he came across your story, he knew that he had found exactly the right property.

"As for me, I live in Manhattan. I'm a graduate of the University of Pennsylvania with a BA in Journalism. I have written a lot of nonfiction, but I have never published anything. I have been told that I'm a pretty good editor. This is my third assignment."

Harry asked me to read my story out loud to him. I had never read any of my stories aloud before, and it was quite a moving experience—nearly as emotional as the first time I had heard the story from my grandfather. My voice thickened, and my eyes teared up as I read the Rabbi's response. Harry was spellbound.

"My God, that's a powerful story," Harry finally said. "Now I understand why Mr. Davis liked it. How did you ever conceive of such a story?"

"Actually," I replied, "my grandfather told me the central story. It's about his sister in Lomza, in The Pale. I changed some things around to give it a setting and a beginning and an end, but the core of the story is from my grandfather. But it's just a story, and it will never be enough for a book. That's what I told Mr. Davis."

"I see what you mean, but that's not what Mr. Davis is looking for. He wants a kind of historical novel about Jewish life in The Pale. He likes your story, and he would like us to make it the centerpiece of a novel, but he is more interested in the history and the atmosphere. He wants you to write a few additional stories that can be tied together and that will capture, in an informal way, what it was like to live as a Jew in The Pale at the end of the century. He wants some history, some fiction, and a lot of emotion. We can do the research on the history together, but it will be up to you to supply the emotion. Do you think your grandfather has more stories?"

"Oh, he's got lots of stories," I said, "but they're usually folk tales from the books that he reads. I can try to get him to tell me some personal stuff that he remembers from when he was a child in Lomza. Stories are easy, it's the historic material that I don't know."

"That's easy," Harry said with a smile. "The New York Public Library on Forty-Second Street has a fantastic history section, and the librarians know every source. It will take some time, but we can get all the information we need."

We, I thought to myself. I liked the way that sounded. I had never been a "we" before. I had gone out on dates to the theater, and gone to dances, and even went boating in the park, but it had always been "you" and "me," never "we."

"It's going to be a lot of work, Ruthie," Harry said, "but I'm sure we can do it."

"But I'm hoping to go to college next fall. Do you think we can get it done by then?"

"Sure. We'll just have to work extra hard during the summer. When do you graduate from high school?"

"The beginning of June, but I really don't have any important classes after the middle of May, so I could probably start working on the book then."

"How about Sundays? Are you seeing somebody?"

I involuntarily blushed and was immediately embarrassed. "No," I said softly, "not just now."

"Good. Then we can spend our Sundays together. Mr. Davis will be very pleased."

And so will I, I thought to myself.

CHAPTER 12

Harry was a cosmopolitan—a *bon vivant*—living the good life. He was the only son of an affluent German-American Jewish family and had been raised to enjoy life, rather than to earn a living. His wealth, excellent manners, and good looks provided an easy entry into the postwar cultural world, and, though he spent his days working as an editor, he spent his evenings in the artistic demimonde. He attended private art openings, art gallery shows, museum previews, concerts, Broadway theaters, jazz clubs, and every other sort of cultural experience that his mother could suggest. His circle of friends with whom he attended these events consisted of young, unmarried men and women from similar Jewish backgrounds, all of whom seemed to be seeking appropriate matches. Harry often attended these events in the company of some wealthy and eligible young woman, but he never developed any long lasting romantic attachments.

He was an observer and an outsider rather than an active participant—more interested in the motivation of the artists and musicians he befriended than in the value of their work. He enjoyed his relationships with the artists, and he frequently dropped into their studios just to talk with them and watch them work. He was non-judgmental and a good listener, and he encouraged the artists to share their ambitions and frustrations with him.

He had no personal ambition, and, for the artists like me that he spent time with, the fact that he would never compete with them or copy their style was reassuring. He was both supportive and discreet. He had never thought about "what he would like to be when he grows up" because he never planned to grow up. There simply was no compelling reason for "growing up." He had found a comfortable niche in both the social and artistic worlds, and he was content to remain there as long as possible.

Although he was ostensibly a writer, he had been exposed to a variety of other cultural experiences and was conversant in many. His personal preference was for jazz. He did not sing or play an instrument, but he appreciated the freedom and creativity of jazz musicians. For the most part, he avoided the big band concert stages and halls and stuck to the small jazz clubs and speakeasies. His parents did not approve of this, and they aggressively encouraged him to spend his time in more socially acceptable company. This was a source of endless conflict, and eventually Harry moved out of his parents' apartment and rented a small apartment in Harlem near 125th Street, where several of his favorite jazz clubs were located. He spent many late nights and early mornings in the clubs, waiting until after they had closed to the public and the musicians played for themselves. That was when they would try new sounds and orchestrations, and Harry wanted to be there to enjoy their creativity and to encourage them.

Harry was a third-generation American. His grandfather had come to the United States in the middle of the nineteenth-century. The family had owned a large candle factory in Germany on the Swiss-German border, and his grandfather, as the oldest child, had been sent to the New World charged with the responsibility of establishing a branch of the family business there. He had traveled throughout the country and finally decided to open a candle factory in Philadelphia. This was before electricity, and candles were an important household item. Harry's grandfather, however, realized that candles also had a romantic quality, and so his factory not only produced utilitarian candles, but, in a departure from the German parent company, it produced decorative candles as well.

Harry's father, who had inherited the factory, had recognized the potential market for electric lamps and had converted the factory to manufacture electric table lamps. His timing was perfect, and the factory thrived. In 1920, having survived the post-war recession, Harry's father had sold the factory to a competitor and had become an early full-time investor in the soaring stock market. He also was involved in the workings of Temple Emanu-El, the enormous Reform synagogue that was being built on Fifth Avenue. He was very proud of his German-Jewish heritage.

Harry's mother was a "trophy wife." She was tall, strikingly beautiful, and spoke with a velvety southern accent. She had been born and raised in Charleston, South Carolina and was one of the few Jewish girls to have attended a finishing school there. These schools gave girls training in social graces and proper etiquette. Although some academics were taught, the primary goal of such schools was to help girls learn to be good wives and more interesting women overall.

Unlike my parents, Harry's parents were bright, inquisitive people who knew a great deal about a large range of subjects, but were always trying to learn more. They never raised their voices, and they never spoke about things that they were not familiar with.

When I got to know Harry better, I visited their home on Fifth Avenue, which occupied a full floor. The elevator opened directly into the entry hall, with the kitchen and servants' quarters on the left, the living room straight ahead, and the dining room also to the left. There was a large balcony outside that ran the full length of the dining and living rooms, and faced Central

Park. All of the furniture in the living room was upholstered in French silk moiré, with Italian marble topped tables. There were gold drapes on all the windows.

But I am getting ahead of the story.

That spring and summer, I spent most of my time in the Fifth Avenue Library doing research on the Jewish communities of The Pale. I would take the West End subway every morning from the Fifty-Fifth Street station in Borough Park to Times Square and then walk east on Forty-Second Street to the central library. That library and its wonderful reading room became my home for the summer. The librarians at one end of the room and the wooden tables with their green lamps were my daily summer companions. I studied every book on the subject I could find, plus every book the librarians recommended. As I read, I took copious notes, which I integrated into my book. By the end of the summer, it seemed to me that I knew everything there was to know about The Jewish Pale of Settlement.

Every Sunday afternoon that summer, Harry and I would meet, and review and edit the additions that I had made that week to my book, which was getting longer and more complex. Inevitably, just by proximity, and biology, and the occasional intentional touch, an unmentionable undercurrent of sexual tension developed between us. In all fairness, we foolishly and futilely tried to overcome it, but Harry and I were both healthy, attractive people, and we were both young and . . . human.

We did nothing to satisfy this inexorable force. In fact, we fought valiantly against it, but it remained lurking in the background, waiting to be explored once the book was finished.

By September, when we took a break for Rosh Hashanah—the Jewish New Year—we had been working for four months, and the book was over 300 pages long. It had chapters on the Polish Jewish community, the Polish governmental structure, the growth of the cities, and the writings of the *King James Bible*. I also devoted a great deal of effort to a description of the academic life in Westminster University in the early seventeenth century and the selection process for the fifty-four scholars who would actually do the translation of the *Hebrew Bible*. I even had a chapter on the disruptive effects of the Renaissance and the Industrial Revolution on the Jewish community. I had tried to cover every aspect of Polish Jewish history that I thought might have had an effect on the circumstances that surrounded the characters in my story.

Although I was very careful to maintain the storyline throughout, I tried to include as much of the information as I thought was relevant to the story, and to present it in as clear a way as possible. Harry and I agreed that we had done a herculean job and that the book would certainly satisfy Mr. Davis's requirements. We had worked extremely hard that summer, and we had come to the end of our task. The draft of the book, we felt, was ready to be submitted to Mr. Davis. I was ready to start my college career, and Harry, I thought, was ready to begin a romantic relationship with me.

Just as a last step before submitting it, we decided to reread the book from cover to cover during the days between Rosh Hashanah and Yom Kippur. I gave Harry the typewritten original, and I read the carbon copy.

Perhaps it was as a result of the clarity that comes during a time of self-examination, but I realized, quite definitely, that my book, although scholarly and informative, was, in fact, terrible. I had taken a good short story and turned it into a tedious historical dissertation. I actually fell asleep out of boredom reading my own book.

On Yom Kippur night, after the break-the-fast, I called Harry. Not surprisingly, he had come to the same conclusion. "I can't imagine what we were thinking," he said. "It seems like somewhere along the way we lost all perspective."

The problem was that I was scheduled to begin my college career that week, and I would no longer have free time to work on the book. We had wasted the summer and produced exactly nothing! Harry was worried about his job, and I was just plain fed up with the project.

I hadn't wanted to do it in the first place. I had allowed myself to get talked into it by my father and Mr. Davis, and now it was time to move on. After all, I was close to eighteen-years-old, and some of my friends were even starting to get married.

I packed up the manuscript and sent it to Mr. Davis, along with a note explaining that I had tried my best and that, although I was not particularly satisfied with the manuscript, I had warned him in the beginning that I was not an experienced novelist. I told him that this was, in fact, my best effort. I made it clear that I was about to start college and that I would not be able to do any further work on the book.

A few days later, Mr. Davis made a special trip to Brooklyn to meet with my father. Both Harry and I were present at the meeting, but we were not given an opportunity to speak. Mr. Davis was angry and threatening.

"Mr. Rubin," he began, "I have invested a great deal of time and money in your daughter's book. So far, although the progress has been quite slow, she and my assistant have started developing a theme that shows some promise, but it needs to be reworked and it is certainly far from finished. I understand that your daughter has chosen to attend college rather than continue working on the book. This is most unfortunate.

"Now, don't get me wrong, she has the right to go to college, and Brooklyn College is a fine college for immigrant children, but I have invested a good deal of money in this book, and I cannot wait until she is ready to continue. As a business man, I am sure you understand my position."

My father visually bristled at the word "immigrant," but he kept his silence and dignity. His anger, I knew, was simmering just beneath the surface.

"Mr. Davis," he replied in measured tones, "I am a man of my word. I understand your concern and appreciate all the effort and expense that you have sustained on behalf of my daughter. You have my word; she will finish the book even if that means that she must delay her college."

I was sitting in my usual place at the dining room table, and I heard it clearly—it resonated in my head. "Delay her college," he had said. Just like that. Delay her college. I had fought for my parents' permission to go to college. They had said that girls didn't need an education like boys. "Girls," they said, "just have to get married." But I had fought, day after day. And finally they had agreed. I would have been the first in our family to go to college. And now, in a meaningless effort to impress Mr. Davis, my college dreams were dashed. Perhaps forever.

My father and Mr. Davis shook hands. They even shared a *shnops* to seal the agreement. Then the maid brought Mr. Davis's hat and coat, and he left, and just as quickly my dreams were destroyed. Harry stood at the door for a moment and looked at me sadly, and then left with Mr. Davis.

I remained seated in the chair in which I had been sitting during the discussion.

I went into my office, carefully closed the door, and lit a cigar. Ruthie was still sitting at the table.

I knew what I had done. I knew how important college had been to her. She was going to be the only one of her friends to go to college. But a deal is a deal, and I had made a deal with Mr. Davis. Besides, how long could it possibly take for them to write the book? Another six months or a year? And then she'd be a famous author. In fact, it wouldn't be such a tragedy if she didn't go to college. Why couldn't she just get married like the other girls?

But I knew the answer. Ruthie was not like the other girls—she never had been. She was tough, a ball buster. She deserved to go to college—she had earned it—unlike other kids who thought that it was just coming to them.

Well, she would just have to wait, that's all. A man's word is a man's word.

But I knew I had failed. Again.

I opened the door a crack and saw that Ben Zion was there, talking to her. I watched them—so intimate. And I was the outsider across the threshold.

I remained seated at the table, alone. I didn't cry—I was beyond that. New forces were taking control of me. Some people call it maturity: the acceptance of fate, of powers stronger than you, the realization that you cannot always control the outcome. I had been a dreamer. I had dared to imagine the future as beautiful and poetic. I had expected that I would become an artist among artists, responding only to my own creativity. I had believed that I could soar to the outer limits of society through my art. But now I was on a leash. The collar pressed against my neck, and no matter how I strained I could not escape. The free spirit was now under control. Ruthie the child had been replaced by Ruthie the woman.

My grandfather slipped into the chair across the table and took my hand. "You know, Ruthie," he said, "things have a way of working out. It isn't so bad that you might have to delay going to college, maybe you'll meet a nice Jewish boy in the meantime. Maybe even this Harry Berger. He seems to be a nice man, and I can see that you like him."

And then, as usual, he told me a story.

"There is a story by Rabbi Nachman of Bratslav that I would like to tell you," he said ever so gently. "Maybe I told it to you before, but you should listen now because it has a good moral."

I nodded sadly, and he began.

"Once a Jewish man who lived in a small town in Austria had a dream, and in that dream he saw that there was a valuable treasure buried under a bridge in the city of Vienna. He traveled from his little town to Vienna where he found the bridge exactly as in his dream. He stood on the bridge wondering what to do. If he searched under the bridge during the day, people would see him searching and wonder what was going on. If he waited until night, he wouldn't be able to see.

"After a while a soldier came by and saw the Jew standing and wondering. He asked him, 'What are you doing here and what are you looking for?'

"The Jew thought about it. If he told the dream to the soldier he would have to share the fortune, but if he didn't tell him then he might not be able to find it at all. So he told his dream to the soldier and asked him to help search for the treasure. He offered to share the treasure 50/50 when they found it.

"But the soldier replied, 'I feel sorry for you, you crazy dreamer! I also have dreamed about a buried treasure. But in my dream the valuable treasure lays buried in the cellar of such and such a Jew in such and such a town. But I'm not going to journey all that way for a stupid dream!'

"The name of the town that the soldier had named was this man's town and the name of the Jew was this man's name!

"So the Jew hurried to get two fast horses, and he hitched them to his wagon, and he set off in a rush to his town. He went down to his cellar and there he discovered the treasure.

"At the sight of it the Jew declared, 'Now this mystery has been revealed to me. The treasure had always lain buried in my house, but I had to leave my town and journey so far to Vienna in order to discover that the treasure was always in my house.'

"The meaning of the story is this: you, Ruthie, have been given a treasure—your writing skill. It is right here, in your head, and you don't have to journey very far to find it. You just have to dig deeper into yourself. It might take more time, and this Harry will help you, but it is your treasure, and all you have to do is to find a way to uncover it."

I watched Ben-Zion and Ruthie through the open door of my office. They appeared to have such a close, intimate relationship. It's true that I envied Ben-Zion and his easy relationship with Ruthie, *but*, I rationalized, *I am who I am.* And right at that very moment, I was very sad.

I waited for Ben-Zion to leave and then, uncertainly, I walked over to Ruthie. "I know you're disappointed," I began hesitantly, "college was important to you, and a year seems like a very long time.

"Listen," I said with greater energy, finding my way, "I'm not such a good talker, but I am a good businessman, so I'm going to offer you a deal. One of the most important things about going to college is going out into the world on your own and taking responsibility for yourself. It's like you walk out the door for the last time as a girl and the second you are outside, you're a woman. So I'm telling you now that it's going to be exactly like that even if you delay going to college for a year. Today, from this moment on, you have crossed the threshold to becoming an independent adult. From now on, the decisions that you make are yours alone. Your mother and I will be here to give you advice if you ask for it, but only if you ask for it. Otherwise, you're on your own.

"So here's the last bit of unsolicited advice I'm going to give you: right now, writing this book is your job. If you do a good job, your book will be published. And then, having had a book published, you'll be able to choose whatever college you want. And whatever college you choose, I agree to pay for it. So, sit up, square your shoulders, and go ahead and write the best book you can. The college world will just have to wait a little longer for Ruthie Rubin."

I'm not sure where that came from because I hadn't planned to say it. But when I did, and after I did, I felt good. I felt that it was right.

Mein Liebe Rivka,

Your beautiful granddaughter has met a man, but he is the wrong kind of man. He has no Yiddishkeit *at all. He comes from a Reform family, and I don't even think he owns a* yarmulke. *But as they say in America, love is blind, and I can see already that Ruthie loves this man. I can only hope that Jack will put an end to it quickly, but I am afraid that he will wait too long, and then it will be too late to stop it.*

I wish you were here; you would be able to talk to her. Rose tries, but she has no idea of what a young girl thinks, and Jack is so worried about how he looks and sounds that he never thinks about what he says.

I think it would be better if I don't try to stop her. I want her to trust me in all things so that I can maintain my influence over her.

God's ways are not always known to us. I can only hope for the best.

May God protect and bless you.

I worked very hard with Harry, Sundays at first and then some evenings too. We made slow progress. Harry kept trying to get me to loosen up, but my writing had become stiff, and formal, and pretentious. I would write in the afternoon and evening, and then reread what I had written the following morning and decide that it all was terrible and tear it up and start over. I repeated the process over and over: write all afternoon and evening—much better this time. Reread it in the morning, and it was the same terrible, formal, phony stuff.

My writing was stiff and getting stiffer. But Harry was like a sports coach, cajoling, teasing, and encouraging me at every opportunity. "Forget about whether it is good or bad," he told me. "Just write whatever you want, it doesn't all have to be perfect, just write whatever comes into your head. You're a natural writer, so don't fight it." And slowly my confidence returned.

But there was new issue, one that neither Harry nor I was able to overcome: I had fallen deeply and irretrievably in love with Harry, and it was clear that the feeling was rapidly becoming reciprocal.

It had started, as so many romantic affairs do, with seemingly innocent intentions. In an effort to get me to "loosen up," Harry had begun taking me to some of his favorite night spots. These jazz clubs had a seductively seedy aura of permissiveness which was attractive to the young socialites of the time and especially to Harry and me.

Harry took me to the best of the dance halls. We danced the shimmy, the breakdown, the black bottom, and the Charleston to the great uptown bands. I wore my hair bobbed, my breasts flat, and my legs exposed with the shortest, swishiest skirts. The tall, narrow figure that I had inherited from my mother was perfect for the new fashions. For Harry, who, until that time, had been mostly an outside observer, being with me was an eye-opener. For the first time in his life, he was now an active participant rather than a passive observer. He now had someone he cared about to go with him, and it made all the difference.

Under Harry's guidance, I rapidly became a jazz fanatic, and together we sought out the best of the lot. Our favorite place for listening to jazz was a small speakeasy on 125th Street, not far from Harry's apartment. Most of the club's patrons were jazz lovers who had heard about it through the underground reputation of its musicians. Harry had been a regular listener almost from the start, but now, as a result of our frequent visits, and late night stays, Harry and I had developed a close friendship with the musicians.

We liked this particular club because the musicians were serious about what they played. We developed an easy camaraderie with the musicians which had started as a friendly nod of recognition and had developed into a full-blown, after-hours friendship. To Harry and me, the players' creativity was astounding and very subtle, and a listener had to pay careful attention to hear the changes they made from session to session.

The music, for the most part, was soft and gentle and romantic. Sometimes the intensity of the feelings that I sensed in the music brought me to tears.

Late at night, after most of the customers had left and the band had finished their last set, the musicians would wander over and sit at our table. "Did you hear when I came in?" the bass player boasted. "I was fast—it changed the whole set—ahead of the beat—really messed Charlie up." Charlie was the drummer who rarely spoke.

Their enthusiasm was infectious, and I loved being with them. Most of all, I loved that they included me in their inner circle. They encouraged me to listen to the rhythm. That was their specialty, rhythm—drums, a bass, a guitar. They would sit at the table working on the rhythm for hours, late into the night. They beat a bass, then syncopated it, then an overlay—no words—just melody. A sax, sometimes a guest trumpet. Plaintive, pleading, and passionate. There was no singer—the words didn't matter. Sometimes, because I was so focused on words, I would put words to their passion. At first the words made sense, then they were just random words, and then they were not even words. I learned to imitate the speaking sound of every instrument, but I couldn't sing, I could only say the rhythm.

They called me Bessie because they said I reminded them of Bessie Smith. Of course that was just a joke—Bessie Smith was the greatest black blues singer that ever lived, and I was a very white Jewish girl from Brooklyn who could barely carry a tune. But they teased me, and I loved it. Sometimes, late at night, when only the regulars were there, and when I had had enough to drink and smoke, I spoke my rhythms into the microphone in front of the band. And I was good at it, and they encouraged me, and they laughed at me and with me, and they flirted with me, and I flirted with them. It got so that I didn't hear the melody—didn't hear what they were playing—just the rhythm. I could hear the overlays, breaks, and segues. I heard rhythm in my breathing and walking and writing. I would talk and shout and laugh and tell stories, and, for the first time in my life, I understood what it was to soar. I was so happy; I laughed at everything, and they teased me and laughed with me and listened to my stories, too.

And under the table, with our fingers interlocked, Harry and I communicated wordlessly. Questions were asked, answers given, conclusions derived, and decisions made.

In my eyes, Harry was perfect. He was tall, smart, Jewish, a good dancer, and very good looking. We had rapidly proceeded through all the sexual preliminaries, and, although we had exhausted most of New York's romantic private spaces, I had resisted going to Harry's apartment because I felt that it might lead to "going all the way," which I was not about to do until we were married.

By that winter, I had already begun planning our wedding. My new fantasy was that Harry and I would get married before I was 20. We would finish the book, which would become an instant success, and then we would both go to an Ivy League college somewhere in New England. I would study English literature while Harry got his law degree. And then, after Harry became a lawyer, I would get a job writing for the *New York Times*. We would specialize in helping needy people. Harry would represent poor people, and I would draw attention to their plight. We wouldn't need much money because we would live in the slum alongside the people we were helping.

We never actually talked about it in so many words, but we both knew that we had a plan. We were certain that we could do anything. Of course, that was during the 1920s, when young people still believed that anything was possible. We could see only good things ahead, and we shared the belief that because we had been fortunate enough to be born into rich families, we had the responsibility to help people who had not been so lucky.

And just as Harry had anticipated, once I became more relaxed, my book started to take shape. Slowly I began to fit all the elements together. I started to think of the book as a developing story rather than the epic book that it had become in its first iteration. Although I was never completely happy with what I wrote, Harry thought it was good. We sent the completed chapters one by one to Mr. Davis, and he said that he was satisfied with what we had accomplished so far.

For Harry and me, this was an especially happy time. So we kept working, slowly, chapter by chapter, but, nevertheless, making progress.

CHAPTER 13

"'In the spring a young man's fancy lightly turns to thoughts of love,'" Harry said quietly. We were sitting on the steps of the New York Public Library between the lions, watching the traffic on Fifth Avenue, holding hands. "Alfred Lord Tennyson said that about fifty years ago," he said softly, so only I could hear. "Well, it is spring, and I'm a relatively young man, and my thoughts have turned to 'thoughts of love.' In fact, my thoughts have gone far beyond just thoughts of love, they have gone to action. Ruthie, you know that I love you. This last year has been the best year of my life. And I think that I know that you love me. So, here's the thing, will you marry me?"

I smiled and put my head on his shoulder. "That was so romantic," I whispered, "and my answer is a definite yes! But shouldn't there be a ring?"

"Oh my God," Harry said. "I was so nervous I totally forgot." And, reaching into his jacket pocket, he produced a small, red velvet box. The ring, pretty and delicate, was inside. I slipped it onto my finger. "It's perfect."

"It was my grandmother's," Harry said proudly. "I hope it's OK."

"OK? It's perfect, and I love it, and I love you, and I can't wait to be married."

"Me too, but there's a lot of stuff that we have to do first."

"Like what?" I said impatiently.

"Well first we have to get permission from your parents. You're still underage. And then, we'd have to speak to my father. He's kind of traditional about things like this and even though I'm old enough, he would want us to formally ask for his blessing."

"I don't think it would be a problem with my parents," I bubbled enthusiastically.

"OK. When should we do it?"

"How about today?" I said, standing up and pulling Harry up alongside of me. "I know they're home, and it's a beautiful day so they should be in a good mood, and we could just take the subway, and we'd be there in no time, and then you could ask for their permission, and then we could all celebrate, and then we could pick a date for the wedding and make plans, and . . ."

"Hey! Hold on," Harry laughed. "One thing at a time. OK. I agree that we can go talk to your parents today. Do you think I should do it by myself or do you want to be there?"

"I wouldn't want to miss one second of this. I want to see their faces, but I promise not to say a word. This will be all your job. What are you planning to say?"

"I don't know. I'll think about it on the subway."

And so, as if on the wings of eagles, we flew, running and skipping and laughing and loving down Forty-Second Street to the subway. Once on the train, though, and on our way to meet with my parents, we had the sober realization that, in fact, my father might not approve of the marriage. He was so unpredictable, I explained to Harry, and he always needed to be in charge. We made a quick list of my parents' possible objections to the marriage, and then we listed all of Harry's strengths, and all the reasons why the marriage was going to be successful. We felt that we had logic on our side, but we weren't sure. And so, with some anxiety, we climbed the stairs to my house.

"Mr. Rubin," Harry began after the usual greetings, "I have something very important that I have to ask you and Mrs. Rubin."

"Sit down, Harry, I'll get Mrs. Rubin," my father said kindly, and he went into the kitchen where he stayed for an unexpectedly long time. Harry and I just sat, not talking, not even touching.

Rose was pacing nervously when I came into the kitchen. "Close the door," she said, "we need to talk in private."

"You do understand why they're here!" she said matter-of-factly after I had closed the door.

"I think he wants to marry Ruthie," I replied excitedly.

"So do I. What do you think we should say?" Rose asked.

"I'm not sure. On one hand, he's a nice boy from a well-to-do home, and I'm sure he can support her, but on the other hand, he's not one of us."

"What do you mean?"

"His family is Reform. I know all about Reform Jews. They don't keep kosher. They don't even wear *yarmulkas* in shul, and they pray in English. I bet he doesn't even know the words to the Shema. He's almost a *goy*. Ruthie's so beautiful and so smart and so young. Why should she throw herself to this half-Jew? She should wait for a better match."

Rose sat down at the kitchen table. "I never thought of that," she said quietly. "Of course you're right. He would lead her astray. She is our only child, and we have a responsibility to make sure that she marries a religious man and that she continues all of our traditions. But he's a nice man and he's rich and he can take care of her and he will make her happy."

"Yes, yes, yes. Yes, to all of that," I said, pacing. "But still, we have raised her in a certain way, and we have an obligation to see that she continues along that path. We are part of a tradition that goes back thousands of years, and we have an obligation to make sure that that tradition continues. Even though this is America and a new world, we are still Jews, and we must remain Jews."

"So what will you tell them?"

"I'll tell him no, and I'll give him the reasons."

"Jack, don't lose your temper," Rose said grasping my hand. "Be nice to them, but make it clear that it is impossible."

***

My parents came into the room looking solemn. My father sat in the big chair facing Harry and me. My mother sat stiffly on the edge of one of the upholstered dining room chairs.

"So, Harry, we're here, what is it?" my father asked.

"Mr. Rubin, I would like your permission to marry your daughter," Harry said in a clear voice.

My father looked briefly at my mother. Something was wrong, and I felt my stomach muscles twinge. "Yes, Harry, go on," he said gently.

This was not the initial reaction that I had hoped for. I had expected a smile and a big hug, and now I sensed trouble on the horizon.

"Mr. Rubin," Harry persisted, "I will be a very good husband to her. I will take good care of her. I have a good job and a steady income." He paused uncertainly and glanced at me. "And I love her."

My father remained silent, focusing all his attention on Harry, who was now becoming nervous. We had hoped for some sort of response so that Harry could press his argument, but my parents just sat and didn't say a word.

"I have some savings," Harry continued, with increasing dread, "so we will have some money to start off our marriage." I could hear a tone of desperation creeping into Harry's voice. This was not what we had anticipated. "Mr. Rubin," he declared, a little too forcefully, "I will take good care of her. I promise you that. We love each other. We will be happy together." Then he fell silent. He couldn't think of anything else to say, and my parents still had not responded. Silence dominated the room.

Dramatically, my father rose from his chair, walked into his office and shuffled some papers.

Everyone was waiting to hear what I would say, and I wanted to appear to be thoughtful, although I had already prepared my response. I had waited years for this moment. This was my time to do my parental duty, and I wanted to be sure to get it right.

Slowly I walked back into the room from my office and stood facing them.

"And you will take good care of my daughter?" I asked as gently as I could.

"Yes, sir," Harry replied, looking up at me.

"And will you keep a kosher home?"

"If that's what she wants."

"And will you send your children to yeshiva?"

"Yes, sir. If that's what she wants."

"And will you *daven* with them and study *Talmud* and *Torah* and *Rashi* with them? And can you guarantee that your home will be filled with yiddishkeit?" My voice was now rising uncontrollably.

"And will you take them to shul on Shabbos," I nearly shouted, "and teach them to make a *motzi* and *Kiddush*?

"Can you say yes to this?" I shouted, standing over him. "You don't even know what I'm talking about! How can you have a proper Jewish home when you know nothing—nothing!"

I was feeling good. Being aggressive brought back all of the instincts of my youth. This was what I had grown up with. This was what I really knew. This was what being a parent was all about! I looked over at Rose proudly, but she was not happy—I had been too aggressive, and she was signaling me to take it easier.

I walked over to where she was sitting and took her hand. She shook her head inconspicuously. I took a deep breath and slowly walked back to my chair.

And then in a quieter, more reasonable, almost pleading tone, I said, "Listen to me, Harry, we are Americans just like you, but we are something more. We in this family carry with us our souls, hundreds of years of history, the teachings of the great Rabbis and scholars like Hillel, and Shammai, and Rabbi Akiba, and Yehuda Ha-Nasi, and Rashi, and Maimonides, and the Baal Shem Tov. We have a heritage of *pogroms*, and life in the shtetle. This is in our blood.

"Although we both are Jewish, Harry, our family is Orthodox, yours is Reform. We are at different ends of the religious spectrum. Frankly, we Orthodox Jews do not consider you Reform Jews to be authentic, and I suspect that you Reform Jews consider us Orthodox Jews to be fanatics. You and your Reform family have turned Jewish practice on its head, and you, Harry, know so very little about Jewish history and family and traditions, that this marriage would be doomed from the start. Believe me, Harry, I would like to say yes because you are a nice fellow, and Ruthie is so happy when she is with you, but I am so sure that this will not work out that I must say no."

Harry and I had certainly not expected this reaction. After all, we had felt, we're both Jewish, certainly that should be enough. But now it wasn't, and I realized that I should have anticipated this response from my father.

Without raising my voice, without showing emotion, I said, "Mom, Dad, Harry and I intend to get married, with or without your blessing. It would be very unpleasant for us if we got married without your blessing, but we will. We will just have to wait a little longer until I am legally of age. So now, it is up to you. Will you give us your blessing? Or will we just get married eventually without your blessing?"

This surprised my father, and he reacted slowly. He took off his glasses and began polishing them with his handkerchief, obviously buying time to think.

"Yes," he said finally. "I see. What you have said is certainly logical, and it makes our situation much more difficult. You see, religion has always been an important part of our lives. Speaking for myself, I was born into a religious home in Minsk, and I went to a religious school—what we called a *cheder*—as soon as I was old enough to read. My mother raised me in this country by herself. It was very hard for her, but she did it. The main thing that helped her get through it was our shul, our synagogue, and our yiddishkeit. We went to shul every Shabbos and every holiday. It was the only thing that we had that was the same as all those families with two parents; the same as what we had in Poland. And the shul took care of us, and the Rabbi and the *Rebbitzen* visited us, and the sisterhood brought us food and clothing. And we survived. And now, we are an integral part of the Orthodox community, and, as you very well know, that is a very important part of our lives."

My father stopped speaking and looked at my mother, waiting for her to speak.

"Harry, Ruthie," my mother said gently, "love is very important, and I can see how much you love each other. And that is very beautiful and very romantic. But in a marriage, you need more than love. You need to have shared values. Those values are transmitted to you by your parents in subtle ways and in steady doses. That is the difference between romance and marriage. Yes, you have romantic love, but you have very disparate values.

"Harry," she said, focusing on him, "we love Ruthie very much, and, though she is now an adult, we still have a responsibility to protect her from danger. Her father and I feel that marriage to someone who is so far from our Jewish traditions and values would put her in harm's way. We only want the best for her, and I'm sure that you do too. I know that you both feel very strongly about this, so now, all we can ask is that you please take some time and think about it."

My mother paused and looked around the room, focusing on each of us. She seemed to be weighing, very carefully, what she was about to say.

"So now, Harry," my mother finally said, with great sadness, "I think you should leave. And Ruthie, you should go to your room. Maybe, after we all have had some time to think, we can talk again."

I ran to my room, but I couldn't throw myself on the bed because my grandfather was sitting there. He had been waiting for me, and he jumped to his feet as I came into the room.

"Ruthie, I have to ask you an important question," he said in his most scholarly tone.

"Oh no, please, not now!" I cried.

"Ruthie, listen carefully," he insisted, "this is very important. I can help you, but first you must think very hard about the question I'm about to ask you."

With gathering tears in my eyes, I turned to face him.

"Ruthie," my grandfather said, putting both hands on my shoulders, "I know you love this man very much. So now, here is my question, and I want you to think very carefully about your answer before you respond. Ruthie, do you love him enough?"

"I don't understand," I mumbled.

"I know—this is a very hard thing for a young girl to understand. Let me try. When you marry a man, you split yourself in half, and so does he. You give up part of yourself to join with him, and he gives up part of himself to join with you.

"This is very hard. Half of you and half of him join together to make one whole person. In most marriages the couple learns to match his half to her half and make a whole. That is because they are willing to give up the remaining half of themselves in order to make a new unit. But sometimes, like your parents think it might be with you, the other half of each personality tries to pull the couple apart. So if your marriage is only made up of the two halves that joined in the beginning, then it is doomed because the other two halves—your leftover half and his leftover half—will try to pull you apart.

"When these leftover halves are similar they eventually blend together and pretty soon instead of being four halves, you are one whole.

"But when the leftover halves are very different, it is much harder to make a whole. They will pull on each of you and try to get their other half back. Do you understand?"

"I think so . . . but I love him, and he loves me. Isn't that enough?"

"You ask if that is enough. That is what I am asking you to determine. It is going to be very hard. You come from two different backgrounds, different values, almost a different religion. You will have to teach each other. In order for your father to give his blessing, Harry will have to learn how to be Orthodox, and you will have to learn how to accept him. And then you will have to learn how to be Orthodox all over again. Do you think your Harry would be willing to do this?"

I nodded dumbly, tears rolling down my cheeks.

"This kind of marriage," my grandfather went on, "is not easy to do. Only people who are very sure of their love can do it. Only people who are willing to give up half of themselves can do it. Think about it. This is not your father's decision—it is yours."

"But he is so mean—he won't let me marry Harry."

"You don't really mean that," my grandfather said, releasing me and sitting down on my bed. He patted the space next to him.

"You know I always tell you stories, this time I want you to remember the story of Ruth and Naomi. Naomi was Ruth's mother-in-law. They were very different, even more different than you and Harry. Naomi was Jewish from Bethlehem, and Ruth was a Moabite. Both Naomi's and Ruth's husbands suddenly died. Naomi told Ruth that now that her husband had died, she planned to go back to her family in Bethlehem. She recommended that Ruth return to her family as well. But Ruth refused to leave her. She told Naomi how much she loved her. She said, 'I love you so much that "where you go I will go, and where you stay I will stay. Your people will be my people and your God my God. Where you die I will die, and there I will be buried."'

"This is the kind of commitment that I am talking about. One hundred percent; nothing held back. It is very difficult to make, but it is the sort of commitment that Harry must make to you before your father will give his approval. And also, Ruthie, it is a great responsibility for you to accept such an intense commitment.

"Ruthie, think very hard about the question I asked you. Do you love Harry enough? And does he love you enough as well? I have to tell you that very few people in your circumstances have enough love to say yes to this question. Perhaps you do. Only you and Harry can decide. And then, if you are sure that you have enough love, go speak to your father, tell him what you have resolved. He will understand. But Ruthie, you must be sure."

CHAPTER 14

To say I was upset would be a great understatement. I realized, while I was sitting there, that Jack and I had made a bad decision. We were now, I was afraid, in danger of losing our daughter.

I couldn't sleep, and, late that night, I tapped on Ruthie's door. "Ruthie," I whispered, "are you up?"

"Yes."

"Put on your bathrobe and come into the kitchen," I said. "I want to talk to you."

Obediently, and a little dazed, Ruthie shuffled into the kitchen. Only the light over the stove was lit. I was at the table in my bathrobe and curlers. Ruthie looked shocked when she saw me—I can only imagine what I looked like.

"I made you some warm milk, and here's a plate of cookies," I said softly. "I wanted to talk to you about what happened tonight, and I want you to listen to me very carefully. Sometimes your father gets a little too emotional. It's the way he was brought up. He's used to fighting for everything, especially if it is something or someone that he really cares about, like you. He only wants the best for you, but sometimes he doesn't express himself as well as he should.

"But that's not what I wanted to talk to you about. Or rather, that's not all I wanted to talk to you about. This is hard for me, and I hope you hear it with all the love that I can give you. You are a mature, grown woman," I said, "and it's time for you to take charge of your life. I know that you are planning to go to Brooklyn College in the fall. That would have been a good idea because you could live here, at home. But right now I don't think it would be a good idea for you to live here.

"I would like you to go to City College, which is all the way uptown in New York City, instead. I want you to get an apartment and live near the college instead of going to Brooklyn College and living at home. You know I love you very much, but you need to get out of this house and live on your own now. I know it's not the same, but when I was your age, I had already opened the shop, and I was also supporting your grandfather.

"I'm not telling you to do this because of what happened tonight or anything else. I just want you to be on your own, and I am very confident that you will be able to manage very well. Of course we will pay for everything, but it will be better for you to live uptown. We're only a subway ride away so you can visit here whenever you like, and your room will be exactly as you left it, but right now you need to be independent—and the sooner the better. We can go next week to look at apartments. I'm sure that we can find something that you really like."

It was painful, and I wasn't sure what to expect, but Ruthie hugged me and rested her head on my shoulder. She had not sat like that since she was a child. I should have been better prepared for that moment.

I phoned Harry the next morning and told him all that my grandfather and my mother had told me, and we agreed to meet on the library steps that afternoon.

"I've been thinking about this non-stop since I left your

parents' house," Harry said as soon as we met. He had been pacing in front of the library waiting for me, and he seemed extremely anxious and agitated.

"Your father and your grandfather are right," he said. "We're really nearly two different religions. It's a giant step, and it's possible that we are making a big mistake. What happens if we are wrong? What happens if your father was right and that our values are too far apart? And what happens if your grandfather is right, and we can't fit together? Then what? If we marry and it doesn't work out, then we will suffer for the rest of our lives!

"Look, we love each other, and we know a lot about each other in the present, but we know very little about the different worlds that we came from. That's the problem. Look, I know I love you, I know I want to live with you for the rest of my life. But I don't know what's in the blood that runs in your veins and in the air you breathe. And you, you don't know much about me either.

"After I left your house on Sunday, I was very upset. But then I started to think about what your father said. He was very harsh, but what he said was honest emotion. He told me that I didn't understand your culture—that you and I come from opposite sides of the spectrum. For you, keeping kosher is natural, for me, it's unnatural. For you, sending your child to yeshiva is natural, for me it's unnatural. And there are a million other ways in which we are different. Here's the thing, Ruthie, your parents are right. We are very very different. But we are in love, and that's got to balance all the other things."

"Look," I said, taking his hand, "my grandfather said that we could become whole—that it's up to us to decide. He said that we have to have enough love. I think we do, what do you think?"

Harry looked a little bit happier. He could hear the anxiety in my voice, and he smiled at me and squeezed my hand. "I think we do, Ruthie, I think we do. The burden, it seems to me, is mostly on me, and I am willing to give it a try. Look, being a Reform Jew is not so important to me and being Orthodox is really important to you and your family. So I will learn the laws about keeping kosher, and from this moment on I will eat only kosher food according to Orthodox Jewish tradition. And I will rest on the Sabbath and go to services at an Orthodox synagogue. These things are pretty easy because they're all surface stuff. But I'm willing to do the hard part too: I will find a teacher and begin to study ritual, and *Torah*, and *Talmud* so that I can learn what to do and also learn the background of the laws. I want to feel the same passion about Judaism that you and your family feel. I probably won't be able to do all of this right away, but I promise to start. And once I start, I promise to finish."

I took Harry's arm and led him up the library steps, to our usual place, between the two lions. I smiled to myself remembering their names: Patience and Fortitude.

That's what we need, I thought to myself, *patience and fortitude.* I held Harry's hand very tightly, afraid to let go, and we sat there silently, but together, for quite a while, watching the pedestrians on Fifth Avenue. They say that if you sit between the library lions long enough, all the world will pass by.

"I don't know your family at all," I said finally. "I have to get to know them. How should I do that?"

"That's easy. We can just go to the apartment and talk to my mother. She loves to talk."

"This is so strange. You have met my parents a million times, but I have never met yours."

"That's because I always come to your house to work on the book. But we can easily fix that. The only problem is that my mother's kind of formal, and she likes to invite people rather than have them just drop in. I'll ask her to invite you next week. Is that OK?"

The following week, on my first visit to Harry's parents' apartment, Mrs. Berger was in a chair reading when the maid admitted us. She looked up, hesitated slightly, and then, in one graceful motion, rose from her chair and walked to us with her hand outstretched.

"You must be Ruthie," she said in her elegant drawl. I made an instant evaluation: she had perfect manners, perfect diction, a perfect face, a perfect body, and perfect clothing, and I immediately felt intimidated. I had never been good at meeting people, but the ultra perfect mother of the man I intended to marry was more than I could handle.

Surprisingly, it was OK. Mrs. Berger did all the talking until I could get over my fright. We had tea and little breads with cream cheese and sliced olives.

I tried to talk with her, but all I could think about were the instructions that I had learned in school. Sit up straight, knees together, ankles crossed, don't forget the napkin, plate on your lap, and don't talk with your mouth full. Speak when you're spoken to. Make eye contact.

Mrs. Berger did all the talking, and Harry didn't say a word. Soon, surprisingly, I found myself telling Mrs. Berger about my writing and how much Harry had helped me. Mrs. Berger seemed interested in everything I said, and she kept asking questions to encourage me to speak. And eventually, the floodgates opened. I told her about my early stories, and the magazines, and Mr. Davis, and the progress we were making on the book.

Mrs. Berger was a voracious reader. And, like me, she liked to read the same books over and over. We talked about books we enjoyed, authors we preferred, even favorite characters and quotes. I loved her; I loved being there, and I decided that when I got older I would be just like her. I began to relax—the afternoon was wonderful—everything was going to be OK.

And then, Mr. Berger came in. He had been at a meeting, and he apologized for being late. He was a large, impressive man, and he called greetings and apologies from the front door. The maid helped him off with his suit jacket and helped him into another jacket. Mrs. Berger rose to greet him as he came into the room, and she pressed her cheek to his briefly. Harry and I stood as Mrs. Berger introduced me to him. We shook hands and Mr. Berger bowed slightly, and then he went to the large chair.

All conversation had stopped. After the introductions, we had resumed our seats, and we waited for Mr. Berger to initiate a topic for discussion. The room was now uncomfortably silent and expectant. Rather than speak immediately, as my father would have done, Mr. Berger reached into a humidor on the side table, removed a cigar, rolled it briefly between his fingers, smelled it, snipped off the end, and finally lit it.

"So," he finally began, "Harry tells me that you are from Brooklyn. What synagogue do your parents belong to?"

It was such an abrupt and direct question that I was shocked. "Shomrei Emunah," I replied, without trying to put the name into a sentence as I had been taught.

"Guardians of the faith. Orthodox, I suppose."

"Yes."

"And your parents, do they speak English"?

"Yes."

"And your father, in the garment industry?"

"No, he owns houses."

"Owns houses? Really! What sort of houses?"

"He owns some apartment houses on Parkside Avenue in Brooklyn."

I could feel the tension in the room; no one spoke. It seemed to me that Mr. Berger somehow did not approve of me. The friendliness that I had felt just moments before seemed to have turned to hostility once Mr. Berger had entered the room, and I wondered to myself why he was being so aggressive. Was this his natural tone? Or was there something particularly objectionable about me?

And then, before I could even explore these doubts, Mr. Berger changed his tone. To me, it was like a sudden thunderstorm that was followed by beautiful clearing skies.

"So, Harry tells me that you are a writer," Mr. Berger continued in a noticeably warmer tone. "Fiction, eh? I don't read much fiction—not enough time. It's a pity you're not a reporter. You could write something about the politics in our temple; there is such controversy." And with that, he turned to Mrs. Berger.

"They sold the building today. That's where I was. It's going to be the end of Temple Emanu-El."

"Yes, I heard. It's a sad day. But the new location is very nice, it's still Fifth Avenue, after all, and it's even closer to us. It'll be all right. Times change, we're growing so fast; we need more space. I just hope they make it as beautiful as the sketches."

"That's going to be our job: making sure that they stick to the plans. But how will you feel worshiping at Beth-El while the building's being built? It's going to take years before we have our own synagogue again."

I was trying hard to follow the conversation, and I was relieved that Mr. Berger seemed to have forgotten about me. I knew that both Temple Emanu-El and Temple Beth-El were Reform synagogues, and I didn't understand why they would consider one preferable to the other. In my mind, they were both the same. Even though I didn't understand the differences, I definitely got the feeling of a subtle prejudice—first against my parents and then against Temple Beth-El.

The conversation eventually settled into a surface discussion of current events, which I participated in only when asked and only in the most neutral way. I was wary of Mr. Berger's volatility, and wanted to make a good impression on him. I felt that I was succeeding when, all of a sudden and without warning, Mrs. Berger stood up, and Harry stood up too.

"Come Ruthie, let me show you the apartment," Mrs. Berger said, and without waiting to see if I was following, she started across the room toward the dining room. We did a quick tour, with me struggling to keep up. And then, just as quickly as it had begun, the tour ended at the front door, and Mrs. Berger was holding out her hand to me.

She thanked me for my visit, thanked Harry for bringing me, and said she was looking forward to talking with me again soon. And then she opened the door and Harry and I found ourselves out in the hall ringing for the elevator.

I was confused. *Had I done or said something to offend Mr. or Mrs. Berger?* But when I looked at Harry, he was beaming.

Out on Fifth Avenue, after our visit with Harry's parents, I breathed a sigh of relief. Harry was overjoyed. He said that his parents had obviously liked me, and that I had overcome a major hurdle. He said that I had done my part, and that the rest, now, would be up to him.

As soon as we were out of the doorman's vision, I stopped and confronted him. "Are you sure you want to do this?" I asked.

"Yes," he said with intense conviction. "My moment has come, and I am ready. It is definitely going to be a challenge, but rather than feeling anxious, I feel euphoric. I finally have something and someone that I care about enough to make a change. Let's face it," he said introspectively, "I have been a passive observer all my life. I have been the audience rather than the player, the editor rather than the author. But now, for really the first time in my life, I am making a commitment to a cause."

He said he could feel the adrenaline rush, that he would do this for me, and that he would show me and my father and my grandfather. He told me that we would see how powerful his drive could be once he set his mind to a task. And most of all, he said, stopping mid-block and taking me by the arm, he had finally found someone who would encourage him and stay with him and reward him through his struggle. The burden, he said, was on him, and he welcomed the challenge.

"I have always felt like an outsider," he said sincerely, "an observer. But now, I can devote myself to my new religion. I plan to learn as much as I can until I can feel Judaism in my soul. The truth is," he said, "that I like the dedication of the Orthodox Jews. I like that they pray so often, and that they fast so many times throughout the year, and that there are so many controls and restrictions on their behavior, and that the weight of the world sometimes seems to rest on their shoulders. I plan to start slowly, to learn all the rules, and all the rituals, and then as I learn to do them, they will become part of my life pattern, just like you."

I went to speak to my father to ask if Harry and I could meet with him, and we set a time for the following Sunday.

This time I did most of the talking. I explained to my parents that I understood their concerns, and that I understood and appreciated that they had those concerns only out of love for me. I confessed that I had been very upset, and that I was surprised that when I had discussed it with Harry, he had agreed with my father.

My father turned to Harry and focused all his concentration on him.

"So, you agree with me! And what do you agree with me about?"

"Mr. Rubin," Harry said, "you and your family have a long and wonderful history. You have beautiful traditions, which I now realize are very important to Ruthie. She and I talked about them after we met with you, and, frankly, we hadn't thought about those very important issues until you brought them up. I have made a commitment to Ruthie that since they are so important to her, I will try my best to honor them and follow in your footsteps. I may be somewhat naive in the beginning, and I may do it in my style and in my own way, and it might take longer than you would like, but we will do it. We will do it together—Ruthie and I. You might not agree with every decision we make, but I promise you that we will make every effort to do things right, and we will welcome your guidance whenever it is offered."

⸻

Rose and I had not expected this. We had expected a battle, and we had been prepared to relent. I took my glasses off, slowly folded them, and put them in my breast pocket. I suddenly felt older—tired. I had fought a battle and won, but somehow, I didn't feel good about it. I felt that there was something missing—that there should be something more—but I couldn't tell what it was. It had been too easy, something was off kilter, but I couldn't tell what. I stared at Rose, hoping for inspiration. Something was wrong, very wrong, and Ruthie, I sensed, was at risk. I needed time to think, but they were here now, and they were waiting for my answer, and I had to give it. But still, I needed time to think.

"Ruthie is our pride," I said aloud. "You must promise to take care of her always. She is a special person with a special gift. You must honor that gift.

"Here," I said, standing up, "give me your hand. Promise me now."

I stood and Harry stood and we shook hands. Formally.

"Harry," I said, still holding his hand, my mind racing for guidance, trying to buy time. "You have pledged to learn the Orthodox way. I don't expect you to do everything that you promised. But I am a businessman, and I want to make sure that you are going in the right direction, so here is my offer: you study and show me that you are serious, and I will give you and Ruthie my whole-hearted blessing. We should make a deadline. How about Chanukah?"

Harry freed his hand and looked at Ruthie, who was anxiously watching him. "That sounds like a good plan, Mr. Rubin. We can then arrange for a spring wedding, maybe in June."

"Chanukah, it is," I said, taking Harry's hand once more. And then Harry and I embraced, and then we all hugged each other. And Rose began to cry.

CHAPTER 15

With a song in our hearts, we made our way into New York to celebrate. We had decided to treat ourselves to the best and most expensive kosher restaurant in the city, Lou G. Siegel. On the subway, going to Manhattan, we talked sporadically about the future. The rest of the time on the subway, and on our walk to the restaurant, we just held hands and dreamed.

The restaurant was crowded, and we were finally seated at a small table near the kitchen. Normally, Harry would have complained, but tonight he was too elated. We sat quietly, holding hands, with our fingers intertwined, sipping our cream sodas and waiting for our pastrami sandwiches.

As I sat there, amid the noise and excitement of the Sunday night crowd, holding Harry's hand, I was thinking about my father's remarkable change of heart. I just couldn't believe that he had completely changed his mind on the basis of Harry's promise to become more Orthodox. It was a kind of miracle, and it was not like him, not at all. He was cautious and methodical in everything. Why this abrupt change of heart?

And then, I understood.

Tears of anger and frustration involuntarily welled up in

my eyes, and I freed my hand from Harry's and searched in my pocketbook for a handkerchief. Harry looked at me with uncomprehending alarm.

"What is it?" he asked.

"I just thought about it," I said through my tears, "and now I understand what he did."

"Who?"

"My father. I'm sure that he's not going to agree to our marriage. He just said he would agree in order to delay the decision. He's hoping that in six months we will have parted ways."

"And if we don't?"

"He'll just delay it again."

"Until we give up."

"Exactly. Until we give up. That's his way of doing things."

Harry reached across the table and took my hand again, but I took it back.

"Why do you think he'll say no?" Harry asked.

"He's always interested in *maris ayin*."

"What's that?"

"Appearances. He's always worried about what other people will say about us. If I marry someone from outside our community, he will look bad."

"No matter who it is?"

"Well, not absolutely. If I married some famous person or some rich guy from Fifth Avenue, that might make it OK."

"I'm a rich guy from Fifth Avenue. Doesn't that count?"

"Yes, but, and don't take this the wrong way, you're an editor. You are coaching me. You don't have the right kind of *yichus*."

"Yichus?"

"Unique quality. If you were a published author, for example, that would be yichus, or if you came from a family he heard of, that would be yichus."

"What if I came from an impressive family that he never heard of?" Harry asked.

"Then the family would have to do something to impress him."

"That's the answer then! There is no one more impressive than my parents—especially my father. You said so yourself. Suppose we set up a meeting between my father and your father, or my parents and your parents. You want yichus? I'll ask my parents to invite your parents to the apartment! That will impress them."

And suddenly, once again, our mood changed, and our joy returned. This was going to be even better than we had envisioned! We sat, each reveling in our own imaginations of how well such a meeting would go.

Harry telephoned his parents. He told them that there was something important that he and I wanted to discuss with them, and they arranged a time to meet.

"Let me handle this," Harry said with a worried look as we rode up in the elevator, "they are very formal, and they insist that there's a proper way to do everything. I think I know what they want to hear."

I could hear the anxiety in Harry's voice, but I let it pass without comment. *Maybe*, I thought, *it will actually work out*.

When we were seated in the living room, each in our accustomed places, Harry told his parents that he and I would like to get married. He explained carefully, and a bit deceptively, that even though he and I were planning a very small wedding, it was important that his parents invite my parents to their apartment so that they could all participate in the planning of the wedding together.

Harry explained, with a proud smile, and a quick glance at me, that he intended to learn how to get more deeply involved in Jewish ritual, and that he looked forward to experiencing, with my family, the increased intensity of Orthodox observance.

While Harry was speaking, I watched Mrs. Berger, hoping for a clue as to her reaction. She seemed pleased and had just the slightest hint of a smile. But then Mr. Berger said the words we feared most. He spoke slowly, clearly, and distinctly, so as to avoid any misinterpretation.

"Harry," he said, "based on what you have just told me, I

must tell you that I disapprove of this marriage."

Then calmly, without emotion, he explained, "Unlike Ruthie's parents, and the Orthodox in general, our status as Reform Jews is not something that happened by accident of birth, it was a conscious decision that my parents made after great study. We, in this family, have chosen to be Reform because it represents the future, and I would not be faithful to our family's values if I allow our only son to slide backward into the superstitious Judaism of the past.

"Judaism," he said with increasing passion, "is a rational religion that has always adapted itself to the present. Judaism, throughout the centuries, has been a leader in forward-thinking social responsibility. This is the twentieth-century, and I will not let my son marry someone whose family values are stuck in the Middle Ages."

He rose and stood proudly, ramrod straight, right in front of me. "Ruthie, you and your family represent the past. It is interesting as history, but it is not life. We are in the beginning of the twentieth-century. The world is ahead of us, not behind us. We Reform Jews live in the present and look forward, you Orthodox Jews live in the past and look backward."

"Ruthie, Harry," he said, "listen to me carefully. This marriage cannot be allowed to happen, and I promise to use all my energy to stop it."

We saw ourselves out of the apartment, down the elevator, and out into the street. Harry was shocked and furious, I was surprisingly calm. It was almost as if I had expected this. Nothing that Mr. Berger had said in the past made me think that he would act this way. And yet, I was almost relieved. The conflict that I had dreaded would never materialize.

We left the apartment and walked down Fifth Avenue, looking in the store windows without seeing. Eventually we ended up at the Forty-Second Street Library. We had spent so many happy hours there that that's where our feet automatically took us. We sat on the steps, in our usual spot, among the lovers, between the lions, warmed by the spring sun. We didn't speak.

In fact, we had hardly spoken since we left the Bergers' apartment. We sat for a long time in silence—holding hands.

"A penny for your thoughts," I finally said.

"No, you go first."

"OK," I said, "I think we should move in together."

"I was thinking the same thing, but I was afraid to say it because I was afraid it would shock you," Harry said.

"I don't shock that easily," I laughed. "Remember, I write romantic fiction. I have thought about every possible attachment."

"Wait," Harry said, laughing, "am I going to be in your next story?"

"Not unless you do something really out of the ordinary."

"Do you think we should tell our parents?"

"No."

"How can we do that? You still live at home."

"Yes, but my mother wants me to go to City College rather than Brooklyn, and she said that they will help me get an apartment. So it looks like I'm going to be living uptown in Manhattanville, way above Harlem. It's probably an hour and a half by train from Brooklyn so I'll be pretty much on my own, and they will never just drop in. Once they get me the apartment, you can move in."

"But you're a virgin."

"Not for long!"

"It'll be just like being married."

"Just like being married."

"Can you cook?"

"No."

And just like that, we had a plan.

Although it had seemed exciting and romantic when we had first discussed it, the actual act of moving in together was still a big step, even in those racy times. And, although I was the one who had suggested it, I was getting cold feet. For a while, I tried to tough it out, but then, as I had always done with all of the decisions that I had previously made in my life, I consulted my grandfather.

I wasn't sure how to introduce the subject, and so I decided to just jump in. I went into his bedroom and closed the door behind me. And then, without taking time to think about the consequences, I laid my cards on the table.

"I need to ask you an important question, but it is about sex and marriage and forbidden things. Before I say anything more, I want to know if I have your permission to ask, and before you answer, I want you to know that I won't be upset if you say no."

"It's hard for me to know whether to say yes or no until I hear the question," he said, looking up from his books.

In spite of my anxiety, I smiled to myself—this had always been my grandfather's typical Talmudic answer to every question that I had ever asked.

"That's fair," I said. "Here's the introduction: my father told Harry that he would only give his permission for us to marry if Harry became Orthodox. Becoming Orthodox is not a black and white situation, and I'm afraid that, no matter how hard he tries, Harry will not be able to become Orthodox enough to satisfy my father. There is no test, you know, so it's all going to be up to my father to judge.

"There are only two possibilities," I said in my most Talmudic tone, "one is that my father says yes, which I have my doubts about, and the second is that he says no. If he says no, then it is likely that Harry will never be able to satisfy his standards. That is the end of the introduction. Now comes the hard part.

"Harry and I have decided to get married even if my father says no. But, since I'm far from turning twenty-one, I will need my father's permission in order for us to get a marriage license.

We could wait two more years, until I'm twenty-one, and then get married without his permission. But two years is a very long time for us to wait. Harry has already given me a ring so we're engaged, and nobody waits two years after their engagement."

"So what's your question?" my grandfather asked.

"Harry and I might want to move in together. We would still have to wait until I was twenty-one to be legally married, but we would live together as if we were legally married, but without the license."

"So you're asking me for permission?"

"Well, sort of."

"That is something I cannot do," he said with finality. And then, seeing how his answer had deflated me, he motioned for me to sit down.

"Your question," he said, closing his study book, "is not a new one. In the thousands of years of Jewish history, this question has come up many times. In fact, there is a whole book of the *Talmud* devoted to questions pertaining to marriage. The name of the book is *Mishnah Kiddushin*. As you know, the *Mishnah* is the book of original laws on which the debates in the *Talmud* are based, and *Kiddushin* means marriage. So the name of the book is *The Laws of Marriage*. But the laws are only the beginning. The important part of the book is in the Talmudic discussion that follows the *Mishnah* in which the Rabbis debate the interpretation and application of the laws. I am not very familiar with those debates, but I am sure that we can find an answer to your question there. Unfortunately, I don't have those books here, so we'll have to go to the study hall at the synagogue and read them together."

I felt somewhat ambivalent about bypassing my parents and consulting my grandfather, but he had always been my ally in my battles with them, and I hoped that he would be able to find a way for me to do this. Or, alternatively, that he would tell me that it was absolutely forbidden. I was fully prepared to accept his verdict either way. It, therefore, surprised me that he seemed so eager to help me find a way around my parents' authority.

Mein Liebe Rivka,
Today I was finally able to take charge of Ruthie's life. That

man Harry asked her to marry him, and Jack, of course, refused to give them permission. He is such a shtarke, *so full of himself that he completely said the wrong thing. He still has no idea how to be a parent. He should have agreed. That's what I would have done. Agreed and then tried to push them in the right direction. He is an ignorant fool, and this has gone too far. I cannot let him do any more damage. He has no idea how to be a Jew.*

But God has heard my prayers, and now I finally have an opportunity to change Ruthie's life, and Jack won't know until it is too late. I will get her out of the house and away from that ignoramus. They want to get married, and I can influence how they do it and also how they live their lives from now on.

I promise you Rivka, Ruthie will be a frum *woman, and she will raise frum children. I will find a way for Ruthie to get married and become truly Orthodox. I have already taken the first step.*

I wish you were here, but, even now, I feel your hand guiding me.

May God protect you and bless you.

My grandfather and I walked up Fifty-Fifth Street to Fourteenth Avenue and then to Fifty-Second Street to the synagogue. The study hall was in the basement. When we came to the side entrance where the study hall was located, I stopped. Women never went in there.

My grandfather took my hand and led me down the steps. When we came to the door, I refused to enter. My grandfather looked at me angrily.

"Ruthie, why are you stopping?" he snapped.

"Women are not allowed in there."

"Nonsense!" he said. "We have work to do. You and I. They do not permit anyone to remove the books from the library, and I want you to read it in the original yourself. This is your problem and even though we will work on it together, it's up to you to decide what the right course of action is. Now come in here," he said, taking my arm.

The study hall consisted of three rooms. The entrance from the street led down a few stairs and into a long hall. There were closed storage cabinets on both sides of the hall where the special prayer books that were used for the high holidays were stored. Straight ahead were the restrooms and the stairs leading up to the main sanctuary. To the right was a wide corridor that led to the small chapel that was used on weekdays. On either side of this corridor were study rooms. These rooms were lined from floor to ceiling with bookshelves. Each room had two long tables on which were spread open books. There were men sitting at the tables studying.

Their studying took the form of discussion and debate, rather than silent reading, as in a library. Two or three people participated in each discussion, and there were many discussions going on simultaneously so the noise level was quite high. There was a great feeling of energy and enthusiasm in the rooms.

The men in the study hall looked up when I came in. They were surprised. In their memory, no woman had ever been in these rooms.

My grandfather stood defiantly at the door. "My grand-daughter, Ruthie, has work to do. We need to use a table."

The men cleared their books from one end of the table. "Here, Reb Ben-Zion, sit here," they said with deference.

I expected them to leave, but they didn't. I expected them to be offended, but they weren't. They pretended to be studying while they watched to see what my grandfather and I would do.

Reaching into one of the book cases, my grandfather brought out a well-used book with a flaking leather binding and yellowed pages. He expertly thumbed through the book until he reached *Mishnah Kiddushin*, the book on the laws of marriage.

He turned to the proper page and showed me where it says that a wife can be acquired in three ways: through money, through a contract, and through sexual intercourse. In most marriages, the *Mishnah* said, all three of these conditions must be satisfied, but in some cases, only one is necessary to make a binding marriage. They all are, the *Mishnah* went on to say, usually part of the same agreement because they all depend on the bride's consent. The first part, money, is a gift from the groom to the bride. Today, Ben-Zion explained, it is usually the wedding ring. The second is the *Ketubah*, or marriage contract, which guarantees the bride certain rights. And the third is sexual intercourse, which must be voluntary. A marriage that is not consummated by voluntary sexual intercourse may be annulled even though the other two elements are present.

"In some cases," my grandfather said, looking up from the book, "like in war, or in times of national or personal crisis, a wife can be acquired by sexual intercourse alone. For example, if a man is going off to war and doesn't have time to go through the formal wedding process, he can just have sexual intercourse with his wife. In that way, if he was killed in battle, she would inherit his estate. The sexual intercourse must be voluntary and the other elements, the wedding ring and the marriage contract, must follow as soon as possible."

"Well, at least I've got the ring," Ruthie said as she took the little red box that held her engagement ring out of her purse, "that's the money part. We can't get the Ketubah without my father, so that just leaves sexual intercourse. So, are you saying," I asked quietly, "that if I have voluntary sexual intercourse with Harry, that will be enough to fulfill the requirements of a Jewish marriage?"

"It's possible. But I am not telling you what to do, or even what is permitted. I showed you the *Mishnah*, which is the book of declarations. Now you must read the comments and discussions that the Rabbis had about this *Mishnah*. And then you must read the comments on the discussions that more recent Rabbis made. It's all very complicated, and you will see many opinions and contradictions. In the end, you must make up your own mind. That is the reason that you're here. I could have recited the *Mishnah* for you at home, but I could not have told you the contents and language and spirit of the Talmudic discussions. Some of the arguments are easy to understand, and others are open to interpretation. You have to read them yourself, and you have to decide what to do. I am willing to return with you as often as necessary until you have absorbed enough information to make a wise decision."

"Is this what I should tell my father?"

"What decision you make, and what you tell your father, are up to you. I won't try to sway you at all. That is between you and your father."

But my grandfather had planted the seeds of dissent, and I was fertile ground. Even though we spent the time reading the discussions in the *Talmud*, I, under my grandfather's guidance, had already made my decision.

Three major events occurred that first weekend in August. First, on Friday, I sent the final draft of my finished book to Mr. Davis. I had been submitting sections of the book as I completed them, and he had liked them, and then in July he had had his staff retype the entire manuscript and send it back to me for my final author's corrections. Now I had sent back the completed final draft. This time, I was pleased with what I had written.

The book had evolved into a series of vignettes, all revolving around the characters in the original story that my grandfather had told me. I had realized that my strength was in writing stories, rather than in research, and so I had reconceived the book as a series of interlinked short stories. Harry and I were now much more pleased with the results.

That Friday night, for my last Sabbath at home before moving to my new apartment, my mother prepared a festive *"Bon Voyage"* dinner. My mother cried, my father was solicitous, and, just for this occasion, my grandfather, who normally never said anything at dinner, told a story.

"The *Torah*," he began, "tells us that God appeared to the great patriarch Abraham and told him, 'Go forth from your native land and from your father's house to the land that I will show you.' But Abraham's father Terach had already traveled a long distance to get to Charan. The *Torah* says that Terach took his family, including Abraham, and Lot, and Sarah, Abraham's wife, 'and they set out together from the city of Ur of the Chaldeans for the land of Canaan, but when they had come as far as Haran, they settled there.' So the family had traveled from Ur, where Abraham grew up, to Charan. We don't know where these places are anymore, but the fact that the *Torah* tells us about these journeys is a lesson that travel is good. It teaches us that it is a mistake to stay in one place and wait for life to change. You have to make your way, and make your own changes, just as our families did when we left Europe. So it is important for you, too, Ruthie, to be like Abraham and to make your own way—to make your own changes. God was with Abraham when he left his home, and God was with us when we came to this country, and I know that God will be with you when you start your new life in New York."

The second event was on Sunday. Early in the morning, my parents loaded up their car with my clothing and books and typewriter, along with a small set of kosher dishes and pots and pans, and delivered them to my new apartment on Convent Avenue. Together with their chauffeur and maid, they carried the boxes up the three long flights of steps. While my mother and I made the beds, hung curtains, and personalized the apartment, my father and the maid thoroughly scrubbed the kitchen to make it kosher. They spent the day getting the apartment ready, and they didn't leave until dusk. The last thing my father did was to hang a *mezuzah* on the entrance door.

The third event began that night, as soon as my parents left. Harry, who had been impatiently waiting in the coffee shop across the street for most of the afternoon, carried his two big suitcases to the building and rang the bell. I nearly flew down the three flights to let him in. Together we struggled to get Harry's heavy suitcases up the three flights. At the top, just outside the door, Harry put his suitcases down and lifted me in his arms and carried me across the threshold. He kissed me while I was still in his arms, and then gently put me down, back on my feet.

We stood together surveying the small apartment. It looked, we quickly agreed, like my parents' house in Brooklyn.

"This is awful," I said, laughing. "We've got to get those *shmatas* off the windows and let some light in."

Together we removed the drapes that my mother had hung, and we moved the furniture so that it was in a conversational grouping rather than the decorative way my mother had set it, and we removed the decorative shawls that my mother had placed on the back of the chairs to hide where the fabric was worn. Then, we put all of Harry's and my books in the bookcase, and we rearranged the kitchen. When we were finished, tired and sweaty, we fell back, laughing onto the sofa. Harry kissed me, gently at first and then more aggressively.

I put my hand under Harry's shirt, and I scratched his back—hard. Harry reacted in pain and then smiled in pleasure. He reached his hand under my dress and inside my underwear cupping my buttocks and then reaching further between my thighs. I made an involuntary yelp and squeezed my legs together, trapping Harry's hand, and then I moved them apart, welcoming him. The softness of my inner thighs seemed to surprise and delight him, and he caressed them as far as he could reach. I moaned and bit his lip. We had had no idea how stimulating it could be to see and feel your partner respond. We had no idea how much raw emotion we had suppressed. We tumbled off the couch and feverishly tore at each other's clothes until we were sufficiently exposed to make love, which we did violently and ravenously. Satisfied and breathless, we laid next to each other, sprawled on the floor amid the discarded clothing.

"That wasn't the way I had planned it," I said, still gasping for breath. "I bought a new, sexy negligee, and I wanted it to be romantic."

"We'll have to do it again tonight, more romantically," Harry said. "Did it hurt much?"

"No, not at all—it felt great. But I could be pregnant. You didn't use a condom, did you?"

"No, I wasn't quite sure if we should stop so that I could put it on. Sometimes passion and spontaneity supersede prudence and sensibility."

"I'm glad you didn't stop."

That night, we made love—romantic love. Harry got into the bed naked, and I went into the bathroom and put on my negligee (which Harry commented on and then removed), and we made slow wonderful love. We discovered new, unimagined pleasures that were both physical and aesthetic.

We slept naked in each other's arms, and we awoke at dawn in each other's arms. We investigated and discovered the sources of pleasure on each other's body. This time, for the first time, we made love in the daylight, and this time, for the first time, we looked and explored and experimented, and enjoyed.

I made breakfast for Harry, and he went to work, and I went to City College to meet some of my teachers and to start the registration process.

CHAPTER 16

After the rejection by Harry's parents, we realized that we had to win my father's approval to make our relationship legitimate. Although we were now happily living together in illegitimate bliss, we realized that this could only be a short term solution and that the only avenue left open to us, if we wanted to have a family in the near future, was to win my father's blessing.

We attacked the problem of Harry's lack of an Orthodox religious education with manic intensity. It was now midsummer, and we only had a few months until the Chanukah deadline. Harry began studying every weekday night with the Rabbi of the Orthodox synagogue in our neighborhood, and he studied with me on the weekends. We attended services together at the synagogue every Saturday morning—Harry sat among the men on the main level, while I sat among the women upstairs in the balcony.

Harry was learning to read Hebrew so that he could read and recite the prayers properly. In addition to language and ritual, he was also learning the history and meaning of the prayers, and it was making a great impression on him. When we went to synagogue on the Sabbath, Harry was increasingly able to participate, and I, looking down from the balcony, was proud to see him sing with the other men.

One Sunday morning, Harry announced that the Rabbi would be showing him how to put on tefillin that week. "He recommended that I buy a set in a special store on the Lower East Side," Harry said proudly, "and I was thinking that going down there might be a fun excursion for us."

"We should ask my father to come with us," was my immediate response. "It will help convince him that you are really serious about your studies. Besides, I don't think he's been back there since my parents were married."

We agreed to meet my father on Houston Street and then to walk downtown together. The streets were teeming with immigrants—mostly Jewish immigrants—they seemed to be shouting in Yiddish and English simultaneously, and the noise was overwhelming. There were pushcarts everywhere, each one jostling the other for space. In my eyes, it was crowded and dirty. To Harry, it was exciting, and to my father, it represented everything that he had gladly left behind. There were food stands, each with its own unique smell, and dozens of shops and carts selling everything from shoelaces to furniture. Everything seemed negotiable, and everyone was negotiating. As we made our way through the jungle of pushcarts and shoppers to the store that Harry's Rabbi had recommended, my father was obviously resisting the seductive, and, for him, familiar, warm feeling of inclusiveness of the immigrant Jewish community, and, instead, he responded with revulsion to their aggressiveness and squalor.

The proprietor of the Jewish book store, who introduced himself as Reb Shmuel, was huge, friendly, and informative. He spoke English with only a slight accent, and Harry was immediately impressed by his vocabulary.

"Before I show you anything," Reb Shmuel said, "I want to talk to you about *Kavanah*—intention. Do you know where the commandment is in the *Torah* about tefillin?"

"Yes, it is in the Shema prayer," Harry answered hesitantly

with a glance at my father.

"Yes! You know your *Torah*!" Reb Shmuel shouted enthusiastically.

"The paragraph in the *Torah* talks about love—loving your God. And it says that the act of putting on tefillin is an act of love."

"Nobody, my young friend," he said with a wink, "embarks on love without testing the water."

My father, who was listening uncomfortably to the conversation, walked over to the door, to take himself out of hearing. The shopkeeper looked at him suspiciously for a moment and then continued. "Every set of tefillin has its own personality. For a child becoming a bar mitzvah, it doesn't matter what personality the tefillin has, but for an adult, a man who has experienced love," he said, glancing at me, "choosing a set of tefillin is very important."

The shopkeeper encouraged Harry to try each set on to see how it felt. When Harry indicated that he didn't know how to, the man, with apparent, great care, showed him. After a few tries, Harry chose a used set because he said he felt that it had a greater spiritual history. Before we left the store, I ordered a velvet bag for the tefillin inscribed with Harry's Hebrew name.

Harry said that he felt that this proprietor had a special sort of intensity that was both spontaneous and compelling, and he was reluctant to leave the store. He said that this intensity seemed different—more authentic—than the material education that he had been getting from the Rabbi. He resolved to return to the store sometime in the future to learn more about Jewish spirituality.

My father was unusually quiet on our walk back to Houston Street. He told me, while we were waiting for our train, that the Lower East Side had been too familiar, too comfortable, like an old shoe that was out of style but still felt good. He was very tense, and I knew that he was carefully protecting, in his mind, the separation between what he was then and what he had become.

"The peddlers," he said, "were just the same as they had always been: poor, illiterate immigrants. Soon," he told me with conviction, "if they work hard enough, they would no longer be immigrants, they would be Americans. Real Americans."

I asked him how it felt to be back on the Lower East Side.

"That was in the past, a long time ago," he said. He had been there, he said, more to himself than to me, and he had left. He had moved on.

***

Every morning, from that time on, Harry carefully put on the tefillin. The Rabbi had taught him the ritual. First he slid the loop with the box onto his upper arm, then wrapped the strap around once, and then seven times around his forearm and then once around his hand. Then he put the other box over his forehead, hanging in the front, and then he went back to his hand and wrapped the remaining strap so that it spelled out the word Shaddai, in Hebrew—a name for God. The purpose of the tefillin, Harry explained to me, is to connect your head, your heart, and your hand—symbolically uniting intellectual, emotional, and practical human activity.

At first, Harry put the tefillin on, said the blessings, and then took it off. He was very careful to put it on correctly and equally careful to wrap it and put it back in its velvet bag.

He said that putting on the tefillin made him feel good. He couldn't explain it. Just that he felt some sort of connection, like a pipeline to the past. Sometimes he would read his prayer book slowly, asking me to help him with the Hebrew. Sometimes he would just sit by the window in the bedroom and rock quietly.

"You know," I said to him gently one day, "you don't need to know the prayers in order to communicate with God. Rabbi Nachman, who was a Jewish philosopher a long time ago in Poland, said that you don't have to know how to pray in order talk to God, that God understands every language and even understands when you don't say anything at all. You just have to believe. Really, really believe, and then God will hear you and answer you. One time, when I was very depressed, I got very angry at God, and I screamed at Him in my head, and he listened to me, and he made everything work out OK. That's how I came to met you."

At these moments, I felt that Harry was in my world, and that we were one. I could sense his Jewishness growing within him, and I encouraged it as much as I dared. He would rub his hand up and down his left arm, feeling the tefillin. Then he would put his hand over his closed eyes and just sit. I was impressed and proud.

My grandfather and my father put on tefillin every morning, but they did it mechanically in the privacy of their room. It was nothing special for them, but for Harry it was different. It was all new to him, and it had an incredible impact. He said he actually felt the tefillin and the tradition in his soul.

I helped Harry pray as much as I could. And as his Hebrew got better, he started adding prayers until he was able to pray the entire Morning Prayer service by himself. When he felt sufficiently confident, he started going to synagogue on Monday and Thursday mornings, the days when they read the *Torah*. The weekday congregational prayer service started at six in the morning and lasted about an hour, so Harry was back home a little after seven to have breakfast and go to work. Eventually, Harry began attending services every morning.

We fell into a nice, comfortable routine. Harry got up early and went to services. I made the bed and had breakfast ready on the table when he got back. He always brought the newspaper up with him, and we read the paper together silently during breakfast. Then, like an old married couple, we rinsed the dishes together, and we walked down the stairs together. Harry walked downtown to the subway that took him to his office, and I walked three blocks uptown to the college.

The gothic towers of the City College campus exuded academic excellence, and I was initially intimidated by the grandeur of the campus and the seriousness of the students. I was a year older than most of the other freshmen, and I also considered myself an accomplished author. These two factors made a big difference in my attitude. And, as I already considered myself married, I stayed out of the social interaction that was a major part of life on the campus. I was going to be twenty-one at the end of my freshman year, so, if necessary, Harry and I could get married in a civil ceremony without my parents' permission. We believed, however, that once my father realized the solidity and longevity of our relationship, as well as Harry's very real commitment to Orthodox Judaism, he would consent to the marriage. If he was not willing to give us his blessing by Chanukah, the date that we had set, we planned to wait until the end of the spring semester to confront him again. Although we hoped to marry with my father's blessing, we were certain that no matter what, we would be married within a year.

CHAPTER 17

Life, unfortunately, has a way of intruding on even the best laid plans.

On October 8th, five weeks after Ruthie started College, and two days after Yom Kippur, my father, Ben-Zion Perlman, had a stroke.

It was a minor stroke, if there are such things. He had complained of indigestion at the dinner table, and then he collapsed on his way back to his room. We rushed him to Israel Zion Hospital, where they had difficulty determining the cause of the stroke. They assumed that there had been some sort of blockage in the arteries going to the brain, and they treated him with blood thinners. After a few days, he felt better, but he was not able to put any weight on his left leg. Every time he tried to walk, his leg would collapse, and he was relegated to a wheel chair. The doctor thought that the condition was temporary and recommended that he go to a rehabilitation hospital for physical therapy.

The best such hospital was located on the East Side of Manhattan, but they did not have a kosher kitchen. So every night, I brought my father a kosher dinner, and every night I sat with him, and we ate together, and he told me about his day. In the beginning, I didn't pay much attention. As it turned out, although I was his daughter, the most important part of his day, in his opinion, was spent with Ruthie's boyfriend, Harry. I listened, usually without comment.

Although the hospital was a train ride and a walk from Brooklyn, it was only about ten minutes walk from Harry's office. So, starting on the second day that my father was there, Harry visited him nearly every day at lunch time. Unfortunately, Harry did not speak Yiddish, so the first day he just sat next to my father's bed to "keep him company." On the second day, my father said to him, "Zi Ihr Reden Yiddish?"

Harry looked at him blankly. "Do you speak Yiddish?" my father repeated, this time in English.

"No, sir, I don't," Harry replied, surprised.

"Then we will have to speak English. What shall we talk about?"

Harry was dumbfounded. He had not expected my father to be able to speak English, and he was surprised at his fluency.

My father smiled. "I have lived in this country for more than forty years. Why shouldn't I speak English? So, you didn't answer me. What shall we talk about?"

"Ruthie told me that you are a great teacher," Harry said. "She and I are hoping to get married, and I would like to learn the Jewish laws of marriage."

"Good idea. We can start now," my father said enthusiastically. "One thing though, in Jewish learning, the student has to ask questions and debate the response. Can you do that?"

Harry laughed. "It's not the way I was brought up, but I'll try."

"OK. First of all, Jews are required to get married. A man is considered incomplete until he gets married. As I told Ruthie, in a Jewish marriage, the husband and wife's souls merge into a new soul. If a person is not married his soul is considered incomplete."

"What about children?"

"The *Torah* commands us to multiply, but the success of a marriage should not depend upon the children. It is more important for the man and woman to create a relationship in which God is directly involved."

My father and Harry enjoyed these sessions immensely. They became instant friends and conspirators. When other members of the family were present, my father only spoke Yiddish, and Harry sat quietly. Because of this close relationship, my father was able to use Harry to influence the course that his and Ruthie's life together would take, and he chose the topics that they discussed carefully in order to have the greatest impact on her future. He had been concerned that Jack and I had allowed Ruthie to become too liberal—too American. My father told me that he believed that Jack was so focused on being "American" that he had lost all perspective. He was still a Jew, my father said, and Jews have to maintain both their unique character plus their ties to the old country.

"How," he sneered, "could a man be a Jew and not speak Yiddish?"

My father believed that Ruthie was too free—too adventurous—and he told me that too much freedom, especially for a young girl, is dangerous.

"A Jewish girl should look like a Jewish girl," he said, "and more importantly, she should behave like a Jewish woman."

Some days my father and Harry studied together, some days they talked about current events, some days Harry helped my father do his therapy, and some days they didn't talk at all. But Harry was there nearly every lunch hour, as often as he could.

At first, they discussed various aspects of the Jewish laws of marriage, including engagement, betrothal, marriage, marital harmony, conjugal rights, and the obligations of a husband to properly provide for his wife.

But then, my father made a sinister discovery. He realized that while he was in the rehabilitation center, he would be able to have a major impact on Ruthie. He firmly believed that God had acted through his stroke to connect him with Harry. And that through that connection with Harry, he could exert more control over Ruthie than he had ever been able to before.

My father believed that if he could maneuver Harry and Ruthie into strongly religious behavior now, then the inevitable relaxing of observance that they would experience as they got older and more mature would still keep them within the Orthodox mainstream. He, therefore, focused his discussion with Harry on the subject of Marital Harmony, which in Hebrew is called *Shalom Bayit*. Literally, "Peace in the House."

He began by instructing Harry about how a Jewish husband should behave at home, and how a proper Jewish wife should look and behave. He told Harry that the *Talmud* states that a man should love his wife as much as he loves himself, and honor her more than he honors himself. He emphasized that according to the Rabbis, a husband who honors his wife will be rewarded with wealth, and that a husband is expected to discuss with his wife any worldly matters that might arise in his life. He made it very clear that any kind of abuse by the husband, either physical or emotional, is clearly condemned by the Rabbis. My father told him that God counts a wife's tears.

As for the wife, and here my father struggled to make a lasting impact, the greatest praise that the *Talmud* offers to any woman is the praise that is given to the wife who fulfills the wishes of her husband.

"That's all?" Harry asked, falling into the trap. "There is such a long list of obligations that a husband has to his wife, and there's just this one small obligation of the wife to the husband!"

"It is not a small obligation," my father replied with great intensity. "It just sounds small. It means that a wife must be so attentive to her husband's wishes that she can fulfill them without being asked. She must be able to anticipate his needs and respond to them."

"But how can that be in a new marriage like Ruthie and me? She doesn't know me well enough yet to anticipate my needs," Harry asked.

"Yes, you're right," my father replied. "That doesn't happen right away. So, in the beginning, it is the obligation of the husband to tell the wife about his concerns, and it is the obligation of the wife to not only accommodate those wishes, but to listen very carefully so that she understands what emotions are behind the concerns. After a while, after they know each other, she will be able to anticipate his needs, and he will feel safe enough to tell her about his hopes and fears."

"But a new husband and wife like us don't really have a clear sense of what we each should do," Harry challenged.

"Yes, that's a very good point, and the *Talmud* deals with that very clearly. The *Talmud* says that it is good for a wife to express her own opinions, even if these differ with her husband's as long as she does it in a private and sympathetic way. And it is also the obligation of the husband to always be sensitive to the wife's desires. But there is one clearly-stated, public obligation that applies specifically to the wife: a wife is expected to be modest, even if the only other person present with her is her husband."

"Modest?"

"Yes, in her clothing, and in her gestures, and in her demeanor. She shouldn't be brash and noisy and draw attention to herself. And she should wear properly modest clothing."

The discussion had taken a different route and this confused Harry. "What do you mean?" he asked.

"A wife should choose clothing that is modest, and not sexy. Sex is private, and should be restricted to the bedroom. In public, a married woman should make it clear, through her dress and behavior, that she has reserved her beauty exclusively for her husband. If you look around today, you'll see that all of the women are wearing such revealing clothing—even the married ones. They think that it looks good, but it is not proper—too sexual. They should cover themselves more, especially the married ones. After all, God dwells in every family's home, and it is an affront to God to dress seductively."

"But being in style is very important to Ruthie."

"Yes. That is exactly my point. A husband, especially a new

one, must exert his influence to help his wife achieve the high moral status of a married Jewish woman."

My father told me these things at night, every night, while we were having our dinner at his bedside together. I listened, but I rarely commented. It all seemed so innocuous. I didn't, for a moment, believe that Harry would take it so seriously.

But he did.

CHAPTER 18

Harry was now spending most of his evenings learning practical religious practices with the Rabbi of our synagogue, and, although I wasn't aware of it at the time, he was also spending most of his lunch hours discussing Jewish marital laws with my grandfather. Although the meetings that he had with my grandfather had the greatest impact on him, he was not able to tell me about them for fear of revealing my grandfather's secret, so he attributed a lot of what my grandfather had said to the Rabbi.

I adjusted our household schedule to enable Harry to do his nightly studying with the Rabbi. I believed that, as Harry had promised my father, he was learning as much as he could about Orthodox Judaism, and that he was preparing himself for a life as an Orthodox Jewish husband. I was glad that he would be moving into my world and that our two halves would become a whole, as my grandfather had instructed me.

I had decided that, as soon as I passed my twenty-first birthday, Harry and I would revisit Harry's parents and confront them with the nearly accomplished fact of our wedding. I was certain that, faced with the possible loss of their son, they would, however reluctantly, grant their permission. Getting my father's blessing remained the only hurdle, but I was increasingly certain that Harry would pass the test.

In an effort to establish the sort of marital relationship that my grandfather had described, we made a special effort to share all of our day to day experiences with each other. Of course, Harry could not discuss the lunch meetings with my grandfather, but every night he would tell me about his work day and he would dwell on his petty successes and failures, and I would do the same. We fell into another comfortable routine: every evening, before we ate dinner, we would sit in our little living room and discuss our day. For the most part, it was mundane and boring, but we made an effort to make it interesting.

The discussion that Harry had had with my grandfather regarding my behavior and my clothing weighed heavily on his mind, and he hoped to find a way to introduce it without revealing its source. He must have been so insecure in his new Orthodox Jewish skin that he had fully accepted the nonsense that my grandfather had fed him, and now he was about to impose it on me.

I wanted this marriage to happen. We were a good match, I reasoned. We could talk, or we could sit silently together reading a book, and either way, it was good. And Harry liked it too, I was sure of that. But yet, I felt that Harry was withholding some sort of information. That he wasn't being completely honest with me. That there was a hidden part of him that I just didn't know about. There was something, I was sure, standing between us. Some secret, and my anxiety was growing and becoming more compelling. But Harry wouldn't—couldn't—tell me what it was or what its source was.

Harry, as a result of my grandfather's malicious intrusion, tried to steer the conversation in a direction that would make it possible for him to talk about feminine modesty, which was at the core of much of what he and my grandfather had lately been discussing. The unusual emphasis that my grandfather had placed on the matter weighed heavily on his mind because it was apparently an extremely significant issue.

He was unsure how to introduce the subject, and he was grateful when I inadvertently helped him by describing one of the girls in my class who wore her skirt very short and rolled her stockings down below her knees. I said that this girl kept crossing and uncrossing her legs and that the teacher, a young man, couldn't help seeing her bare legs. I told him that I was both jealous and offended.

"Isn't there any sort of dress code in school?" Harry asked.

"Nope, none at all. Most girls dress a little bit sexy, but they still manage to stay a little bit pure. But this girl—there's nothing pure about her."

"Is she married?"

"I don't think so, but that's not the problem. The problem is that because her outfits are so sexy, it makes the rest of us look like dowdy old ladies. I keep looking in my closet to find something that will compete with her."

"Why do you want to compete?" Harry asked. "You've already got a guy."

"That's not why. I know I've got you. It's just that I want to look as sexy as that girl."

"Sexy?"

"Maybe that's not the right word," I said. "How about stylish?"

"But you are beautiful without wearing risqué clothing," Harry protested.

"Thank you, but I still want to look attractive."

"Who do you want to attract?"

'Well, you, I guess."

"If you want to attract me, you should dress more modestly."

"Modestly? Like what?"

"Well, maybe a longer skirt and no sleeveless tops."

"Sounds like you've given this a lot of thought."

"Well," Harry said reluctantly, "I've been thinking about how our relationship will be once we get married, and I was thinking that, like most married couples, we should save ourselves for just us, if you know what I mean."

"I'm not sure I do," I said with an edge.

"It's just that I don't want to share you with other men."

It was an uncomfortable conversation, and, though I agreed to dress more conservatively, I couldn't quite understand his thinking.

Attractive has to do with looks. And sexy has to do with, well, sex. I could clearly see the distinction, but apparently Harry could not. For a moment, we were teetering on the brink of our first fight, but then I relented. If it was so important to Harry, it would be OK with me.

I bought some longer skirts and baggy sweaters and buried the "sexy" clothes in my closet. Winter was coming soon anyway, and it was a natural time to change my wardrobe to a more conservative style.

I needed to find out how Harry's religious training was going. Rose said that I had been too aggressive in dealing with him that afternoon, and now that some time had passed and I had time to cool down and think about it, I had to agree with her. Although I still felt that my sentiments were in the right place, I now realized that I had been too harsh, and I wanted to speak to Harry and try to smooth over some of the damage that I had done. Americans, I was sure, authentic Americans, might have made those same demands, but they would have made them in a more civilized way. I should have found a way to state our differences more sympathetically. Once again, although my intentions had been good, I had failed miserably. The obstacles that I had raised would now only serve to push Ruthie further away from me and deeper into Ben-Zion's sphere.

I was now facing a difficult decision. If I admitted my error, I would appear weak and ineffectual in Ruthie's eyes. If I continued, I would certainly have to face the possibility of losing her to Ben-Zion completely.

"Why don't we invite them to our house for a Sunday dinner?" Rose suggested when I told her of my anxiety. "That way, you can talk to Harry about what he is learning, and I can spend some time with Ruthie."

"I have an even better idea," I replied enthusiastically. "How about if we stop by Gold's Delicatessen and pick up all of Ruthie's favorite food and bring it to her? That way, we can have lots of time to talk to them and also take a walk around the neighborhood and maybe even see the City College campus. We haven't been there since she moved in, and it would be nice for us to see how she's doing. My friends who have kids in out-of-town schools have all been traveling to the schools to see their kids. I know CCNY is not out of town, but still, we should see it."

Rose agreed and made arrangements with Ruthie for the following Sunday. "Make sure that Harry is there too," she said. "Your father wants to talk to him."

That Sunday, Rose and I had our driver park the car two blocks from Ruthie's apartment, as per Ruthie's instructions, and we carried all the food to her building by hand. Appearances were everything in that neighborhood, and Ruthie didn't want to encourage gossip. Inside the apartment, in anticipation of the visit, Ruthie and Harry had tried to restore the apartment to Rose's original layout. They also carefully scoured the apartment to hide all evidence of Harry ever having lived there.

"Before we eat," Ruthie said cheerfully after we had arrived, "let's take a walk on Convent Avenue, and I can show you the neighborhood and also the campus. It's really impressive."

And it was impressive. Ruthie and Rose walked ahead, with Harry and me trailing behind. The brownstone houses with their grand stoops and the apartment houses with their formal gardens were, indeed, impressive, and I made a mental note to find out who the building managers were. As we walked, Harry told me what he was learning. It was substantial, and I was genuinely impressed. I asked a lot of questions and made a lot of comments, and I complimented Harry on his accomplishments.

I felt good about our conversation, and, as was my habit, I was eager to bolster my "American" credentials. I waited patiently until Harry finished.

"You know," I said when Harry paused, "one of the strengths of Judaism is its ability to adapt to the time and situation. We have a core religious belief, but we can modify it according to the situation. That's the main difference between my religious beliefs and those of Ruthie's grandfather. I believe that we are Americans who happen to be of the Jewish faith, whereas he believes that we are Jewish, period. And that being Jewish transcends nationality."

"But isn't being Jewish a way for us to reach out to God?"

"Yes, in a way that is true, but I believe that each of us must find a way to affirm our Jewishness, and if reaching out to God is the most important value to you, then it is necessary to learn how to do that within the context of the American experience. And if social responsibility is most important, then you have to find a way to do that within the Jewish context. Either way, the important factor is that you need to know the mechanics of Judaism, and it seems to me that you are well on your way. And just between you and me, I think that by our Chanukah deadline, we will see eye-to-eye on the important issues."

We had walked through the campus and made a tour of the neighborhood and had returned to Ruthie's apartment.

The dinner was sumptuous and, at the end, I was feeling expansive. So, as had been our family's custom, I told a story.

"There was a wealthy Jew, who, together with his family, had many possessions. Among them was a big boat—a yacht. This Jew was learning not to be ashamed to live his day-to-day life as a Jew, whether before other Jews or before non-Jews, and he had begun to bring those feelings into action. One day he set out, as he did from time to time, for a few days' vacation on his yacht, and it came time for prayers. He knew that the Amidah prayer must be recited facing Jerusalem, so he needed to ascertain which direction was east. At home, and when he was in his boat near the shore, he knew which way was east, but now they were far from any visible landmarks, and he needed to know before beginning his prayers which direction east was in order to face Jerusalem. How can one find this out on a yacht? There was only one option, to ask the captain which way was east. And that's what he did. The captain asked, 'Why is this suddenly important? Are you afraid that I will steer the ship in the wrong direction?' The ship owner was a proud Jew—and when one acts as a Jew, there is nothing to be ashamed of. On the contrary, Jewish pride dictates that we not hide our Judaism. So he told the captain the truth: since he has to pray to God, and the prayers ascend through Jerusalem, through the holy temple which stood in Jerusalem, in order for the prayers to be 'Before God,' he needed to know which way is east.

"The captain said, 'If you, who are so successful in business—successful enough that I am your employee—find it important to think about God so intensely, that even in the middle of the water you turn away from all other matters to ready yourself for prayer, and that you take care to pray specifically facing east, so that the prayer will be proper. If thinking about God is so important to a man like you, I will also start thinking about God!'

"In truth," I concluded, "thinking about God is already a prayer! For this Jew it was a simple act—there were no deep intentions, or mystical secrets. He simply acted proudly and properly. Plus, he had involved the non-Jew with the mitzvah of prayer, and since every mitzvah has the quality of leading to another mitzvah, surely this mitzvah had a continued effect on the captain."

On the way home, I was feeling very good about the way things had worked out, and I was surprised when Rose leaned forward and slid the partition between the driver and the passengers shut so that the driver couldn't hear our conversation.

"He is living there," she said.

"How do you know?"

"I saw his toothbrush in the medicine cabinet, so I did a little snooping. I found some men's clothing in the back of

Ruthie's closet, and some men's underwear under her lingerie."

"That doesn't mean that he's living there, it only means that he is keeping a change of clothing there."

"You wish."

"What does that mean?"

"It means that they are sleeping together. I looked in their night table, and I found a box of condoms. There were only four left in the box."

"Did that surprise you?"

"Not really," Rose laughed. "How about you?"

"I guess if it was OK for her parents, it's OK for her."

Rose put her head on my shoulder and squeezed my hand.

"We can just continue to pretend that we don't know," she said. "They can get married in the spring, just like we planned. At least they're being careful that she doesn't get pregnant."

"America," I said with a smile. "Welcome to the new world."

CHAPTER 19

That November, just weeks before Thanksgiving, my father had another stroke—a setback. He had been making good progress in his efforts to walk, but this new infarction affected both his legs and his heart. He was now experiencing difficulty breathing, an irregular heartbeat, and some dizziness, but, even though Jack and I urged him to, he fought against returning to the hospital. He insisted on remaining in the rehabilitation center at least until he was mobile again. Secretly, though, my father and I both suspected that the end of his life was approaching, and neither he nor I wanted him to spend those remaining days in a hospital. He was lucid most of the time when I was with him, but he complained that more and more he found his mind wandering—uncontrolled.

We continued our dinners together, but there was a new urgency. He told me that his days were now increasingly occupied by fears, dreams, memories, and frustrations. He had lived his life, however well or poorly, and now that he was preparing to join his fathers, he yearned to give his life meaning—to tie up all the loose ends.

"In the end," he told me, "before the pain or the drugs take over, in those last few days or hours of rational thought that I have left, I would like to pass something on—a message, a hope, a dream. Something learned. I want to make an impact, even now. Especially now."

He had learned a lot, he told me, but he had passed on very little. This he now painfully regretted. As a young man he had hoped to write a book—a biography of his hero, Rabbi Nachman of Breslov, the great grandson of the Baal Shem Tov. He had read so much about him and studied so much about him and had never written a word. Not one word.

Maybe one day, he said, Ruthie would write it.

He told me that he was especially concerned about Ruthie. She had so much potential, he said, but he felt that it had been wasted. He said that Jack had destroyed her—destroyed her creativity and her curiosity. He resented, he said, that Jack had control—control of everything—even him.

"I should have tried harder," he said bitterly. "I could have freed her. That's what grandfathers do, but Jack stood in my way. I tried. At least I got her out of the house, away from his tyranny. Harry is nearly a goy, but he has a good soul—he means well. I got Ruthie out from under Jack's thumb, but she needs direction."

I didn't argue with him; I didn't tell him that it had been my decision for Ruthie to leave our house. He was so frail, fading so fast, that I just sat there and listened. I regret that now.

There are so many things that I regret now. There are things I knew—things I should have done. Things I should have reported. I knew that what he was doing was wrong. But he was my father—my only parent.

He told me how he was planning to influence Ruthie's life through Harry. I listened to him, and I did nothing. Nothing to protect Harry. Nothing to protect Ruthie. Nothing. I could have done something. I could have stopped it right at the beginning. But I didn't.

I thought that Harry would reject it—reject it all. But Harry was a *schlemiel*, a naive fool. It is easy now, in retrospect, to see that it was wrong not to say anything. But it didn't seem all that wrong while it was happening. And then, it was too late, and then it didn't matter.

My father told me that he knew that Ruthie and Harry were living together as man and wife. He boasted that he had been the catalyst for that union. When I expressed shock, he told me not to worry, that he had a plan, and that in his final days, he planned to influence Ruthie through Harry. He told me that, when his plan was completed, Ruthie would be a *naarah besulah*, a virgin maiden. I should have protested that this was not possible, but I didn't. I just assumed that it was the morphine talking.

"Harry will listen to what I say," my father said with a wily smile. "He will make her the kind of Jew my parents in Minsk would have been proud of. She will be frum, and she will be modest according to the laws, and she will raise a proper Jewish family. I will teach her modesty through Harry. I will teach her to be a proper wife and mother. And Jack won't be in the way."

My father suffered sleepless nights planning how to return Ruthie to her formerly chaste condition. He knew that it was physically impossible, but, he said, people can change in the eyes of God, and that would be good enough. He said that if Ruthie was to be the sort of woman that he had hoped for, she would have to have a proper wedding and to have a proper wedding there should be blood on the sheet or at least some sort of celibacy. Otherwise people would talk.

The very next day, during Harry's lunchtime visit, my father reached out and took Harry's hand.

"I want to talk to you about the quality of your marriage," he said. "I know that you and Ruthie love each other. That is absolutely certain, and you deserve to have a long and happy life together. But, according to Jewish law, there is something that stands between you and the possibility of a perfect marriage.

"If I may speak frankly," my father continued, "Ruthie is not a virgin. And if you want your marriage to be accepted at the highest level in heaven, she should be a virgin."

"But you encouraged her," Harry protested, withdrawing his hand from my father's grip. "You told her that conjugal relations would confirm the legitimacy of our marriage."

"Yes," my father replied, "and I also told her that it would eventually have to be part of a complete marriage, including a bride payment and a marital contract. But now that I have had time in this bed, I have been thinking about what I told her, and I know now that I was wrong. I was upset for Ruthie, and I was reacting to the terms that Jack had given you for his approval. I think he was unnecessarily harsh and asked too much. Plus, I think that he is lying. I think that even with your Jewish studies, he still will not give you his approval. You don't know him like I do. He is a very rigid man."

"But I love Ruthie, and she loves me. Isn't that enough?" Harry protested.

"It's enough for you. Maybe it's even enough for me," my father replied with a sigh. "And if you lived by yourselves somewhere in the woods, it would certainly be fine. But you live in society, and society has certain rules. You both have parents, and they have expectations. And Ruthie is a proper girl, and proper girls don't have relations without being married."

"But we did it all because you said it was the right thing to do!"

"Yes, I know that. And I still think it was the right thing to do. Jack was being unreasonable, and this was the only way I could see to get you two together. Good marriages are made in heaven, but sometimes they need a push. You are definitely her '*bashert*'—her chosen one—but I am certain that Jack would not have allowed the marriage no matter how much studying you did.

"But the undeniable truth," my father continued with a deep sigh, "is that Ruthie is no longer a virgin. In the eyes of the *Torah* and of the Rabbis and of your family and friends, and even in the eyes of God, she is cheapened. This breaks my heart. When she gets officially married, even to you, she will not be able to say that she is a virgin. She has been somehow 'soiled.'"

Harry was now pacing furiously. Shocked. "Ruthie is the most perfect person," he declared strongly. "She isn't in the least bit soiled."

"Yes, I agree completely, but the fact is that she has been damaged . . . by you."

"Damaged? Not by me. By you!" Harry shouted leaning over the foot of the bed. "How could you have done this to her?"

"It is not my fault. It is Jack's fault," my father whined. "It was clear to me that Jack would not give you his blessing and that you would not be able to be married. He should have given you his blessing right away, but he always wants to be in control. If he had given his blessing, this never would have happened. Now it is too late. With his arrogant manner he has caused the damaging of his only daughter. Blame it on Jack, not me; I could see from the beginning that you and Ruthie belong together, and I was only trying to help."

Harry sank into the chair, his face in his hands. Finally, he looked up at my father. "Sir," he breathed with an icy snarl, "you have destroyed the lives of two people." And he stood and stared at my father with unaccustomed hate and left the room.

CHAPTER 20

Thanksgiving that year was a memorable day. Macy's had announced that it would hold the greatest parade in the history of New York, and there was a community-wide festival in Central Park along the route to celebrate the anniversary of the first colony in America. A spectacular fireworks display along the Hudson River was planned for the evening. President Coolidge made a special radio speech, and New York was ablaze in color in anticipation of the Christmas season. Harry and I went to the parade on Central Park West and then to the community-wide picnic that followed. At night, we went up on our roof to watch the fireworks.

Our fall had been going well, and I felt that this Thanksgiving was a landmark celebration for us too. Harry was improving in his Jewish studies, and I had received good scores on my mid-term exams. My father's Chanukah deadline was only a month away, and I was feeling confident.

I had been looking forward to this evening of fireworks and celebration as a kind of affirmation of our relationship, but Harry seemed slightly withdrawn the whole day. He had been that way for the past couple of days, and I assumed that it was because of the very busy time he was having at work. After all, he was working very hard at his job, and he was still studying evenings with the Rabbi.

The night was clear, with a strong, chilly breeze blowing in from the Hudson. Other couples were on the roof waiting for the fireworks show to begin. My hair was blowing in the wind, and I instinctively snuggled closer to Harry and took his hand and wrapped it around my waist. But Harry pulled away.

"Harry, what is it?" I asked, somewhat alarmed.

"It's nothing. Just something I was thinking about. Something that has been bothering me," he said quietly. Too quietly, as if he didn't want me to hear.

"I thought you had something on your mind," I said. "You've seemed very distant these past few days."

"You're right. I have been worried about something," Harry said into the wind. "But it's too difficult to talk about up here."

"Give it a try," I said nervously.

"I'm sorry," he said over the wind. "I'd rather wait for the fireworks, and then we can talk downstairs."

He sounded so serious that I immediately took his hand, and we went back down the stairs to our apartment.

"OK. Here goes," Harry said ominously, when we were settled. "For the past few months I have been meeting with your grandfather during my lunch hour. It turns out that he speaks English quite well."

"Oh," I breathed a sigh of relief, "is that all?"

"Actually, no," Harry said hesitantly. "That was just the easy part. Your grandfather told me that in the eyes of God we, you and I, are sinners, and that when we get married it won't be a proper wedding. He said that since you are no longer a virgin, the marriage would not be one hundred percent kosher.

"Now I know that he's being old fashioned, and that these are modern times and lots of women who get married are not virgins, but, still, he said that according to the *Torah* and the *Talmud*, you should be a virgin and that makes me some sort of abuser who took advantage of you."

"But that's total nonsense," I said.

"Yes," Harry said. "On the surface it is total nonsense, but in our hearts—and in the eyes of God—it is the truth. We have sinned, and somehow we must pay the piper."

"Harry," I said softly, taking his hand, "it doesn't matter. We have each other, and that's the most important thing."

"But it does matter," he said. "In the eyes of God, it matters."

I could hear the rumble of the fireworks in the background, but our apartment was quiet. Too quiet. We sat at our little kitchen table holding hands, teetering on the brink, and unsure of what would happen next.

"What do you think we should do?" I finally asked.

"Maybe we should make some sort of symbolic sacrifice to demonstrate our good intentions."

"Yes," I brightened, "we could donate some money to charity."

"No, I didn't mean that sort of sacrifice," he said. "I was thinking about a personal sacrifice—giving up something that we both highly value."

I looked around the room. There wasn't much there that we could sacrifice. "What did you have in mind?" I finally asked.

"Maybe we could give up living together for a while," Harry suggested. "That's the thing that I value most highly, and that would demonstrate to God and ourselves the depth of our commitment."

Surprisingly, I wasn't shocked by this. We would have had to wait to get married until June anyway, and then we would be together for ever and ever. *Besides,* I rationalized to myself, *if this had happened during the war, Harry would have been drafted into the army, and I wouldn't have seen him for two years.*

So we decided to live apart for six months. Harry would move back to his apartment, and I would stay in mine. Just to make it that much more meaningful, we also agreed not to telephone, write, or date for the entire time either.

At first, I found the forced celibacy OK, even a little exotic. But then it got to be a strain. But knowing that marriage was in the near future, and that we would then be together for the rest of our lives, made it tolerable.

I continued my routine at City College, which made the time pass faster. My days were measured by the coming end of the semester and finals. My classes had turned out to be more challenging and demanding than I had anticipated. My classes in English literature, which I had expected to be the easiest, now occupied most of my time, and I spent many hours reading. Preparation for my finals was all consuming, and my anxiety level was high. I missed the reassurance of Harry's presence, but I quietly admitted to myself that I was happy to have some time alone.

But Harry, as I was to learn later, was much more concerned about what my grandfather had said than I was. He didn't have the anchor of a family steeped in Jewish tradition, and he didn't understand that there would be no punishment where there was no victim. He had been studying too hard, trying to absorb centuries of culture too quickly, and as a result, he had become too rigid—too absolute. He had not yet achieved the security and confidence that was part of my upbringing, and that now enabled me to move past my grandfather's meddlesome nonsense. It had come so easily to me, but it had never even occurred to Harry.

Now, irrationally, he was worried that he and I had committed a "mortal sin" by cohabiting, and that we would be condemned to Hell after death—he was clearly confusing Catholic and Jewish theology. I wish I had been there to calm him.

My Search for God
Harry Berger

They have told me—warned me—that I might not survive this quest. I am, therefore, writing this brief account of where I started, why I took the route that I have chosen, and where I hope to end up. Hopefully, I will survive. If not, please consider the following as an account of a broken heart and a lost soul.

I am writing this to record my quest to speak with God. I am not sure where this journey will take me, but this is the moment when I can prove myself, and my love for Ruthie. The time has come in my life when I must make the effort. I believe that it is possible, provided I am able to maintain the will, stamina, and dedication.

Ruthie's grandfather, Ben-Zion Perlman, has deceived us greatly, and he has led us down a sinful path. He has taken immoral advantage of our love and naiveté. We can no longer trust his advice. He has ruined my life, and especially the life of his only granddaughter. I cannot forgive him for this.

Ruthie and I are doing what we can to undo this horrible situation, but I fear that our sacrifice will not be sufficient. I believe that the only way that I can undo the damage that we have done is for me to speak directly with God and to ask for his cleansing forgiveness. The rest is up to God. I plan to learn how to enter God's presence, how to speak directly to Him and how to appeal for his kindness and mercy to forgive us for our carnal sin.

I did not know where to start so I returned to the bookstore on the Lower East Side where I had gotten my tefillin, hoping for guidance. The proprietor, who called himself Reb Shmuel, had seemed to be both friendly and knowledgeable, and I hoped that he could assist me in my journey, or at least point me in the right direction.

He greeted me warmly as soon as I entered the store, but he became immediately evasive when I told him that I wanted to communicate directly with God through the study of Kabbalah, and he suggested that I try to increase the intensity of my prayers instead.

When I insisted, he told me that Kabbalah was too dangerous for the uninitiated and should only be pursued by experienced scholars. I asked him if that meant that it was impossible for me to study Kabbalah and eventually talk with God, and he replied that it was not impossible, but very difficult and dangerous.

I asked him where to start, and he reluctantly offered me some books to read, but he again cautioned me that it was dangerous. When I insisted, he gave me the books and a room in the back of the store to read them. He warned me that I could lose my way, and, as a result, possibly lose my mind. He begged me once again not to do it, but when I insisted, he asked me to do all my reading in his store where he could watch me.

I asked him what would happen if I succeeded, and he said that that was unknown.

And so, I began to study intensely and exclusively with Reb Shmuel. Every day, from the moment he opened his store until it closed, I sat in his back room and studied. I was determined to embark, as quickly as possible, on my search for the mysterious *Ein Sof*—the infinite God—who is perfectly simple and infinitely complex, nothing and everything, hidden and revealed, reality and illusion, creator of man and created by man.

I was insatiable and I absorbed each of the books like a sponge. The study of Kabbalah became the center of my universe. It occupied all of my waking time. Every book that I studied opened windows into other books and other facets of Kabbalah. I steeped myself in the process and powers of meditation, and soon I was able to go deeper and deeper. I was now certain that, like the prophets of the Bible, I would soon be able to communicate directly with God.

Now, as I write this, I have stopped studying with Reb Shmuel. I no longer need his advice or his meddling or his constant warnings. I have identified the most important books, and I now have them in my apartment where I can study them freely. I have found the path to *Hashem*. All I need do is to follow that path to the end—to *Ein Sof*. I know that it will be a long and difficult journey. I know that it will take intense work and concentration, but I am confident that I can do it.

I am now on the path, and I am getting nearer and nearer. I think I can see the light. Soon, soon, with sufficient devotion, I will have achieved the ultimate. Soon. Time has lost all meaning to me . . . only the goal exists . . . only *Ein Sof*.

CHAPTER 21

In January, the second month that Harry and I had been apart, I realized that I had missed my period. Again. I had waited another month to be sure. It was now intersession in college, and I had three weeks off. My finals had ended, and I was just waiting for my grades.

On the first day of intercession, I visited the campus nurse to confirm my suspicions. The next day, I took a taxi to the rehabilitation center where my grandfather was being treated. I had been there frequently and the staff recognized me. I rushed past the reception area, barely returning their greeting, down the medicinal smelling corridor to his room. My grandfather was in bed reading, and he looked up happily when I came into the room.

"I need your advice," I blurted out after we had finished our greeting. "It concerns Harry and me. I need to know what are the rules concerning having a family."

"Are you and Harry getting married?" he asked.

"No, not yet," I said somewhat annoyed. "I just need to know what a family does when a baby is coming."

"Why do you ask?" he asked.

I didn't want to face him so I walked over to the window and looked out at the East River hoping for some sort of inspiration, but none came. So I turned back to him, and in as matter-of-fact voice as I could, said, "I'm pregnant, and I need to know what to do."

"Oh my God," my grandfather breathed. "I didn't think about that. Don't you young people have ways of preventing that?"

"Yes, but they're not one hundred percent reliable." I had planned to simply discuss this with him, but I suddenly became uncontrollably angry.

"We should name the baby after you," I snapped. "You're the real reason I'm pregnant. What in the world were you thinking? And why did you tell me what you knew I wanted to hear rather than the right thing?"

"I did tell you the right thing!" he whined, now clearly defensive. "If I didn't tell you that, you would never have gotten married."

"I'm not married!" I shouted in Yiddish. And then in clear, Anglo-Saxon English, "What the hell were you thinking?"

"Listen, Ruthie," my grandfather said in Yiddish, trying to calm me down, "your father was not going to permit you to marry Harry, no matter what he did."

"How do you know that?"

"Ruthie, listen, I know. I have known this man since long before you were born. He promises things, and then he does whatever he wants. Look at what he did to me. He promised me that I would be a teacher in the synagogue, and in the yeshiva. But he thought that I would be too much competition for him, and so he made them erect hurdles. He always has to be in charge, and he would never allow you to marry a man that you chose. It would have to be someone that he chose for you. I was trying to save you from that."

I stood at the side of his bed breathing hard, trying to control my anger. This man whom I had loved all my life— this man who had encouraged me to write when no one in the family supported me, this man who had helped write my book, this man who had shared his stories and his dreams and his knowledge with me—had taken advantage of our intimacy and misled me, and I was angry. But I was guilty too. I had wanted this marriage so much, and my father had put up obstacles, and maybe my grandfather was right and my father would have found another reason to block the marriage.

But the fact remained that I was pregnant. That could not be denied.

The other undeniable factor was that I could not go to Harry. He and I had made an agreement, and I was sure that if I confronted him now with my pregnancy, that he would say that my condition confirms what he had predicted.

I stood there, at the foot of my grandfather's bed and listened with tears in my eyes. The three most important men in my life had betrayed me. Harry, by insisting on six months of celibacy to satisfy his need for proper appearances, my father, by erecting insurmountable hurdles to our marriage, and my grandfather, by giving me the worst advice.

And the strange thing about it was that they all claimed that they did it for me—that they had all made sacrifices to satisfy my needs.

"Ruthie," my grandfather said with great compassion, "come here. I want to hold your hand, and tell you a story."

Another fucking story? I thought to myself, but reluctantly I moved closer to the bed, reached out, and took my grandfather's hand. He was so feeble, his hand was so thin, and he was still my grandfather, and no matter how angry I was, he was still my grandfather, and we had our own history.

"The ways of God," he began in his storytelling voice, "are strange, and very often they are unknown to us. But God has His own plan for the universe and for each of us. We must assume that everything that happens in life is part of the grand scheme and is for the better. Sometimes the future is hard to see. Sometimes God's plan seems cruel. But we, as humans, must accept His will.

"Ruthie, do you remember when we studied about the strong women of the *Torah*? One of those women, maybe the strongest of them all, was Abraham's wife, Sarah. The *Torah* tells us that when she realized that she would have difficulty bearing children, she encouraged Abraham to sleep with her handmaid Hagar, so that he should have a son. That son was Ishmael. And then she had her own son, Isaac. And when the two boys grew up, Sarah was afraid that Ishmael would dominate Isaac, so she told Abraham to send Hagar and Ishmael into the wilderness. So Abraham listened to her, and he sent them out into the wilderness. This was the cruelest thing because there was nothing for them to eat in the wilderness, and they would surely have died. But God told Abraham not to worry about Hagar and Ishmael.

"In the wilderness, Hagar was worried about her son. They had run out of food and water, and Hagar did not want to see her son die, so she went some distance away and cried. And God asked her why she was crying, and she said because she was worried about Ishmael. God told Hagar not to worry, that her son would give birth to a mighty nation. And God opened her eyes, and she saw a well of water, and she went, and filled a bottle with water, and gave Ishmael a drink. And God was with Ishmael, and he grew, and lived well. And, in fact, he did become the father of a great nation.

"Ruthie, the ways of God are hidden from us. We do the best we can, but in the end, we have no choice but to accept his word, and to trust that everything will work out for the best in the end."

My grandfather leaned back against the pillows, exhausted. I stayed with him, holding his hand, until he fell asleep. This was the last conversation I ever had with him.

I left the rehabilitation center and walked slowly, quietly, pensively across town to the subway. I knew I would have to discuss this with my parents—there was no alternative. On the train, I rehearsed what I would say and how I would say it, but when I came to my parents' house, I felt my assumed maturity falling away. I climbed the steps that I had climbed so often as a teenager in the past. When I came into the living room, everything was as it had always been, and I was surprised. I had been expecting something different—something that would reflect how different I was now than I had been.

My mother was on the phone when I came in and she waved to me happily, surprised to see me during the week. My father was in his usual place at his desk shuffling papers, chewing on his ubiquitous cigar.

I told them everything; they didn't ask questions. It was as if they had been expecting this news—as if their worst fears had been confirmed. I told them that Harry and I had been living together, and that now we were apart, and that I was pregnant. I told them about how Harry had been studying and how that had changed him. I told them what Harry had said, and that even though my father had said otherwise, I now suspected that the marriage would not happen. I spoke for more than an hour. Not emotionally, not pleadingly, almost like a newspaper reporter. I told them all the facts as best I could remember them, but I didn't tell them how I felt.

When I finished, my mother went into the kitchen and returned quickly with a glass of tea.

My father spoke first. He was obviously taking charge, as he usually did.

"Don't worry, everything will be OK, Ruthie," he said in a syrupy tone. "There are doctors who do this sort of thing. I'm sure this can be worked out. I'll start making some discreet calls right away. No one need know. You can stay here while we're finding a solution. I'll do whatever you want me to do. It will be OK. You'll go away somewhere. We'll get good doctors. We can figure it out. Just don't worry. We'll help you."

Then he didn't say anything, and I didn't say anything. It was quiet—eerily quiet.

My mother was breathing heavily, taking in gulping breaths as if she couldn't breathe. My father looked at her with concern, but her returned look was icy.

"This is all your fault," she said to him. "You and your American ideas. 'We want her to be a real American' is what you said. Well, I'm not sure that having a *mamzer* baby is being a real American. So now, mister real American, you have destroyed two lives, your daughter's and her baby's. And maybe ours too."

She gulped some tea, grimaced, and turned to me, her eyes blazing. "This is terrible," she snapped. "You are pregnant. No man will marry you. How could you do this? Who do you think you are? A real American? Hah! Feminist equality? Hah! You don't claim equality, you earn it! And when you have it you take care not to boast, not to make other people feel bad. I worked, I struggled, I sewed at night until my hands bled. And for what? To support a family! Sure I was equal—I could work just as hard as anyone else. But I worked harder. And I was successful, maybe too successful. Maybe if I had struggled a little more then you would appreciate what you have and not spit on it.

"Your father and I have worked very hard to give you a fine Jewish home and all the privileges we never had. You want to go to college? OK you go to college. You want to write a book? OK you write a book. You need a new dress? OK you get a new dress. Just like that! And everything you think is coming to you. We are rich, and we can afford things because we earned them. And you have the nerve to turn your back on that! You hate your beautiful clothing, you hate our 'fancy' furniture, you make fun of everything that we earned. Earned! Do you hear what I am saying? We earned this. And you, you were born into it. Luxury should be something you enjoy, not something you are embarrassed about.

"And now, you gave up the only thing that was yours. What man from a good family will marry you now? What are we going to do about the baby? What will everyone say? How can we show our faces in the shul again? Everyone will talk. What were you thinking? Thinking? You weren't thinking at all. You free thinkers. Hah! You have ruined us. Ruined!

"I worked to give you every opportunity—especially the

opportunity to marry someone important who can provide for you and give you the freedom to be someone, and you throw that in the trash. So now what should we do?"

My father looked up as if to say something, but my mother stopped him with a look.

"First of all, you will move back here," she snarled. "It was a mistake to trust you to live by yourself. Your father will stop paying for your apartment, so don't think you can go back there. You will go away somewhere to deal with the baby. We will find you a husband, and you will go out into the real world and struggle—and you will appreciate everything that you earn. You are nearly twenty-one years old. I was married when I was your age. It's time."

My father, sheepishly castigated and feeling embarrassed, came over to me and took my hand. We both felt awkward.

"Listen," he said, "I know this isn't the best time, Ruthie, but there is a man I know, he's an older man but still much younger than me. I play pinochle with him. He has lived a rough life, but now he's ready to settle down. He's looking for a wife. I will call him tomorrow to make arrangements. Then I will find you a doctor, and we will do whatever is necessary."

And then, for the first time in my life, I saw my mother cry. Right in front of everyone. She put her hands to her face, and doubled over with great, body wrenching sobs.

"Ruthie," she said gulping air. "How could you do this? Our *shaina maidel*, our dream. You are so smart, so beautiful. How could you do this?"

Great sobs, gasping for air. My father went over to hold her, and she leaned her face into him.

I sat immobile on the couch, and slowly my mind began to clear. My panic had passed. I now knew what I had to do; it was suddenly obvious. I heard them speaking, but I was no longer listening.

My father knelt next to my mother, holding her face in both his hands. "Ruthie," he said quietly, not taking his eyes off my mother, "you will stay here tonight. Tomorrow we will find a good doctor."

"I can't, not tonight." I said. "I need some time. Everything has changed; everything is different. I need some time."

"I understand," my father said, struggling to stand up. "This is a difficult time, and we didn't mean to press you. Take whatever time you need, think about it. I know that you will make the right decision this time. But Ruthie, don't take too long. You're in your third month, and we need to take care of this soon."

With increasing clarity, I now knew what I was going to do. It was a long-term plan, and it was risky, but when I finished— when I achieved my goals—they would no longer be able to control my life. Not my father or my mother. Or my grandfather. Not even Harry. I was a woman and an author. Now I could be the bohemian I had always wanted to be. Unwanted child? Of course I wanted this child! Lots of bohemians had illegitimate children. This was my badge of courage!

Like a flash, I could see my life plan in front of me.

I stood up and slowly walked over to the chair where my mother was still sniffling. I stood above her, looking down at her. Proudly. Defiantly.

"I am a writer," I snarled, "not your *shaina maidel*."

I grabbed my coat and pocketbook and ran down the stairs before they could stop me. Out in the cold night air I felt refreshed, energized. "I can do this," I kept repeating to myself. "I can do this, and they can't stop me."

I felt exhilarated, renewed, as if a great burden had been lifted from my shoulders. I had been perspiring in the house and now in the cool night I felt a chill that added a bounce to my step. I practically ran to the elevated train. "I can do it," I kept repeating. "I can do it."

The train arrived just as I got to the station. Friendly and familiar, its green walls and rattan seats felt so good. I was nearly alone in the car. Fort Hamilton Parkway, Thirty-Sixth Street, Pacific Street. Change trains. It was all so familiar and comfortable, but this time it also felt new. I saw things I had never noticed before. I delighted in the squeal of the wheels on the tracks, the loud roar of the train in the tunnel, the lights dimming, blinking off and on. So exciting. So exciting! The wheels seemed to be saying, "You can do it, you can do it," as they clicked along the tracks. And I repeated, "I can do it, I can do it, I can do it."

West Fourth Street, Washington Square Park. So beautiful and dangerous in the dark. "I can do it, I can do it." The express run in upper Manhattan, the stations flying by. "I can do it, I can do it."

Finally, my apartment. I ran up the stairs, key in the lock, lights on. So beautiful, so cozy, so private. "They can't get me here. They can't control my life here."

I put some water on the stove, made myself some tea, and sat down at the metal kitchen table.

I had no doubts; I didn't need their help—any of them. *After all*, I reasoned, *I was writing stories long before they even knew*. I had written a book, and I would write another, and then another. I could go on speaking tours, give guest lectures, people would pay to hear me, artists and society people would flock to my parties. It was all so easy, so clear. My fantasy was fully renewed, but this time it was possible. This time it was possible.

I couldn't sleep that night. Plans and images were running through my head. "Exhilarated," I kept saying. Exhilarated—with a strong accent on the "H"!

By morning I had a plan. I would call Mr. Davis, the publisher. After all, my book was done, and it was pretty good. I would ask him if he had read the completed, final edit yet. I would ask him when he was planning on publishing it. I would ask him what I could do to help him promote the book, and I would ask him for an advance. I didn't need my father's money! I was an author and Mr. Davis would give me enough money to live on and maybe even a lot more.

At promptly nine-o'clock the next morning I called the publisher, Davis and Hart.

The switchboard operator, with an Irish accent, was cool

and formal when I told her who I was. She asked me if Mr. Davis was expecting my call, and she refused to put me through directly to him. Instead, she connected me with his private secretary.

"Oh, you're the young Jewish girl who is writing about her family's roots in Europe," the secretary, a Miss Winauker, said. "Mr. Davis is in a meeting now, but I'll tell him you called. I'm sure he would like to speak with you. Where can he reach you? Are you in your home in Brooklyn?"

"No," I said, a little disappointed,

"Well, what number can he reach you at?" she chirped.

I gave her the number, but I offered to call back later. "When is a good time that I can be sure of reaching Mr. Davis?" I asked.

"It's hard to say, he attends so many meetings, but your best chance would be early in the morning, just before nine."

I called the following morning promptly at ten minutes to nine, and I was put through immediately to Mr. Davis. He was very nice and courteous, and he suggested that we meet in his office. Then he transferred me back to his secretary to make an appointment.

An appointment! I had never been to his office, and now I wondered what to wear and how to present myself. Should I be artistic? Intellectual? Sophisticated? Naïve? I finally settled on a conservative business suit. I rehearsed the meeting in my mind for days. This was my big moment—author meets publisher.

Mr. Davis's office was in the Flatiron building on Twenty-Third Street. At that time, the triangular Flatiron building was one of the most famous buildings in New York. It had been the tallest building in the world once, and it still had great prestige. The lobby was covered with mosaic tile and the elevators were golden. The operators wore dark green uniforms and white gloves. It was very elegant and very intimidating.

Davis and Hart occupied the whole top floor of the building, and I was nervous about where to go. But when I got off the elevator, the Irish receptionist was right there. I told her who I was, and she asked me to wait. After a few minutes, Mr. Davis's secretary came out and ushered me into another waiting room. "Mr. Davis is just finishing a call, and he will be ready to see you in just a moment."

There were magazines on the table and books lining all the walls. I had been wondering if I should sit there without moving, read a magazine, or get up to examine the books when Mr. Davis himself came out to greet me.

"Ruthie," he said, extending his hand. "I have heard so much about you. I am so pleased to meet you." Of course he didn't remember, or he chose to forget, that he had come to my house in Brooklyn to meet my father.

I was too frightened to speak. Mr. Davis's office was in the corner of the building facing up Fifth Avenue and Madison Square Park, right on the Ladies' Mile. I had shopped there with my mother many times.

The office was just what I expected. Dark paneling, books everywhere, and an enormous desk in front of the window. Mr. Davis led me to a chair in front of his desk, and, rather than sit behind his desk, he sat in the chair next to mine and crossed his legs. We talked briefly about nothing. Small talk. My parents, the weather, politics. Then Mr. Davis asked me if I had seen Harry recently. I told him that I had not, and that we were no longer working together. Yes, Mr. Davis said, he was aware of that. Then he told me that Harry was no longer working for him. This surprised me, although I made an effort to hide it. Mr. Davis said that Harry had suddenly disappeared, and that no one had been able to reach him.

Eventually, the conversation got around to my book. Mr. Davis took a deep breath, rose from his chair, and walked over to the window.

"You know, Ruthie," he said with his back to me, "times change. When you started this project, it seemed like there would be interest in the background of the Jews who had recently come into this country. But now that there are so many Jews in New York, and they are so visible, there is less interest.

So my editors have decided to drop the project.

"Unfortunately, I have spent a great deal of the company's money on this project, and I regret that there is nothing left of the assigned funds to disburse to you. But it is a good book, and I think that if you spoke to a publisher who specializes in Jewish books, you will be more successful. It is, as I said, a good book, and you should be proud of it."

He returned to his desk, looked through his personal phone book, and jotted down a name on a piece of paper. "This is a friend of mine. If you like, I can send the manuscript over to him along with my recommendation."

It would have to do. I really had no alternative, and I tried to hide my disappointment. "Thank you," I murmured. "Do you really think he would be interested?"

"It's right up his alley. And he's a good friend so my recommendation holds some weight."

And then, in the most elegant and gentlemanly way, Mr. Davis escorted me to the door. "Thank you for coming. My secretary will give you all the information. And please don't hesitate to call me and let me know how things work out."

———————

Three weeks later I received a call from an assistant editor at The Hebrew American Publishing Company.

"I asked you to come in because I was concerned about discussing this on the phone," the assistant editor said as he led me into his office. "I'm not sure how much you know about the material you used in your book, and my boss wanted me to go over it with you.

"May I ask you where you got the story that is central to your novel?" he asked when we were seated.

"My grandfather told it to me," I said defensively, sensing something threatening in the assistant editor's tone. "And it's not a story, it's what happened to his sister in Lomza, in the Pale of Settlement."

"I'm afraid that your grandfather may have misled you," the assistant editor said. The problem is that the story that you have used is a traditional Hasidic Jewish folk story. It didn't happen to his sister; it's just a story that he must have heard growing up."

I sat, shocked. "Are you sure?"

"Yes." And with that, the assistant editor reached across his desk and handed me a children's Yiddish-language story book that was open to the page where my story, or should I say my grandfather's story, appeared. "Do you read Yiddish?" he asked.

I nodded, staring dumbly at the book. Of course I had never read it. I had gotten all my Yiddish education and exposure from my grandfather.

"I'm surprised you never read this," the assistant editor said. "It's a very popular children's story."

I sat there dumbfounded, unable to speak.

"I am sorry to have taken so much of your time," I finally mumbled, as much to myself as to the assistant editor. "I had no idea."

CHAPTER 22

The following morning, I went to the rehabilitation center to confront my grandfather. He had made a fool of me, and I was angry and intent upon some sort of retribution. But when I arrived, I was surprised to see my parents there.

My grandfather had taken a turn for the worse during the night and was now in a nearly comatose state. The resident doctor told them that the rehabilitation center did not have the proper facilities to care for him. He implied that my grandfather did not have long to live and that my parents should move him to a full-service hospital. My parents were waiting for our family doctor, who was on his way.

I waited with them until the doctor and the ambulance arrived. Then, since there was nothing else that I could do, I returned to my apartment.

The Super was waiting for me in the hall. He told me that my parents had been trying to reach me and had called him in the hope that he knew where I was.

"Yes," I said. "I just left them. My grandfather is dying."

I thanked him and walked up a flight of steps, just to be away from him, and sat down on the top stair of the landing.

It had been an adventure, this book writing, and now it was over. Curiously, my mind was blank—without emotion. I tried to force myself to think about the future, about alternatives, but nothing came to me. After a while, I stood and continued up to the apartment. I did not have a plan anymore. Somehow things had always worked out for me in the past, and, in spite of everything, I expected some sort of knight in shining armor to save me now. I had been a dreamer all my life. My earliest stories had been filled with women in distress who were facing all sorts of imminent dangers that were averted at the last moment by the arrival of a hero. *Where is my hero now?* I thought to myself. A line from Psalms that is often read at funerals popped into my head, "I lift up my eyes to the hills. From where will come my help? My help comes from God who made heaven and earth."

I put some water on the stove to make tea and sat down at the tiny kitchen table. The apartment now seemed dark, dirty, dingy, and oppressive. How long I sat at that table, with my head in my hands waiting for I don't know what, I didn't know.

"Tomorrow," I said aloud, struggling to stay focused. "Tomorrow I will go to see Harry."

I had promised that no matter the circumstances, I would not make any effort to meet him until the six months of celibacy had passed, but now, things had changed, and I was certain that he would understand when I told him what had happened. I spent another sleepless night rehearsing what I would say and trying to anticipate his reaction.

In the morning, I decided to phone him first so that he would be prepared, but, surprisingly, his phone had been disconnected. I called the phone company and asked to speak to a supervisor, and they told me that the phone had been disconnected for non-payment. This in itself shocked me more than I expected. Harry had always been conscientious and punctual about his debts, and it wasn't like him to not pay the phone company. I dialed Harry's mother but hung up before she answered. *What would I say?* I thought.

On the way to Harry's apartment, I once again rehearsed

in my mind what I would say to him. I hoped he wouldn't be angry. I didn't think he would notice that I was pregnant, and I decided not to talk about it until we resumed our courtship. It was certain to be a hurdle, but, after all, it was his child, and we would be getting married and becoming parents at almost the same time. Right now, I just needed to see him and talk to him and tell him about Mr. Davis's rejection and how the entire book was now unacceptable. I was hoping that he would have a solution—maybe some sort of rewrite, maybe presenting it in a different way. Harry was good at that, and I was sure that he would know what to do.

I also wanted to tell him about my grandfather. Harry had been friendly with him, and I knew that he would want to know that his condition had worsened.

But, most of all, I just wanted to see him—to be with him, even at a distance. I could no longer stand his absence. Life without Harry had become intolerable.

The brownstone in which Harry lived was similar to my own, but Harry's apartment was on the street level, just a short flight up. I hesitated at the stairs. I knew the building, but I had never been in his apartment. A wave of panic overwhelmed me, and, rather than go up the stairs, I walked down to the corner and then back to the stoop. *What if Harry gets angry and calls the whole thing off?* I asked myself. *He wouldn't do that,* I reasoned, *he loves me too much. I wish I had been able to get him on the phone. Maybe if I just wait around outside the stoop he'll come out, and I can say that I was just in the neighborhood.*

As I entered the public hallway at the top of the stairs, I could feel the tension building inside me. A shudder of fear went through me. *Somehow,* I thought to myself, *this is not going to work out well.*

But I was there at his house, and I had made a commitment. Timidly, I knocked on the door. There was no answer, and my hopes rose instantly that maybe he was out. I rapped again, this time louder, more confidently. Still no answer. And then, his next door neighbor came out.

"I'm looking for Harry Berger," I said. "Do you know if he's home?"

"Yeah, he's home," the man said with a hint of bitterness. "He never goes out. You really gotta bang 'cause he doesn't hear too well." And with that, he went over to the door and banged on it with an open hand. "Harry!" he shouted. "You've got a visitor."

Eventually, after a long wait, I heard rustling behind the door. Harry opened the peephole and then he opened the door. He didn't react to me as I had expected. In fact, he didn't seem to recognize me at all.

"I'm sorry," he said formally. "I was studying, and I didn't hear the door."

He looked so thin, and dirty, like he hadn't shaved or bathed in a long time. There was so much that I wanted to say to him, all the words that I had rehearsed on the way over, but now it all seemed wrong. I stood there for a long while looking at him, not sure what to do.

"Harry," I said tenuously, "I had to talk to you. I know we promised, but I had to talk to you. Many things have happened. I hope it's OK." I was short of breath, and my heart was pounding as if I had been running.

He stood in the entrance, his eyes glassed over, and for a moment I was tempted to tell him who I was. Then he smiled—a crooked, halfway smile.

"Ruthie," he said, with the tone coming from his chest. "Ruthie."

We stood like that, he on the inside, I on the outside, without speaking. Harry seemed confused, disoriented.

"Ruthie," he repeated. "I should ask you in. Yes, please come in." And he stepped aside so that I could enter the room. I wanted to rush to him, to hug him, to press my face against his chest, to feel his arms around me. I had expected that. All that we had been to each other all those months flamed up inside me. But the man I was seeing now was not my Harry. Not the Harry I remembered.

We stood uncomfortably, somewhat apart. I didn't know what to say. Harry said nothing.

"I went to see Mr. Davis," I said breathlessly, in a rush, "and he told me that he's not going to publish my book because it's too Jewish, and he sent me to another publisher who publishes Jewish books, and he told me that the story that my grandfather had told me was an old folk tale, and that I would have to completely rewrite my book if I wanted them to publish it, and I don't know what to do, and my grandfather's gotten worse, and I really needed to talk to you."

I was out of breath, but Harry just looked at me.

"Fiction is the work of the devil," he said finally. "I don't know how I ever let myself get tempted into doing that. Here," he said, picking up a book from a chair, "look at this. Here is all the book anyone ever needs."

He handed it to me—a massive, well-worn, and falling-apart edition of the *Zohar*, the central book of Kabbalah. "This is all the reading I need. All of the meaning in the entire world is here, in the relationship between the unchanging eternal, the mysterious Ein Sof, and the mortal and finite universe. And the more I study, the closer I come to peeling the *kliphos* and discovering God. Like Rabbi Akiva said, 'The words fly off the page and soar to the heavens.' I'm learning to fly to heaven with the words."

We were still standing just inside the door. I looked around desperately. Harry was so thin, so tired looking, so dirty. There were dishes in the sink, food on the counter, books and papers and uneaten food everywhere. And the stench!

We stood as if frozen in time; Harry holding the book of the *Zohar*, the guide book to Kabbalah, I standing with my coat still on. I asked him if he was OK, and he said that he was never better—that his eyes were finally opened. He said that he thanked God every day for sending me and my father and my grandfather to him, for showing him the way to truth. He said that the synagogues just didn't understand. That prayer was just phony poetry. That the only way to God was through meditation, and that he had already advanced past the *peshat*, the *remez*, and the *derash*, and now he was embarking upon the study of the *sod*, the core: the inner, esoteric, and metaphysical nature and purpose of existence.

He said that he was getting closer to finding God, and that soon he would be able to talk directly to God—that he just needed a little more time and the right circumstance.

He was becoming more and more agitated as he spoke, his words running into each other. He was drooling, and he kept wiping his mouth with his sleeve as he spoke.

Desperately, bravely, I went to him and took both of his hands in mine. "Harry," I nearly screamed. "I'm pregnant. Harry! I'm pregnant with our baby."

His body relaxed. I could feel it in his hands. "Pregnant? We are going to have a child?"

"Yes, we are going to have a child."

Slowly, I could see the old Harry, the Harry I loved, emerging. He held me tight by the shoulders, concentrating on my face.

"We are going to have a baby," he repeated.

"Yes, Harry, a baby," I said softly.

He took a deep breath, and then the old Harry began to take over. "Have you seen a doctor?"

"No, not yet," I said, with a twinge of guilt.

Harry looked around the apartment as if seeing it for the first time. He brushed some books aside on the couch. "Here, sit down, you and the baby must rest."

"Only if you will sit here, next to me," I said, patting the couch.

So we sat, there on the couch, in the middle of the chaos of the room, quiet at last.

"When will the baby be born?" Harry asked finally.

"I don't know, probably in August or September."

Another long pause. Something was not right. I tried to think of something to say, but everything I had prepared now seemed wrong. And Harry didn't say anything. Nothing at all.

Then finally he asked, "What will you do?"

"Well, I guess we'll have to get married."

"Yes," he said gravely. "We should do that right away."

Silence again. Painful silence.

And then Harry said, "Ruthie, I have to think about this."

"What do you mean?" I asked with unintended panic in my voice. "I don't understand. Why do you have to think about it? This is our child, born out of our love."

"Love, yes. And I love you, and I will marry you. But there are issues that I have to think about."

I could feel my body relaxing. It was going to be alright. Images of a home and a child flashed through my mind. It was going to be alright. Harry would marry me, and we would raise the child together, and we would live "happily ever after."

"What sort of issues?" I asked hopefully. "Maybe we can work on them together."

"OK," Harry said as he stood up. "Here's the problem. This is a child born of sin. Hashem will not accept me if I am the father of a child born of sin."

He had said "accept me." I didn't understand, and now I could feel Harry slipping away. He had been with me for only that brief instant. And now . . .

Harry returned to his desk. He was repeating a phrase over and over again. "Kadosh, Kadosh, Kadosh." Three times then a pause, and then over and over again.

"Harry! What are you doing?" I asked as calmly as I could manage.

"I'm calling Hashem. It's the way the angels called Hashem. I need to speak to Hashem now. We need his permission."

And just like that, Harry was gone. I couldn't reach him. I called out to him, "Harry, listen to me! Come back! I need you! We are here, now, together, you and me. You and me. We are together!" He didn't even hear me any more. "I can help you!" I screamed.

Finally, I lowered my voice, walked over to him, and tried to reason with him. I tried to tell him that this child was a blessing from God. That God wanted us to be happy together.

But Harry wouldn't listen. He was murmuring to himself as if I was no longer in the room. He was manically studying his books, rapidly turning pages and going from one to another while I just stood there, helplessly.

"Harry," I pleaded. "Talk to me. We're here together. I can help you if you talk to me."

Harry finally turned to me, and, in a very patient voice, as if he was speaking to a child, he explained to me, with the certainty of someone who knows absolutely what he is talking about, that the way to God is through suffering—that the Christian martyrs were right—that God demands suffering.

He told me that he had been fasting—one or two days at a time. He said that the longer he fasted, the more he could feel God speak to him, and the more he could feel the spirit of God in his body.

Then suddenly, Harry's face brightened. "Here," he said, nearly knocking me down in his enthusiasm, "look at this!" There was blazing fire in his eyes, and it frightened me.

"Here is the lesson," he nearly shouted with joy, "it's right here in the *Torah*. Now I know what we will do.

"Here's what it says: You know the story. Hashem tests Abraham. He tells Abraham to sacrifice his son. To tie him up and then take a knife and slit his throat. Hashem never gives Abraham a reason for His commandment to sacrifice Isaac, and Abraham never asks for an explanation. That's the test! Hashem demands complete devotion! Sacrifice your child!

"Well I am ready for the test!" he shouted. "Ein Sof!" he shouted to the ceiling. "Listen to me! I am ready to be tested. I will sacrifice my child. Show me the way!"

"Ruthie," he said passionately, returning his gaze to me, "thank you. You have finally given me a way to demonstrate my love for Hashem. Soon, you will have a child. Together we will sacrifice that child. And just like Abraham, Hashem will tell me when to stop. We will get married today, Ruthie, I am ready!"

I protested that what Harry said couldn't be true. But Harry insisted that the only way to feel your true love for God is to dedicate your life, and the lives of your loved ones, to God. He said that the love of God was not intellectual or emotional. He said it was physical. You had to make some sort of sacrifice, give up the things that you valued most. He said that there was an intensity—a devotion—something that could only be experienced through pain and sacrifice. He said that you must never take God's love for granted, that the more pain you experience and the more you sacrificed, the closer you would be to God's perfection.

I could feel tears running down my cheeks. I reached out and tried to put my hand on Harry's arm, but he brushed it away. He said that I was a fool if I thought that we could ever return to the same life that we had had together. He said that I had to accept the yoke of my religion and only then, only then would my heart be open enough to accept God. He said that he prayed every day for me, that I would soon accept the burden of God's love.

Burden.

I tried to have a conversation with him, to tell him of the joy that this child would give us, but he wouldn't even look at me. Every time I said something about our relationship, Harry turned it back to his relationship with God.

I was now becoming increasingly frightened. Harry was irrational, and now I was afraid he might hurt me. Slowly, so as not to seem threatening, I inched my way to the door. It was good that I still had my coat on. But Harry rushed to the door, blocking my way. He took my hand in both of his and brought it to his lips, bending his head down to my hand as in a very deep bow.

And then he held me by my shoulders at arms length. He told me that I was God's vessel. That I was his angel. That God had sent me to bring him into the light. That someday, when our souls were pure enough to be accepted by God, we would walk together in the path of righteousness and accept God's burden. Desperately, I twisted away from his grasp and rushed out the door.

Back outside in the street, I collapsed on the top step, drained. I sat waiting for my tears to stop and for my breathing to return to normal. Where had my love gone? What had happened to my life? Where could I turn?

When I got home, I called Harry's parents. His mother answered the phone.

"I went to see Harry today," I told her, "and he was not well. I think he needs medical attention."

"He doesn't need medical attention," she said. "He just needs to stop seeing you! My husband was right: you fanatical people with your old world superstitions. Look what you've done to my son!"

"Mrs. Berger," I interjected, "I haven't seen Harry in two months. He was fine when I saw him, but he isn't fine now. He needs help!"

"Yes, I know all about it. I spoke to his neighbor. Harry won't talk to me; he says I'm an apostate, and I have you and your father and your grandfather and all of you lunatic religious maniacs to thank for it. Don't you worry," she said with conviction, "my son Harry is a strong man. He'll get a hold of his senses and realize what nonsense you have filled his head with."

"Mrs. Berger," I said desperately, "he needs medical help. Maybe you should call the police."

"And maybe you should just stay away from him."

And with a final, uncharacteristic expletive, Mrs. Berger hung up.

I almost went back to Harry. But I didn't. I almost called Harry's mother back. But I didn't.

And I should have.

I sat in my apartment blankly staring at the wall. My world, the world that I had so carefully constructed, was collapsing, and I was helpless to stop it.

Finally, late in the night, I called my father.

"The baby," my father asked after we had discussed my grandfather's condition and after I had told him about my experience at Harry's apartment, "is it his?"

"Yes," I said.

"Do you want to marry him?" he asked, matter-of-factly.

"I'm not sure. I think so, but he will have to get a lot of therapy before we would be able to get married, and then we would have to start all over."

"So when the baby is born you won't be married?"

"No."

He paused, and I could imagine him at his desk taking out a paper to write notes. "So," he said, "we have three problems. First, we have to decide what to do about the baby. Second, we have to decide what to do about Harry. And third, we have to decide what to do about you. So let's talk about you first. Do you want to move back home?"

"No."

"You're sure about that."

"Yes."

"OK. Next, do you want to continue in school?"

"Yes."

"OK. Now let's talk about the baby. There are three options as I see it: One, you go to a doctor and end the pregnancy. Two, you have the baby and give it up for adoption. Three, you have the baby and you raise it with, or possibly without, Harry. Obviously, the third option will be the most difficult."

"That's easy," I said. "I plan to have the baby and to raise it myself with or without Harry."

"I am not sure that that is a good choice, but the decision is entirely up to you. I'm sure you are aware of the consequences both socially and financially."

"Yes."

"OK. So now let's talk about Harry. What would you like me to do?"

"If you could go over there and talk to him, maybe he'd listen to you."

"What makes you think he would want to talk to me?"

"He said he's doing all this stuff to satisfy you!"

"Satisfy me? I don't know the first thing about Kabbalah. Here's what I think we should do. It's too late now, but first thing in the morning I'll call my friends at the Henry Street Settlement and ask them to send a social worker. Those people will know how to deal with this better than I ever could."

"But he's so sick. He looks like he hasn't had a good meal in weeks. And he said he's fasting. I'm worried about him. What if he doesn't let the social worker in?"

"I'll tell them what the situation is and ask them to send their best person."

"I don't know if that's such a good idea. The person they send might do more harm than good. Couldn't you just go over there yourself?"

"Ruthie," my father said with a deep sigh, "I'd just make things worse. These people are professionals. Don't worry, they'll do whatever is necessary."

When I hung up the phone I finally thought to myself, perhaps for the first time ever, how lucky I was to have Jack Rubin for a father.

———

When the social worker arrived, she found Harry in an aggressively deranged attitude. She immediately called the police, who put him in a straitjacket and called an ambulance. Harry stopped breathing in the ambulance on the way to the hospital. Efforts to revive him were futile. I was probably the last person to see him rationally alive.

CHAPTER 23

Sitting shiva is the week-long mourning period in Judaism for first-degree relatives: father, mother, son, daughter, brother, sister, and spouse. The ritual begins immediately after burial, and lasts for seven days, during which the mourners rend an outer garment, sit on a low seat, and receive visitors. I now thought of myself as Harry's widow, and, although I had not gone to the funeral, I sat shiva by myself for the full seven-day mourning period. During this time, I didn't go out of my apartment, I didn't listen to the radio, I didn't answer the phone, and I had no visitors.

Had I answered the phone during my mourning period, I would have learned that my grandfather, Ben-Zion Perlman, was now gravely ill and on a respirator. My parents, the maid told me when I called, were at the hospital maintaining a vigil at my grandfather's bedside. I rushed to the hospital and arrived just minutes before my grandfather died. He had not recovered consciousness, and he passed away peacefully with his family at his side.

Unlike my private mourning, the shiva at my parents' house was a monumental affair. My mother sat on a low stool and received visitors almost like a queen on a throne. My father acted like the master of ceremonies, greeting each of the visitors, offering them food and a place to sit while they waited to speak with my mother. I oversaw the food situation, making sure that the platters were full and that the soiled plates were quickly removed and washed. This lasted for six days, with the slight exception of the Sabbath and part of the last day.

On that last day, after we had cleaned the house and returned the prayer books and chairs to the funeral parlor, my father asked me to sit with him at the dining room table. It was evening, and we were exhausted. It had been a severely emotional month for me, and I had been eagerly looking forward to returning to my apartment and reestablishing some semblance of normalcy. I had missed nearly three weeks of school, and I was concerned that I might not be able to make up the class assignments. But my father insisted that I sit with him at the dining room table.

"Ruthie," my father began uncomfortably, taking my hand in both of his, "God has been very good to us, but He has been especially good to you. In the prayers at the start of every new month, we ask God for 'a life free from shame and reproach, a life of abundance and honor, a life in which the love of *Torah* and the respect for heaven shall ever be with us, a life in which all the desires of our hearts shall be fulfilled for the good', but we never ask for a life of challenges and opportunities. That is too much to ask for. But you, Ruthie, you have been given this extra blessing from God.

"Maybe it's a blessing, and maybe not," he said quietly. "It all depends on what you do with it. This is what is meant by 'choices'.

"Choices," he said with a sigh. "God does not tell us what to do. God only gives us choices. But he gives us a hint about what choices to make.

"When Moses was about to die—remember, he was not permitted to enter the Promised Land—he stood on a hill, and he spoke to the Hebrews. It is the most moving speech in the

Torah, because Moses is trying to sum up all the teaching that he has done for the past forty years. He says, 'I have set before you life and death, the blessing and the curse; therefore choose life that you may live; you, and your children; to love the Lord your God, for that is your life and the length of your days.'

"Choices," my father repeated. "He tells them to 'choose life,' but he doesn't tell them how to do it. Instead, he tells them that there will always be choices. That's the lesson. That everyone has to make their own choice—choose their own direction. There is no right way, only what is right for you.

"So now, Ruthie, you have to make a choice. God has given you the skills to be an artist. A writer. To add something to the quality of the world. *Tikun Olam*—making the world a better place. But you may have to pay a high price for this honor. Moses says 'choose life,' but he doesn't give instructions. And that path is different for everyone."

I began to cry. I had not cried when Harry died; I had not cried when my grandfather died; I had not cried when my book had been rejected. But now, when my father became a real father, I cried. I had not expected this.

The tears ran down my cheeks, but my father would not let go of my hands.

"When I was a young man," he said quietly, "when your mother and I were building our life together, it was as if we were on a certain kind of boat on a fast-flowing river. I knew what that boat looked like, and I knew what all the passengers on that boat looked like and how they would behave, and I knew where the river, and I, and your mother were going. And we, your mother and I, knew how to get there. But now there is a strange new river, and when I look up that river there is a new boat coming. And even though I try as hard as possible, I can't tell where the river is going, and I can't tell what that boat looks like and I can't tell what the passengers are like, and I can't tell where they are going or what they will do when they get there. But you can."

My father rose from the table and walked over to the

window, pulled aside the drape, and glanced out at the street below. After a minute or two he came back and stood, drumming his fingers on the table.

"All my life, Ruthie," he said, "I have wanted to be a real American, but the harder I have tried, the less I have succeeded. That is the path I chose. It was, perhaps, a foolish dream, but it is my dream. You are old enough, and mature enough, and intelligent enough to choose a path that is right for you. I only want you to know that whatever path you choose, I will support you."

CHAPTER 24

Early that spring, the spring of 1927, eighteen months before the stock market crash and a little over a month after Ben-Zion's death, Ruthie and I met for lunch in a coffee shop near her apartment.

"There are two things I'd like to talk to you about," I said, a bit too brusquely.

"If you have come to talk to me about my pregnancy," Ruthie interrupted, "I just want you to know that with God's help, I am planning to have this baby in a hospital near my apartment, and to raise it myself. It is all I have of Harry."

"Yes, I understand," I said. "But here's the thing, your mother and I would like you to have the baby at a hospital near us, in Borough Park. We would like you to go to a good doctor, and we would like to be with you and take care of you when the time comes."

"But won't you be embarrassed about having an unmarried, pregnant daughter in your house?" she asked.

"That's two questions," I said with a smile. "As far as embarrassed goes, if you ask me, everyone knows where babies come from, so why do they shield their eyes? A baby is a gift from

God, and its arrival should be celebrated, not hidden.

"As far as pregnant and unmarried goes, that wasn't exactly what I wanted to discuss, but as long as you mentioned it, here's something interesting. I looked it up, and according to Jewish law, even though your baby will be born to an unmarried mother, it won't be any different from every other Jewish baby, except that, if it's a girl, she can't marry a *Cohen*."

"That's it? What about all that stuff about being a mamzer? Doesn't that mean bastard?"

"Not really. According to Jewish law, a mamzer is a child who is the offspring of a father and mother who could not legally or morally marry, like a married woman who is having an extramarital affair, or a child who is the result of incest. In all other cases, from a legal point of view, the child of an unmarried Jewish woman inherits from his natural father just as if he were the product of a marriage."

For the first time that morning, Ruthie smiled at me. "What's the second thing you wanted to talk to me about?" she asked with a relieved smile.

"This is more about me than about you," I said with growing confidence. "In the past few months, I have had the opportunity to expand my real estate holdings, and I anticipate that this expansion will continue. It looks like I will have to hire an assistant to help me manage the new properties, and I was wondering if you would be interested in the job after the baby is born."

Ruthie's smile, one of the most radiant that I had ever seen, seemed to well up from the inner depths of her body and spread across her face and neck and even her hair. She was, at that moment, more beautiful than I could ever remember.

"Thank you" she said, although it wasn't clear if she was thanking me, or Harry, or God.

"So you'll take the job?" I asked.

"Let me think about it."

Rose and I dealt with Ruthie's increasingly obvious pregnancy in the most matter-of-fact manner. Ruthie continued to live in her apartment in New York City and to attend classes at City College, although she now spent many of her weekends in Borough Park with Rose preparing for the baby's arrival. At first, Ruthie's presence was difficult for me since some people in the synagogue considered her brazen and whispered behind my back that she should be hidden out of town until the child was born. I passively absorbed their criticism. I honestly believed that I had no reason to make excuses for my unmarried and obviously pregnant daughter. The choices she had made were her business, and I was proud to defend her right to choose. For a while, the gossips gossiped, and the yentas speculated, but once they had tired, Ruthie's pregnancy became "old news."

Ruthie's son, my grandson, was born in the fall just after her twenty-first birthday. He was named for his grandfather, Ben-Zion, and we called him Bentzy. The bris was held in the main sanctuary of the synagogue, which was packed with local Jewish dignitaries and politicians. After her baby was born, I arranged for Ruthie to move to a larger apartment, and I paid for a nanny to take care of the baby during the day so that Ruthie could continue her studies.

To be perfectly honest, I had not done all that well as a father, so now I went overboard in my role of grandfather. I lavished praise and presents on Ruthie and the baby, and perhaps—no, not perhaps—I went too far. Ruthie was uncomfortable about accepting all the generosity from me, and so, not long after the baby was born, and she was settled into her new apartment, she sat me down for a "talk."

"You can't keep giving us things," she said in what she hoped was a light-hearted tone.

"Why not?" I challenged.

"Because I am an adult, and I have to take care of my baby on my own."

"How are you going to do that? You're by yourself, and you're still in college," I said.

"I'm going to try to get a job with Mr. Davis, the publisher."

"That sounds like a good idea, but what makes you think he will give you a job?"

Surprisingly, Ruthie hadn't considered the possibility that Mr. Davis would reject her, but now that I had mentioned it, she wasn't so confident. "I don't really know," she replied hesitantly.

"Would you let me go with you?" I offered. "I'm a pretty good negotiator, and I promise that I won't butt in."

"If you insist on going with me," she said with a grateful smile, "then you might as well butt in. There's a better chance that Mr. Davis will listen to you than to me."

We planned our approach and Ruthie made an appointment with Mr. Davis. She told him that she wanted to talk about Harry, "among other things."

⊶————————————⊷

"Mr. Davis," I began aggressively, as soon as we entered his office, "I think you owe my daughter something."

"Owe her?" he asked.

"Yes. You led her to believe that if her book was satisfactorily written, you would publish it. You never said anything about any sort of contingencies. It is true that you and she never signed a contract, but the very fact that you provided an editor to work with her can be construed as a contractual arrangement with the implied conclusion that at the end, if the product was satisfactory, you would publish her book. Now I do not want to accuse you of breach of contract, but I am sure that you can appreciate the validity of her position."

Mr. Davis still had not returned to his desk, and we stood awkwardly facing each other in the middle of the room. He made an attempt to reach the security of sitting behind his desk, but I aggressively stood between them. It was almost as if

Ruthie and I were the interviewers and he, Mr. Davis, the interviewee.

"What exactly would you like from me?" Mr. Davis asked, directing his question to Ruthie.

"As you know," Ruthie replied confidently, "I'm still a student at City College. As you may not know, I now have a small son. I would like you to suggest a way that I can work in the literary field and continue my education, and also take care of my son."

"Can't your father help you?" Mr. Davis asked, sensing an opening.

"I am not even going to dignify that question with an answer," Ruthie replied with new confidence.

I looked at Ruthie, impressed by her tone and self-assurance, and this time Mr. Davis was able to maneuver around me and return to his desk.

"Please sit down," he said as he assumed his position behind his desk.

I ostentatiously held a chair for Ruthie and then I sat down. I had a feeling that my initial advantage had passed.

"Fortunately," Mr. Davis said, focusing all his attention on Ruthie, "I think there is a way that we both can benefit from this experience. I can offer you a position as a screening reader. What that means is that you will be the first line in the editorial process. Authors, and their agents, send us books all the time that they would like us to publish. We employ screening readers to act as the first filters in the selection process. We pay each reader a fee for reading the book. It is not a large fee, but it is nevertheless a fee. In this manner, you will have some income to supplement the money that your father must be giving you. And you can do most of the work from home."

"What happens after the reader recommends a book?" Ruthie asked.

"Then it is assigned to an editor who determines if, with proper editorial input, the book can be made commercially viable."

"And then?" Ruthie persisted.

"And then, we have an editorial meeting and we decide, as a group, whether or not to offer the author an advance and whether or not to begin the long, tedious process of bringing the book to market."

"Mr. Davis," Ruthie said with a brief glance at me, "I do not want to be a reader. I would like to be an editor."

"I'm sorry, but I don't think you are qualified for that. My editors have worked their way up to that position and bring years of experience to the task."

"Well, Mr. Davis, you might consider my situation in the opposite direction. I would like to have the opportunity to prove myself as an editor, and if, after I have been at the job, you feel that my work is not up to your editorial standards, then I will leave and not ask for any other position."

"But Mrs. . . . . I'm sorry I don't know your married name."

"Ruthie is just fine."

"But Ruthie," Mr. Davis said, obviously flustered, "you have no experience as an editor."

"Yes, but I have been a successful short story writer for quite a few years, and I have written a novel which, by your own high standards, was considered good enough to invest in and publish."

"You make a good point, and you drive a hard bargain, and so I agree. I'll have to run it by my board, but I don't think there will be any objection. The only question that I think might come up is the legal ramifications of your doing the work at home."

And so, completely without my help, Ruthie became an editor at Davis and Hart. Her skill was apparent from the moment she started, and eventually she specialized in a new category of novels that targeted young women—the same market that had read her steamy short stories.

After she graduated from college, Ruthie moved to a two-bedroom apartment on West End Avenue, on the far west side of New York City. The year was 1929 and she was twenty-three-years-old. She had been working for Davis and Hart for two years. Perhaps it was her age, or perhaps it was her experience as a pulp magazine writer, but within her first two years at Davis and Hart, she had established a reputation as a rare editor who was able to recognize and develop new, raw talent. She had also resumed her career as a short story writer, but this time she was targeting college age girls rather than teens.

And then, on October 24th, 1929, on a day that would be known throughout history as Black Thursday, the stock market crashed. And nearly everything in the world changed.

Less than a year earlier, when Ruthie's son was still an infant, unemployment in the United States had been 4.2 percent and the economy was booming. Four years later, unemployment soared to 23.6 percent, the stock market had crashed, and many banks had gone out of business, stranding their depositors. Nearly one out of every four available workers in the country was unemployed, and many of those who were able to keep their jobs were now working at a small fraction of their former salaries. Typical annual income of the average American family declined by forty percent, and the Gross Domestic Product—the value of all goods and services produced in the United States—tumbled from 103 billion dollars in 1929 to 58 billion dollars in 1932.

It was a painful time in America, and, although the income statistics were shocking, they did not come close to describing the complete horror of the time, especially for the middle class. In the roaring twenties, as the stock market and the real estate market had soared, many people had borrowed more and more money on their homes and businesses in order to have sufficient cash to invest in the booming stock market with the hope of "making it big."

Commercial banks, life insurance companies, and mutual savings banks encouraged this borrowing by offering tempting, five-year balloon mortgages which allowed the speculating public to borrow against their home's value and just pay the interest on the loan. Many homeowners refinanced every year, continually borrowing more and more. The suckers borrowed on every one of their assets, and they invested that money in the inflationary dream that they were fueling through their own borrowing. They dreamed that they could earn enormous profits on their investments, but as a result of their speculation, stock prices rose rapidly, and the carrot of easy money constantly loomed just out of their reach. So they borrowed more. And, in an irrational, nearly maniacal dream of their potential future wealth, they spent their anticipated profits lavishly. And that lavish spending, plus their increasingly risky speculation, fueled the "boom." And so, with optimistic abandon, and caught in the powerful inflationary spiral, they borrowed more, hoping to make more.

As in a poker game where there are a few big winners and many big losers, American wealth was becoming increasingly concentrated in the hands of a few players, and the other players had to continue to borrow aggressively to stay in the game. They borrowed against all of their assets, and they even borrowed against their future income, and the more they borrowed, the fewer assets they had left to borrow against. When they ran out of assets and were no longer able to borrow, the game ended. And with the end of the game, came the end of their dreams.

Sharp warning price breaks had occurred several times during the boom, and each of these price breaks gave rise to dark predictions of the end of the bull market and the end of easy, speculative profits. But until that fateful day in late October of 1929, these predictions turned out to be wrong. With blind faith, the suckers continued to believe that stock prices would continue to rise indefinitely, and they invested with greater and greater abandon. In March of 1928, for example, 3,875,910 shares, the most ever, were traded in a single day on the New York Stock Exchange. A few months later, five million shares being traded in a day was a common occurrence.

There was a feeding frenzy in America as the suckers tried

to get on the bandwagon of the rising stock market. Unfortunately, by the end of the decade, most of them had fallen off and had been seriously injured.

The real estate partners with whom I had purchased my tenement houses after Rose sold her shop were caught up in the easy money frenzy and were among the most seriously injured. Fortunately, I had been too timid to join them, and I cautiously gave them loans which were secured by their real estate. When they were not able to repay the loans, I became the sole owner of a number of attractive apartment houses on Ocean Avenue, just across the street from Prospect Park. I was now in the uncomfortable position of having benefited from another's grief.

As an immigrant, I had always looked up to the real estate developers with whom I had invested, and when they became involved in the soaring stock market, I was painfully ambivalent. On the one hand, I wanted to participate in their investments, and to be part of the "American Dream," and on the other, I still had the poor immigrant's fear of losing. I chose to be "safe, rather than sorry," and I justified my position by pointing with pride to my role in growing Rose's business.

"We didn't have the proverbial pot," I liked to say, "but we were tough, and we did whatever was necessary to survive. And with hard work and cautious investment, we survived just fine. I never borrowed a penny," I told them, "never in my life. Not when my mother and I were struggling, not when Rose and I were building her business, and not even when we bought and furnished our house, and I'm not about to start now. I can go anywhere with my head held high," I liked to say, "because I don't owe anybody anything."

As The Depression deepened, Rose and I continued our life in our beautiful house in Borough Park, and although my term as vice president of the synagogue had expired, I remained one of its primary financial and moral supporters. My studies of ancient Jewish texts now occupied most of my day, and I increasingly enjoyed the seclusion of becoming a scholar.

Rose, who was much more social than I, had become active

in Zionist causes and spent a large portion of her time at meetings in New York City. She was enthusiastically involved in the development of the Mizrachi Women's Organization, which was a women's organization that was especially devoted to the needs of religiously observant Jewish girls in Palestine. They were working on the creation of the first vocational high school for girls in Palestine, which was opened in Jerusalem in 1933. Rose's generosity and business experience were important factors in its development.

I had invested the proceeds from the sale of Rose's store wisely and conservatively, and while others had made and eventually lost fortunes speculating in the stock market, I had continued to upgrade our properties, which were now considered prime locations. I had installed every modern convenience as soon as it became available, and my buildings were now especially attractive to the former "millionaires" who had fallen on hard times and were now grateful to have an affordable and attractive place to live.

Ruthie was living in a beautiful part of New York and was supporting herself. Bentzy, our grandson, who was now a toddler and our great joy; he was walking and talking and said he that he loved us very much.

highly respected member of both the business community and the religious community, and I was involved on the national level in the development of the Mizrachi Women's Organization. I now spent a great deal of time out of the house attending and organizing meetings, and supervising publications and mailings. I traveled on the train down to Washington DC to meet with congressmen and other politicians on a nearly regular basis.

Ruthie was well on her way to becoming successful both as an editor and short story writer, and Bentzy would soon be starting nursery school.

We were, for all intents and purposes, living the American Dream, but surprisingly, now that we had achieved this level of success, Jack was intensely unhappy. He suffered from periods of depression and unpredictable emotional outbursts. He no longer slept through the night, and he had taken to having a glass or two of wine at dinner and a brandy or two before bed.

I understood what the problem was—we had discussed it many times. Jack had always expected that once he reached a certain age of maturity, once he attained a certain level of affluence, once he achieved a certain level of knowledge, he would finally be an authentic American. He had accomplished all of this, but, still, in his mind, he wasn't authentic.

He had been successful in nearly all of his business endeavors, as I often told him, and he was accepted on every social level. And yet, he felt, somewhere deep inside, that he was a pretender, and that he really didn't fit in. I was aware that he resented my social ease. Whenever we went to public events, he felt that I was the person everyone greeted, while he was merely my companion. He occasionally referred to himself sarcastically as Mr. Rose Rubin.

Because I was often away at meetings, and Ruthie was fully occupied with Bentzy and her job, Jack now had too much time to think about his dreams and his failures. His dream had been so simple: to be an authentic American. But now that he had reached middle age, and now that there was nowhere for him to advance to—no dragons to slay—he felt unfulfilled and frustrated. He told me that he knew, without any doubt, that he was still not a real American. This discontent, which had languished so long in his unconscious, now dominated his thoughts.

He had been financially successful—more than he could ever have anticipated—he had learned *Talmud* and *Torah*, and he was one of the most charitable, if not the most charitable man in the community. And yet, he believed that he wasn't yet an American—not an authentic American. He believed that he was merely an actor, going through the motions, playing the part, and reciting the lines.

So now I am going to tell you about the Americanization of Jacob Rubinowitz.

It began, as most momentous events do, very slowly, without fanfare, and completely unnoticed. On a Sunday evening in November of 1933, Jack and I were sitting in our car stuck in traffic on the Brooklyn Bridge on our way home from visiting Ruthie and Bentzy in Manhattan. As we had done every time we traveled home from Ruthie's apartment, we had passed the Hooverville on the far west side of Manhattan, just a few blocks from Ruthie's apartment. There had been a thunderstorm earlier in the day, and the conditions at the Hooverville seemed worse than anything that we had read in the newspaper. Both Jack and I had been depressed by it. Although some of the more resourceful men in the Hooverville had been able to build structurally sound houses, most people had resorted to building their residences out of wood from crates, cardboard, scraps of metal, or whatever materials were available to them. Their huts usually had a small stove, some bedding, and a couple of simple cooking tools, most of which were outside their sleeping hut. They slept under "Hoover blankets"—old newspaper used as blanketing, walked on "Hoover leather,"—cardboard used to line their shoes when the sole wore through, and, in the depths of winter, they lined their coats with "Hoover liners,"—old newspapers which they tied to their bodies with rope.

"We should find a charity to send money to help them," I said.

"We already do," Jack said with some bitterness. "That's always our solution, 'send money and let the other guy do it.' I'm getting tired of sending money to some organization and then hoping that something good comes of it. All they do with the money is hire secretaries and administrators to help them raise more money so that they can hire more secretaries and administrators. There's got to be a way that we can help directly."

"I guess you could give some of them jobs, or maybe help them find jobs," I offered.

"What do I know about finding a job? I haven't worked for anyone in years, and I have very few employees."

"Well, what do they need most?" I asked.

"Everything, I guess," he said glumly.

We sat quietly, inching along in the traffic. "The way I see it," Jack said after a while, "giving them a loan would be better than charity, because it helps a person to help himself. Maybe we should give them a loan so that they can start something and get their dignity back."

"That sounds like a really great idea," I said encouragingly, "but where would they get the money to pay it back?"

"They could start some sort of service business, like sewing or tailoring. The money might help them buy supplies," Jack said optimistically.

"But it would take some time before they could start making enough money to pay the loan back."

"Suppose they didn't have to pay it back until they had enough money?"

I turned to face Jack. "I think you're on to something," I said. "A loan would let them keep some of their pride, and if they didn't have to pay it back until they were on their feet again, it wouldn't make them feel so bad."

"We could have them sign IOUs just like a real loan so that

they wouldn't feel like they were on the take," Jack said, brightening. "We'd have to put together a fund of some sort so that there would be enough money to make a difference."

Jack's idea of a Borough Park Free Loan Society was met with instant enthusiasm, and many donors came forward immediately to contribute to the fund. One of the members of the community who was a retired banker—one of the few Jewish bankers in a typically anti-Semitic field—offered to manage the fund, and two retired accountants and a lawyer stepped in to make sure that it was legal and fair.

And so, without much more planning, the Borough Park Free Loan Society was launched. They decided to offer a maximum of five hundred dollars per loan, per family, with no pre-conditions. The loans were to be paid back at the rate of five dollars per month with no interest. Jack, who had been the source of the program, had declined to participate in its management, and was given the job of researching any relevant Jewish Laws.

He was both relieved and disappointed to be relegated to this seemingly secondary responsibility, but he was proud that his work in Talmudic Studies was being recognized, and he was grateful for the opportunity to do some specifically directed research. He worked diligently on the research, and, after only two weeks, he produced a paper entitled "The Talmudic Laws of Lending Money."

Here, briefly, are his conclusions:

1. There is a Positive Commandment (mitzvah) in the *Torah* to lend money to anyone who needs it.
2. The mitzvah to lend money is even greater than the mitzvah to give charity, because a person is much less embarrassed to receive a loan than to receive charity.
3. The lender has a right to demand proper collateral for his loan to guarantee that it will be paid back in a timely manner.
4. If two people approach you for a loan, and you are only able to lend to one of them, you should give precedence

to the poorer person.

5. If you have been approached by a number of people for loans, and one needed a very large amount, to the extent that if you would lend him what he is requesting you would be unable to lend the others at all, it is preferable to provide a few loans of smaller amounts than to give it all to one person.

6. If you told someone that you decided to participate in a free loan fund, it is considered as if you had taken a vow to this effect, and it is forbidden to change your mind.

The members of the Borough Park Free Loan Society thanked Jack for his careful and informative research, and they quickly began the important work of distributing their funds as judiciously as possible. Although he remained an advisor, by his own choice, Jack's involvement with the fund, other than his original idea and his financial contribution, had essentially ended. He was secretly proud to have been the originator of the Free Loan Society, but, with his usual reticence, he was uncomfortable about being publicly credited for its existence.

The night after the official launch of the Borough Park Free Loan Society, Jack and I went to our favorite restaurant, a kosher delicatessen called Gold's, on Thirteenth Avenue in Borough Park, where we considered ourselves "regulars." Jack had been depressed all day since the launch, and I knew that only a good pastrami sandwich could cheer him up.

We liked the rough atmosphere in the delicatessen because it reminded us of both our origins on the Lower East Side and how far we had come. Hymie Gold, the enormous, barrel-chested owner, delivered our sandwiches himself without waiting for us to order.

"Mind if I join you?" he asked as he sat down without waiting for a reply.

"So," he asked in his gruff, Brooklyn accent, "what's goin' on? I heard about the Free Loan Society, not a bad idea. I could use a free loan," he laughed. "But all kidding aside, it sounds like a good idea. Do you think it will help?"

"I'm not sure," Jack said slowly.

"Whadaya mean?"

"Well, the money will help them get some food and supplies, but the whole idea is for them to be able to invest it in something, but I don't think there's much out there to invest in."

"You don't sound all that enthusiastic," Hymie said with a half smile.

Rather than answer, Jack took a big bite of his pastrami sandwich and looked at me.

"You've got to excuse him tonight," I said with a smile. "He's just depressed. The poverty, the things we saw, I can't explain."

Hymie waved to the waiter who brought over a knish. "Here," Hymie said, pushing the plate in front of Jack, "maybe this will cheer you up."

"It's not that I'm depressed," Jack said between mouthfuls. "It's just that I think that there has got to be something more that we can do."

"Like what?" Hymie challenged.

"Like here I am eating this pastrami sandwich, and there they are standing on line for a bowl of soup."

"You want they should eat Pastrami?"

"Yeah, I guess that's what I'm saying," Jack mumbled glumly.

"OK, then maybe I got an idea," Hymie said. "Every night, when we close, we throw out a lot of food, and on Friday night, because we close for Shabbos, we throw out even more. What do you say we send our leftovers to one of the Hoovervilles?"

Jack brightened. "There must be a half dozen restaurants right in this neighborhood that do the same thing. What if I get a truck and pick up the food from each of them and deliver it to the Hooverville?"

"It's a nice idea," Hymie said, "but there wouldn't be enough food to make a trip during the week. It only would make sense before Shabbos, and you couldn't get there and get back before the Sabbath begins. Besides, where would you get a truck?"

"You can leave that up to me. Just have the food ready this Friday."

"That's a good idea," Hymie laughed. "You and I will both get a mitzvah for it. I'll tell you what, I'll get the other delis to deliver their stuff here too so then you'll have enough leftovers to make it worth doing, and you'll be able to get it done before the Sabbath."

⊢————————————⊣

I arranged to borrow a panel truck from one of the companies that serviced my buildings, and just after lunch on that Friday afternoon, I showed up at Gold's delicatessen. Hymie was waiting for me with a huge amount of partially sliced meat, sliced bread, and nearly a full barrel of salad. He also had similar leftovers from the other delis. They filled the entire truck, and I merrily drove off to the Hooverville near Ruthie in New York.

I was euphoric. For once, I told myself, I was doing something direct—and it was physical, just like it used to be. But unfortunately, I soon ran into forces that were beyond my control. The moment I reached the Flatbush Avenue approach to the Brooklyn Bridge, I knew that I was in trouble. Traffic had come to a complete standstill. At first, I was concerned that the food in the truck might spoil, so I opened all the windows to keep it as cool as possible. But then I came to another realization: I would not be able to deliver the food and return home in time for the Sabbath.

I thought that I had allowed enough time to make the delivery and return home, but I had been inching along in traffic for over an hour, and I was stuck at just about the midpoint of the trip. I could turn back, but I would arrive at home after sundown, or I could continue to the Hooverville and deliver the food. I decided to keep going, so I pulled the truck over to the side of the road, got out, and began to recite the psalms welcoming the Sabbath. "At least I can say the prayers," I said to myself, but then, in the middle of the prayers, I stopped.

"This is nonsense," I said aloud, "it doesn't feel like the Sabbath when I'm standing on the side of the road saying prayers welcoming the Sabbath because then I'm going to have to get back into the truck and drive on the Sabbath. At least I'll be doing a good deed while I'm breaking the Sabbath."

Back in the truck, I laughed at my efforts at rationalization. "God probably doesn't care if I'm breaking the Sabbath or not; it's just my problem. And God probably doesn't care if I'm doing a good deed either. He's certainly got much more important things to worry about. This is just between me and them."

Saying this aloud made me feel better, and, as traffic started to move, I turned my thoughts to the coming presentation of food that I would make at the Hooverville. I smiled to myself with satisfaction as I visualized the residents gathering around the truck. But then I realized that I had not thought the process through very well. I had a truck full of deli meats, fish, breads, and vegetables, but I had no way to slice them or serve them. I had not even thought to bring a table, nor had I brought any serving utensils. In a panic, I decided to stop at Ruthie's apartment and borrow serving utensils from her and from some of her neighbors.

It was pitch dark when I arrived at the Hooverville on the Upper West Side of Manhattan. There were candles flickering in some of the shacks, but there was no one there to help me, or to take advantage of my generosity.

I was now very disappointed, and I parked the truck near the Hooverville and spent the next half hour walking around in the field trying to find someone—anyone. I had expected my generosity to be received with open arms and overwhelming gratitude, but night had fallen and the residents were in their tar paper huts with their families. I was now not only disappointed, I was angry. I knew that my anger was unreasonable, but I had felt so good in anticipation of this mitzvah that my let-down was steep.

I walked through the Hooverville, through the winding lanes between the huts, shouting, "Haloo, I have free food." Eventually people started to come out and gather at the truck, but they seemed excessively cautious, and some even seemed to resent my generosity, as they picked very carefully and suspiciously at the food that I had brought.

When most of the food was gone, I repacked the truck and returned, dispirited, to Ruthie's apartment. It was after ten, Bentzy was asleep, and Ruthie was in her bathrobe, in the kitchen, reading.

"What did you expect?" she asked when I had told her of my disappointment. We were sitting in the kitchen drinking tea from the kettle on the stove that had been simmering for the Sabbath.

"They didn't know you were coming," she said gently. "And they didn't know what you were bringing, and they don't know you well enough to trust you. There are all kinds of conmen out there, you know, trying to take advantage of them."

"But I was only trying to help, and they treated me like some sort of thief. What should I do?" I whined.

"First," Ruthie said, like the mature mother that she now was, "you should take a hot bath and sleep here. Second, you should come for a walk with me tomorrow, up to the Hooverville, and talk to them."

"But it's the Sabbath," I said, "and I've got to go to synagogue tomorrow morning."

"This is more important," she said, putting her arm around my shoulders. "You'll see."

I called Rose and told her what had happened and what Ruthie and I had planned for the next day, and then I took Ruthie's advice one hundred percent—took a bath and went to sleep.

In the morning, after a cold breakfast and some playtime with Bentzy, Ruthie, Bentzy, and I set off for the Hooverville, about a mile walk north. It was a beautiful morning, and I enjoyed pushing Bentzy's stroller and walking with Ruthie up Riverside Drive along the side of the construction of the new Henry Hudson Parkway.

Jack was surprised to see, what appeared to him, to be a thriving, animated village. Children were playing baseball in a nearby field, women were hanging out wash, and men were working on the construction of new shelters.

Jack, Ruthie, and her son stood on the edge of the Hooverville looking around, and then walked hesitantly across the field toward us.

"Excuse me," Jack called out to me from a distance, "do you have a few minutes? I'd like to talk to you."

"Unfortunately," I replied with a smile, "I've got all the time in the world. What's on your mind?"

"I was here last evening to distribute some food, but there weren't many people here to give it to."

"Yeah, I heard about it," I said, turning back to my work.

Jack stood uncomfortably. He didn't seem to have expected such a cold shoulder. He walked around me so that he was now facing me again.

"There's no need to be rude," he said, taking a step forward.

I tried to look like I was concentrating on what I was doing, but what I was doing didn't need that much concentration. Jack, who did not seem accustomed to being slighted, cleared his throat loudly, rounded his shoulders, and aggressively took another step forward.

Ruthie looked surprised. He suddenly looked like a local hooligan, and she seemed afraid that her father would physically attack me, so she reached out and put her hand on his arm.

Jack brushed it away. "You got some kinda problem?" he asked me. Ruthie looked like she had never heard him speak that way. "I'm tryin' ta help yez."

I stopped what I was doing and put my face just inches from Jack's. "What do you want, some kind of star or a medal or something? Listen, just because you've got a job and we don't, doesn't give you the right to patronize us."

"I'm sorry," Jack said, still standing his ground. But then, with a more reasonable tone, said, "I didn't mean to be patronizing."

"Well then, what the hell do you want?" I snarled, seizing my advantage. "You came here in the middle of the night with leftovers from some fancy restaurant—stuff that they can't give away—and you think that we want it? I can't stand all you goody goodies."

Ruthie now stepped between us. "My father," she said to me, "is just trying to help, and I think you owe him an apology for your tone." And then, turning to Jack, she said, "What were you thinking? These are people, not pets, you can't give them leftovers and expect them to be grateful."

"The point is," she said, turning back to me, "that my father wants to help. He is accustomed to being in charge and making all the decisions. But he's out of his area of experience now. So please tell us what we should do to help feed all these people."

The tension had been palpable, but then, after Ruthie spoke so reasonably, it broke.

"Is this your son?" I asked, turning to Bentzy.

"Yes, he is," Ruthie said defensively.

"I've got a boy just about the same age. Listen," I said, turning back to Jack, "you're Jewish, right?"

Jack barely nodded.

"*Vus macht a yid?*" I said in Yiddish with a grin.

"I'm sorry," Jack replied stiffly. "I don't speak Yiddish."

I now turned to Ruthie. "Is he kidding? Everyone in New York speaks Yiddish. Even the goyim speak Yiddish."

"Yes," Ruthie said with a smile, "most Jews in New York speak Yiddish, but my father doesn't. What exactly would you like us to do? We have good intentions, and my father has a little money. We will do whatever we can, within limits."

"Limits?" I challenged.

"I misspoke. We will do whatever we can. What do you suggest?"

I turned to Jack, and in a more conversational tone, asked, "Are you familiar with a Jewish philosopher named Maimonides?"

Surprised, Jack barely nodded.

"Well, this guy Maimonides, back in the fourteenth century, said that there are different levels of charity. The lowest form is giving money to a beggar, the highest is giving a person the equipment to satisfy his own needs.

"So here's what I'm telling you. If you want to help, get us a decent stove that we can cook on and an ice box, and get us the ingredients so that we can make our own soup and bread, and coffee. We don't want leftovers, or some charitable institution's stale bread and watery soup, we just need a little leg up."

Jack stared incredulously at me. There I was, well over six feet, broad shouldered, with an open shirt and rolled up sleeves. And there he was, in a suit and vest, if you can believe. We stood, still in combative mode, staring at each other.

"You are Jewish," I finally said, "aren't you?"

Ruthie smiled to herself as she listened. No one had ever questioned her father's Jewish identity.

But Jack didn't reply as his hostility slowly faded to compassion. "I think we can do that," he said finally. "At least we can try."

And then, Jack the hooligan disappeared completely, and Jack the elegant gentleman returned. He took a step back, squared his shoulders, and put out his hand.

"Jack Rubin," he said, shaking my hand. "Thank you for not being too offended at my bumbling efforts. I just didn't think it all the way through."

"Your suggestions," Jack said studiously, "make sense, and I will see what I can do."

Jack turned to go, but Ruthie lingered. "How can we get in touch with you?" she asked.

"That's my house right over there," I said. "Me and my kid."

"And what's your name?" Ruthie continued.

"Aaron."

"Pleased to meet you, Aaron," Ruthie said, shaking my hand. "My name is Ruth, and my son is Ben-Zion."

It was if Aaron had injected me with a gallon of adrenaline. I paced like a caged lion all through Sunday, and when Monday morning finally arrived, I was at my roll-top desk at dawn, with renewed vigor. I was about to reinvent myself. Again.

I had no idea where to get a commercial stove and an ice box. My first effort was to contact the contractors who had worked on my buildings in Brooklyn. Most of them were now out of the construction business, and the few that remained were unfamiliar with the sort of commercial restaurant equipment that I was looking for. I was both relentless and tenacious, and I worked the phone tirelessly. Every rejection that I received led to a recommendation of someone else to contact, and slowly I began making headway. I didn't want to invest in a new stove, and it was hard to find a used stove that was in reliably good condition. Eventually I was able to find both a commercial-size, coal-burning stove and an enormous ice box. I borrowed a truck from one of the contractors who periodically worked on my buildings and drove it myself to pick up the stove and the ice box. Driving the large truck was much more difficult than I had anticipated, and, with some difficulty, I parked the truck in my driveway in Brooklyn. That was a pretty strange sight: a huge commercial truck in the middle of our very quiet, residential community.

The next morning, with the stove and the ice box sitting on the truck in the driveway, I started to look for reliable suppliers of coal and ice. One of the members of the synagogue had contacts in a fuel company, and I was able to arrange for them to deliver coal directly to the Hooverville. Ice was a more difficult problem because the ice had to be stored in a properly designed area and had to be replenished and drained on a daily basis; someone at the Hooverville would have to take responsibility for its maintenance. The ice company was not willing to sign a contract until all the pieces were in place, and I was reluctant to sign a contract as well. I struggled with myself about the risks, but refrigeration was the key to the success of my self-feeding venture. I finally managed to delay the contract signing for a week while I worked on making arrangements at the Hooverville.

In the early afternoon, I carefully backed the truck out of my driveway and set off to the Hooverville. (I am very proud of having been able to do this without destroying Rose's hedges.) This time, I planned to take Ruthie with me to act as a "moderator."

Driving the large truck in Manhattan was a lot more challenging than I had anticipated, and I was tense and sweaty by the time I arrived at Ruthie's apartment. I was in a rush to go, but Ruthie insisted that we have a glass of tea and a snack before we proceeded to the Hooverville.

When Ruthie, Bentzy, and I arrived at the Hooverville, we immediately went to Aaron's hut. There was no door on the structure, just a bedspread that was pulled to one side. When I went to knock on the doorpost, I was surprised to see that there was a hand-carved mezuzah mounted on it, and I stopped for a moment to admire it. Before I had a chance to knock, Aaron, who was even larger than I had remembered, emerged from the hut with his son. He greeted us warmly and introduced us to his son who promptly and very properly, shook my hand, after which he and Bentzy ran off to play.

"I was able to find a pretty good commercial, coal-burning cooking stove," I said, continuing our conversation from the last time we met. "We can see how well it works out, and then I can try to get another."

I gave Aaron the name of the company that would be supplying the coal and asked him to make sure to have someone on hand to receive the delivery of coal that was coming the following morning.

"The ice box," I said, "is a much bigger problem. I was able to find a commercial grade one with a pretty good storage capacity, but it will need constant supervision to replenish the ice and drain the water. Plus, it's a safety hazard with all these kids here. So I'm going to leave that up to you. Everything's on the truck which is parked right over there. The ice box and the stove are both pretty heavy, so you'll need some strong men to unload it.

"I brought Ruthie with me," I said, "because she is a writer, and I thought that she could write about what we're doing here so that other Hoovervilles can do the same thing."

"Hey," Aaron laughed, "take a breath. Let's talk about this a minute. First let's say hello," he said with a broad smile. And then, focusing all his attention on Ruthie, as if I wasn't even there, "So, you're a writer. I knew you would be somehow connected with the arts. What do you write?"

"Short stories mostly," Ruthie said. "But my real job is as an editor."

"Like for magazines?"

"No. Actually, I work for a book publisher," Ruthie said with a smile. "I work with the authors to help them make their books better. My stories, though, are in magazines, so you were not far off."

I was getting impatient, and I took a step forward. "I hate to break this up," I said, "but I've got a truck waiting. Where should we put the stove and what about the ice box?"

"I think we should keep them close to each other and central to the community," Aaron replied. "I can get some guys to unload the truck and to dig a pit that we can line with burlap to keep the ice cold. It should last at least a week, that way."

"OK. So the next question is, once we get the stove and ice box off the truck, what sort of food do you want me to get?"

"I'm not big on cooking," Aaron replied, with a glance at Ruthie, "but beggars can't be choosers. So we'll take what-ever you can get, but it should be as fresh as possible. We both looked expectantly at Ruthie, who shook her head vigorously.

"Don't think I know how to cook just because I wear a skirt!" she laughed. "I'm a writer, not a cook."

"Every Jewish girl knows how to cook," Aaron said with a twinkle, "it comes with the territory. What about your mother?

Didn't she teach you how to cook?"

"My mother?" Ruthie laughed, rolling her eyes. "You've got to be kidding. Trust me. I don't cook. But I do write, and here's what I can do: I can be here nearly every day to write about you and the rest of the people who live here. We, the people on the outside, only hear stories about how bad it is and how people are suffering. It would be good to show that some people have figured out a way to make things better."

I smiled as I thought about Rose in the kitchen. To tell the truth, I was so focused on the task at hand that I didn't notice the chemistry that was developing between Aaron and Ruthie.

"I'm not sure I can back that truck up," I said, trying to get Aaron to focus on the task at hand. "Maybe you have someone here who can do it."

Even though we were a generation apart in age, Aaron and I developed a close working relationship. We seemed to be able to communicate with each other without discussion. I returned to the Hooverville several times to deliver food and more equipment, and to report on my progress, and especially to get Aaron's feedback.

It turned out that most of the commercial food companies who supplied the local restaurants loaded their trucks in the morning with enough food to satisfy their customers' needs. Their trucks then followed a standard route, going from restaurant to restaurant in the city. When they arrived at a restaurant, the chef would come out to the truck and select the food that he would need for the day. The truck would then go on to the next restaurant. Each of these food companies specialized in one particular food category: vegetables, meat, fish, dairy products, or fruit, and their trucks followed nearly the same route to all of the restaurants in the area. The trucks always carried more food than they needed because they wanted to be able to fully supply their customers. As a result, there was always food left over on the trucks after they had made their last stop. This food was usually disposed of at a dump at the end of the day.

I contacted all of the restaurant food suppliers in my area and arranged to take their leftovers. I set up a central collection point where I had a truck waiting every afternoon to take whatever was left on the trucks after they had made their rounds. Pretty soon, I had a team of drivers and truck workers, all of whom came from the Hooverville, who unloaded the suppliers' trucks and loaded mine. It made me smile when I remembered that my first real job, so many years—lifetimes—ago, had been on the back of a truck delivering newspapers.

The food distributors liked this arrangement because they didn't have to worry about getting rid of the leftover food, and their trucks could now return to the terminal empty and ready to be washed and prepared for the next day's load.

We usually finished the transfers by noon and my truck would arrive at the Hooverville every day at around four in the afternoon where Aaron would have a crew ready to unload it.

Although I probably should have gotten personal pleasure out of being philanthropic, I never quite thought of myself that way. I saw myself more as Aaron's partner than as his benefactor, and I was glad to be doing such meaningful work. While I was working on getting the food and equipment, Aaron was organizing a series of cooking stations throughout the Hooverville. He posted cooking schedules so that individual families would have access to the equipment on their own, as well as in groups. We supplied coal stoves and ice boxes, which were placed in accessible locations in the Hooverville, and we created a central distribution facility where my food deliveries could be distributed on a daily basis.

Throughout my business career, I had always worked alone, but now, thanks in great part to Aaron, I discovered within myself hidden interpersonal skills. Although I was naturally reticent, when it came to the Hooverville cause, I was aggressively outgoing and usually convincing. I tirelessly promoted Aaron's cooking stations with the restaurant supply houses, and

I also sent my drivers out to local truck farms for fresh produce. We now had two trucks on the road with two full-time drivers.

Aaron and I were ubiquitous. Aaron and his son went from station to station making sure that there was a sufficient supply of coal and that the equipment was being kept in good repair. I now spent most of my days on the road or on the phone, finding and cajoling new suppliers.

Eventually, we branched out into other products as we sought to satisfy as many of the needs of the Hooverville as possible. We supplied clothing, books, and even bedding. It was always Aaron, the gentle giant with his sleeves rolled up and his son next to him, and me, the short, bespectacled, round-barrel of a man with a never changing frown.

Ruthie, who had begun writing a novel based on the history of the people that she had met in the Hooverville and the services that Aaron and I were providing, was often part of our team. Aaron and I, although we were neither business partners nor friends, had developed the kind of shorthand that long-married couples have—anticipating each other's needs, concerns, and even comments. Although we enjoyed working together, we never pried into the other's private affairs.

But then, just before Yom Kippur, without intending to pry, I asked a very personal question: I asked Aaron for the Hebrew name of his wife.

"Why do you want to know?" Aaron answered brusquely.

Taken slightly aback, I explained that in our synagogue, during the Yom Kippur memorial prayer, the Rabbi gave the worshipers in the synagogue an opportunity to mention, out loud in Hebrew, the names of the departed souls that he was praying for. I told him that I would like to mention his late wife by name.

Aaron stopped and considered me for a long moment. "She's not dead," he said with finality.

But I had already committed myself, and so I asked, "Then you're divorced?" I hated my tone and regretted having asked.

Aaron answered matter-of-factly, "No, not quite."

"I don't understand," I said.

"It's a long story."

I was now completely intrigued and also concerned that I had gone too far. "If you would like to tell it to me, I have plenty of time to listen," I said. "If not, that's OK too."

"I told you, it's a long story," Aaron said without feeling. "But, if you're really interested, I'll try to keep it as short as possible."

I looked encouragingly over the top of my glasses at him. I had expected that this would be an especially sensitive topic and that Aaron needed to tell it to someone, but now I wasn't so sure.

"OK," Aaron said. "I come from a little town about fifty miles west of Chicago. I was born there, and I went to school there. There was even a little shul there where I had my bar mitzvah.

"I wasn't your typical smart Jewish kid. I was bigger than all the other kids, and I went out for sports. I was a pretty good athlete, and I got three letters in high school for basketball, football, and baseball. As you can imagine, with all those sports, I didn't have much time for studies, but it didn't matter. The teachers all gave me passing grades so that I could play, and I got a football scholarship to a good college.

"It turns out that I wasn't good enough to make the varsity team in college. I started some games, and I was on the team for three years, but they said that I didn't live up to my potential. The coach threatened to terminate my scholarship at the end of my first year, but I began doing some research with one of the professors in the physics lab, and he stood up for me. He even helped me get my first job.

"But I'm getting away from my story, and that's not what I wanted to tell you. My high school had a reunion every year for the class that had graduated five years earlier. That was the only reunion they had. The idea was that the graduates would have been established by then, but would not have moved too far out of town yet. Anyway, it was a big deal in our town. They decorated the high school gym and hired a dance band. Plus, we were allowed to drink, which we couldn't do in high school.

"I was a kind of hero, you know, what with all the sports. Plus, I had gone to a good college, and I had a good job and was making real money. There was a girl at the reunion who had been kind of my girlfriend in high school. We hit it off really big at the reunion, and we ended up in bed in her apartment. She got pregnant.

"The story might have ended there; we might have gotten married and raised a family. I certainly was willing, but she wasn't. It turns out that she was actually engaged to a nice guy in another town, and they had planned a very happy life together. She really didn't love me, and this fling was just that, a fling—too much nostalgia and too much booze. She wanted to have an abortion, but I didn't want her to. I figured that this was a life worth saving. Plus, she would have had to go to this woman we had heard about in Chicago, and she could die.

"So I made her a deal. I would arrange for her to be hired by my company and be sent on a business trip somewhere where her fiancée couldn't go. She would have the baby. I would pay for everything. And then she would go back to her fiancée and marry him, and I would take full responsibility for the kid.

"And that's the way it worked out. She was away on this business trip for about six months, and she and this guy got married about three months after she came back. And, from what I heard, they are very happy. No one other than she and I, and now you, knows about what happened. Not my parents, not my classmates, not my friends, no one. Just me and her. And now you. I usually tell anyone who asks that his mother died in childbirth."

"What are you going to tell your son?" I asked quietly.

"I don't know yet," he replied.

CHAPTER 26

I had developed an easy relationship with Aaron. I enjoyed his sense of humor, and I always felt secure with him. Our friendship was a mature one of mutual respect with just a touch of teasing and flirting. I am, after all, human, and so I had idly thought about what it would be like to sleep with him as compared with Harry. Aaron was muscular and physical; Harry had been soft and sensitive. Although my father had told me about Aaron's son's mother and the strange agreement they had made, Aaron had never asked about Bentzy, and I had never offered even a clue.

"I have a favor to ask," Aaron said one Friday afternoon. "You know, I was raised in a town that had a very small Jewish population. Even though we had a synagogue, there wasn't much of a Jewish feeling. Although we weren't religious, this lack of a Jewish environment bothered my father a lot. He had grown up in a shtetle in Poland where there were mostly Jews and where preparation for the Sabbath was a big thing. So we, in our home, pretended we were still in the shtetle. The way we did that was to go up on a hill behind our house every Friday night and watch the sunset. When the last trace of the sun was gone, my father kissed each of us and wished us a *gutten Shabbos*.

"My parents are gone now, my brother is on the West Coast, and all I have is me and my son. I try to mark the start of Shabbos, but somehow, it doesn't feel the same as it used to. So here's my favor: will you and Bentzy sit with me and my son and watch the Sabbath sunset?"

And so, that Friday night, we began a ritual of welcoming the Sabbath together by watching the sun set over the Hudson River. The night was clear and dusk had fallen. We were sitting on some packing crates looking out at the river. Our children were playing nearby.

"In case you're wondering," I said quietly, "I never was married. I was in love—very much so—but he died before we could get married."

"I'm sorry. What did he die of?"

"I'm not sure."

Aaron sat quietly, waiting for more, but there was no more. We had both traveled a lifetime of long, winding roads to get to this moment of pure Sabbath peace. The last remnants of sunlight glittered on the Hudson River, and then suddenly they were gone.

"A gutten Shabbos," Aaron said softly, wishing me a peaceful Sabbath.

"Yes," I said, "it is."

Instinctively, I took Aaron's hand. It had been meant as a gesture of friendship or consolation, maybe reassurance, but something else had happened, and it meant something more. We both knew it.

The "self help" supply chain that Aaron and I had developed was working smoothly. We had equipped complete kitchens in a number of central locations in the Hooverville, which the residents now referred to as "villages." Once these kitchens were in operation, a bunch of other charities began delivering food supplies to them on a regular basis, and the only task remaining for Aaron and me was to keep the stoves burning.

These stoves were coal-fired, and they required two grades of coal and enough kindling to start the fire each morning. Our responsibility now was to keep them supplied with coal and to remove the ashes. Through one of my connections, we were able to save a substantial amount of money by buying the coal nuggets directly from a coal mining company in Pennsylvania and avoiding the middleman.

Once a week, the Hooverville's driver would pick up a truckload of coal from the mine and deliver it to the various kitchens in the Hooverville. The problem was that we didn't need all the coal that we brought up to the Hooverville, and it was too expensive for us to buy less than a full truck load. Although it was still cheaper than buying the coal from a middleman, we had to find a way to dispose of the excess coal.

At first, we resold the remaining coal at a loss to a local distributor, but this was awkward and way too expensive. Then we looked into renting a storage facility, but this was too costly. We were faced with the real possibility that, because of the excess coal, we would not be able to afford to continue the coal delivery service.

"This is crazy," Aaron said as we were paying our bills. "This process is costing us too much money. You're a generous guy, but you can't keep on funding it at this rate. I know that you're pretty well off, but I won't let you endanger your family's future."

I was both relieved and offended. It was true that this coal situation was rapidly depleting our savings, but I loved being part of this process, and I didn't want to give it up. And I didn't want to ask anyone else to participate. This was a very personal project between Aaron and me, and I didn't want to lose that.

"It'll be OK," I said. "The economy's turning around and pretty soon we'll be able to stop."

"You're dreaming," Aaron responded. "Even with all that Roosevelt has done, it still hasn't made a dent. For every person who gets a job, two others lose theirs."

We were sitting in the cab of the truck—me behind the wheel, Aaron in the passenger seat. The driver had gone to lunch, and we were just making sure that the coal was safe. "The problem is the leftover coal," I mused. "If we could only find a way to sell it at a profit, or even at cost, then we'd be OK."

"Holy shit!" Aaron exclaimed. "You hit the nail right on the head. The solution was staring us right in the face, but we didn't see it. All we've got to do is find some homes or businesses that will buy their coal from us. Then we might be able to break even."

"You're right!" I nearly shouted. "Coal is coal. The important thing about coal deliveries is reliability. During the winter people don't want to risk being without a reliable delivery of coal. They don't really care who they buy their coal from as long as they are certain that it will be there when they need it."

Enthusiasm is infectious and Aaron was nearly jumping out of his seat. "We've got more reliable drivers than you can shake a stick at. All we've got to do is convince some of your neighbors that we will always be there on time with their delivery. I bet you know plenty of people in your neighborhood who would give us their business—especially if we tell them that all the profits will be going to charity."

"That's it!" I said. "That's the key: charity! I can tell the people in my synagogue that buying coal from us is a doing a good deed—a mitzvah. They get coal to heat their house and a mitzvah too!"

And just like that, "Share the Heat Fuel Company" was formed, and Aaron and I were equal partners. It was, as they say, a marriage made in heaven. Aaron—outgoing, friendly, and larger than life—was the outside man, and I was the inside man.

We were careful not to take on more customers than we could comfortably service, and every month, when we sent out our bills, we indicated on the bills the amount of money that we had donated to charity that month and the cumulative total for the year. Since neither Aaron nor I was being paid a salary, and we had no real overhead other than the truck rentals and the Hooverville drivers, our charitable donations were substantial.

Within a few months, word of our new charitable company reached the newspapers and both *The New York Times* and *The New York Sun* did feature stories on our new venture. The business grew rapidly and "Share the Heat" trucks began showing up in residential neighborhoods throughout New York. As our business grew, we were able to hire more and more men from the Hooverville and give more and more to charity.

The rest of the story is family lore, and we tell it freely and happily to anyone who will listen.

On the first anniversary of their new business, Ruthie invited Rose, Jack, and my father, Aaron, to her apartment to celebrate. She had ordered a huge platter of assorted meats from Gold's Delicatessen, mountains of coleslaw and potato salad, and a whole loaf of sliced rye bread.

As we all sat at the table, my grandfather tapped his knife on his glass and rose to speak. He slowly and meaningfully looked around the table, making sure to make eye contact with everyone there, and waiting for quiet.

"I have something I want to say. This is very important to me, and I beg your indulgence to hear me all the way through.

"All of my life in this wonderful country I have wanted to be an American: a real, authentic American. I was never quite sure exactly what that was, but I was sure that once I got there, I would know it. But every time I thought I had reached my goal, I realized that I was not really there.

"One year ago, Aaron and I were sitting in the cab of a coal truck. We were filthy and tired and depressed. We had been working intensely for months, and we were running out of money. And then, Aaron had a brilliant idea, and we changed our point of view from charity to self-help. At that moment, when we were sitting in the cab of that truck, I became a real

American—even though I didn't know it at the time. I discovered that being an American isn't about what you wear, or how you speak, or where you live. Anyone can do that. It's what's in your head and in your heart that makes you an American.

"We Americans argue about everything, but in the end, we always do the right thing. We may like our president or hate him. We may like our neighbor or hate him. That doesn't matter. What does matter is that we Americans understand that we are all part of the struggle, and that we all want to move in the same direction—toward a better world.

"In Europe, and in the rest of the world, there is history and privilege. But in America, everything was new and equal right from the start. And it was a struggle. And it is still a struggle. And it is our responsibility as Americans—real Americans—to help each other in the struggle. And the funny thing is that no one has to tell us what to do. Real Americans see a need, and we do whatever is necessary to make it whole.

"American history is different from the rest of the world. In Europe, the countries are old and they only want to regain their former grandeur. But we are a new country, and we live for the future. And because we live in the present, and not the past, we believe that the future will be better—always better. And we will do whatever is in our power to make it better.

"I'm not talking about charity; everyone can give charity. In church on Sunday morning they pass the plate and people put a few dollars in. That's too easy. I'm talking about involvement. That's what real Americans do: we get involved. *Tikun Olam*—making the world a better place.

"When Aaron and I started the business, we were only thinking about how we could help more people, and hire more people, and somehow figure out how to make life better for people, even if it was only one person at a time."

My grandfather looked down at my grandmother who was sitting next to him. He put his hand on her shoulder, and she reached up and held it.

"When I went to high school," he went on, "there was a

man—a judge—who helped me; helped me make it through, helped me survive. When I finished high school, I asked the judge how I could repay him. And this judge, who had helped me so much, told me that the only payment he wanted from me was that I should make a difference. That's what he said, 'Make a difference.' I didn't understand what he was talking about back then because I was only concerned about myself and my immediate future, but now I understand, and now making a difference is the most important value in my life.

"'Make a difference' might sound like empty words, or some sort of motto, but I want you to remember them. And when the opportunity comes, and I'm sure it will, I want you to remember what I am telling you today: make a difference."

"I almost forgot," Ruthie said as she rushed into the kitchen. She returned with a bottle of champagne and handed it to her father, who, in turn, smiled and handed it to my father.

He proudly and carefully worked the cork out of the bottle until it popped and champagne spilled out over the top. He poured champagne for everyone including us children, and raised his glass.

But before he could say anything, Ruthie stood up. "I know that this is an important event for the two of you," she said with a smile, "but I have something to celebrate too. My book was accepted for publication, and I got an advance of five hundred dollars!"

Without thinking, my father turned to her and kissed her right on the mouth. She recoiled slightly, and then she put her arms around him and kissed him back.

My grandfather said, "Well, it's about time." While my brother and I screamed with embarrassment and laughter.

Ruthie put a record on the phonograph, and we all sang and danced.

They were married, my father and Ruthie, about a year

later at the Brooklyn Jewish Center on Eastern Parkway, less than a mile from where my grandfather, Jack, had bought his first houses. The wedding was an enormous affair with all of the members of Jack and Rose's synagogue and busloads of our friends from the Hooverville in attendance.

And now, here we are, sitting at this table with you, telling a bit of our family history. Thank you for listening.

In keeping with the family tradition of concluding with a lesson, I would like to leave you with a bit of *musar*—an ethical message. It comes from the great Negro Leagues pitcher, Satchel Paige: *"Don't pray when it rains if you don't pray when the sun shines."*

CHAPTER 25

It was almost embarrassing to be living comfortably in such terrible times. I had my nice clothes, and my jewelry, and my mink coat, and we still had a maid although we no longer had a chauffeur. We remained the same as we had been, but the world around us had changed.

It happened so fast. There was the stock market crash—that was the big news. But for a few weeks, or even months afterward, although the newspapers were filled with reports of impending doom, nothing seemed to have happened. And then, slowly at first, and then with gathering speed, the economy started to go downhill. Within a matter of months after the crash, businesses and banks across the country tumbled into bankruptcy and closed their doors, and unemployment soared. In New York, and all across America, formerly employed workers now wandered the streets looking for day jobs and begging for handouts. Farmers abandoned their farms and migrated to the cities hoping for hourly employment in the factories. But there were very few jobs and too many applicants. Families were shattered as husbands could no longer provide for their families and fathers could no longer feed their children.

Many of these men were veterans of the First World War who had married and entered the labor force during the great boom decade of the 1920s. These veterans, who were now in their thirties with young families, had never experienced difficulty finding work, until the Great Depression.

From all over the country, from all walks of life, families who had lost their jobs and their homes, migrated to the cities. Out of necessity, they joined together to establish cooperative communities which they called Hoovervilles in repudiation of President Herbert Hoover, who had, for the most part, stood by submissively and watched his country descend into abject poverty and depression. These rapidly growing ramshackle communities, which were located on the outskirts of major cities, were filled with despair and desperation.

In the spring of 1933, during his first inaugural address, Franklin Delano Roosevelt, the newly elected president, told the nation that the only thing we had to fear was fear itself. But Roosevelt's well chosen words, though eloquent, did not capture the true terror of the time. Even among the people who had jobs, salaries had tumbled and many were earning far less than they had before the crash. Among the self-employed—people who had kept their businesses alive—profits had dwindled to a small percentage of what they had been taking home only a few years earlier. Even Jack's houses, which had always been fully rented, now had vacancies.

Although fear and panic gripped the nation, we, I'm embarrassed to say, were pretty well off. Jack had invested cautiously and wisely during the roaring twenties, and his real estate holdings were now both secure and profitable. Because of our natural caution, he and I were more financially secure than we had ever been in our lives. Jack enjoyed the quiet and solitude of our home, and the management of his properties gave him a feeling of upper class nobility. He attended community board meetings, hob-nobbed with local politicians, and he even became a member of the Real Estate Board of New York.

Jack and I had now achieved a new status in life. He was a

Photo by Izzy Beck

ABOUT THE AUTHOR

Every author draws from within himself: Who am I? And what do I stand for? Well, in his case, Bernard Beck is an American. And he stands for what he perceives as American values, but is also a self-described restless soul. A native of the New York/New Jersey area, Bernie attended Jewish religious school (yeshiva) from kindergarten through the twelfth grade. He then attended City College in the fifties, where he also worked part-time and summers for an advertising agency in Brooklyn. Following graduation in 1959, he spent two years in the army, stationed in Fort Bragg, North Carolina with his wife Judy.

Upon return to civilian life, he joined his father's giftware business which, under Bernie's management over the following thirty years, evolved into a major national importer and distributor of candles and Christmas ornaments.

After the recession of 1988, Bernie closed the business and began his second career as a business consultant and an adjunct professor of marketing at Rutgers University. This second phase lasted for twelve years. Upon retirement, Bernie authored the books *The Bible, The Greatest Marketing Tool Ever Written* and *True Jew, Challenging the Stereotype*, drawing upon his religious school background, combined with his marketing knowledge.

Bernie has been married to Judy for fifty-five years and together they have three children and five grandchildren. Both are very active in their community. They live in New Jersey, about ten miles west of New York, where they have lived nearly all of their married lives.